SAVE THE GIRLS

THE MCGEE CRIME SERIES #1

H. SCHUSSMAN

Save the Girls
H. Schussman
Published and Written by H. Schussman at Smashwords
First Edition 8/11/2020
Copyright 2020 H. Schussman

Discover other titles by H. Schussman at Smashwords.com
<u>Counterpart</u>
<u>El Tiburon</u>
<u>In the Crossfire of Revenge</u>

Smashwords Edition, License Notes

TABLE OF CONTENTS

ACKNOWLEDGEMENTS

It's hard to know who to thank. My husband ranks number one (right after God) because he not only encourages me, but critiques my work too. He catches inconsistencies and technical errors, plus he helps me over dull spots. Besides my friends and family (you know I appreciate you), I want to thank my editors: the hubby, Jeanette Lawson, Isabelle Lynch, and Karen Shipley. This was an emotional book for me to write and it involved several police officers input, and personal experiences. My nephew, Justin Paul, helped with technical details regarding police procedurals.

This is a purely fictional story. Any parallel to real life is unintentional.

CHAPTER ONE

A cowboy leaned over the pool table at the crowded western bar. Music blared from the band in the corner. He tried to line up for his shot, which was difficult considering how drunk he was. The balls on the table under the fluorescent light looked as though they are moving to him, but he'd been drunk enough times to know that was the booze. He whacked the ball and it bounced aimlessly around the table. Several spectators started laughing. Cowboy spun around to see who was mocking him and focused on the closest guy.

Sean McGee watched all this from his barstool. Under-age and all muscle, he eagerly waited for the imminent fight. He didn't have long to wait.

As Cowboy bunched up muscles and fists, an unsuspecting female walked into the tense circle just as the first fist flew. Cowboy connected with his mocker, but not fully because the mocker danced quickly out of range… and bumped into the female.

She fell. Suddenly the mood shifted to serious anger. She was the cowboy's date.

Cowboy roughly grabbed her as she stood, and drunkenly shoved her behind him. Trying to fight off his iron grip, she struggled to maintain her balance. Then her date turned and back-handed her across the face.

All hell broke loose and Sean McGee was right in the middle of it. A pool cue connected here, a barstool there… it was mayhem.

***

The guard unlocked the jail-cell door and, looking at the group of cell-mates, singled out McGee.

"McGee!" he barked as he waved Sean over.

Sean stood up and painfully stretched his knee out before limping over to the guard and exiting the cage. He followed the guard down the hall and entered the room indicated.

The judge was sitting at his desk. He silently pointed at the chair across from his desk.

"Good morning Judge," Sean said politely as he sat.

Judge Standish shook his head as he replied, "Good morning Sean." He slowly tapped his fingers on his desk as he stared at Sean.

Sean squirmed.

"How old are you?" Standish asked. His drumming fingers momentarily stopped.

"Twenty, sir."

"Yet you were at The Boot Scoot?" The judge asked with a hint of frustration creeping into his voice.

Sean squirmed a little again. "Yes sir."

The fingers resumed their tattoo on the smooth mahogany. "This is your third fight in the last six months." He held up a finger to stop Sean from speaking. "This time the guy ended up in the hospital. Actually three guys ended up in the hospital."

Silence. Judge Standish leaned forward and rested his forehead on steepled fingers.

Looking up he continued, "Your father is my best friend... I've known you since you were in diapers. You're not a bad kid, Sean."

"I'm not sure about that sir. When I see a girl get hurt... I, I just lose it," Sean countered.

They sat looking at each other for a moment. Making up his mind, Judge Standish leaned forward and pointed a long finger at Sean. "Let's make a deal. I called Clarence over at the recruiters and told him I had a young man who'd make an excellent Marine. You join the Marines and I'll make this go away."

***

A freshly shaved Sean stood at attention while a drill sergeant screamed in his ear. Sean stared straight ahead.

"We got ourselves a dumb red neck here!" shouted the sergeant.

"Sir, yes sir!" Sean shouted.

"Give me twenty!"

Sean obediently dropped to the ground and executed twenty perfect push-ups. He leaped back to his feet and stood at attention. He wasn't even out of breath. The sergeant glared menacingly at him.

Boot camp was a rapid fire series of physical challenges: Sean running, but not in lead, leaping over a wall and grabbing a fellow cadet who started to fall, a drill sergeant screaming in his ear. More push-ups. Taking apart a rifle, but waiting for someone else to finish before he laid his gun down. Taking a written exam in a room full of cadets. Decking a fellow Marine. More of the drill sergeant screaming in his ear... in pouring down rain.

A classroom full of cadets sat rigidly in their metal seats. Sean was among them. He watched the proceedings with profound interest. Everything interested him. Sean was an obsessive people watcher.

An instructor stepped forward and holding a piece of paper in his hand read, "McGee."

Sean jumped to his feet, eyes staring straight forward as he listened to other names being called while his blood pounded in his ears.

"Jacobson, Lundvall, Lacey... Exit right door."

The four cadets filed out the door into a hallway. A Marine stood waiting for them. She looked them up and down before she indicated they were to follow her. The four silent cadets trailed behind the Marine down the long barren hallway. As she stopped in front of another door with *Lewis* written on a wall placard, she turned to them and said, "Welcome to Recon boys."

They filed past her into an office where Lewis sat waiting for them. Lewis was a wiry, medium height guy with an extremely spiky flat top. His skin was like brown leather and his bright blues eye were barely visible through permanently squinting eyelids.

He stared at them as they maintained full attention. Standing he came around his desk and stopped in front of Randy Jacobson, a nondescript shaved white kid. "Jacobson, do you want to be a Recon Marine?"

"Sir! Yes sir!" Randy barked out.

Sean felt his stomach tighten into a spasm as Lewis approached him. *Please, oh please.*

Lewis looked into Sean's eyes as though taking his measure. "McGee, do you want to be a Recon Marine?"

"Sir! Yes sir!" Never had Sean felt such an emotion. He silently thanked Judge Standish.

Stepping in front of Craig Lundvall, Lewis looked intently at the stiff young man. Craig's eyes twitched nervously. "Lundvall, do you want to be a Recon Marine?"

"Sir! Yes sir!" Craig answered.

The last young man, Dan Lacey, stoically waited his turn.

"Lacey, do you want to be a Recon Marine?"

"Sir! Yes sir!" he answered in a crisp Marine shout.

Lewis turned his back on them and paced the room. "The chances are you won't make it through the training program. But you made it this far... and that's not easy." He leaned a hip against his desk, as he looked at them. "You think you are the best? That's pretty arrogant." Silence. "Report at O'four-hundred tomorrow morning. Dismissed!"

Sean, Randy, Craig and Dan sat together at a large metal table in the mess-hall that evening. They silently ate from portioned trays. Randy glanced up at them a couple of times. He was muscular like Sean, and could never resist the urge to talk. "So why'd they pick us?" He had a grin tugging at his mouth as he chewed.

"Dunno," Sean answered. "I know I'm not the best, that's for sure."

"That's because you choose to not be the best," Dan said. "They can tell though. As for me... this is what I came into the Marines for."

The other three looked at him as they chewed. Randy's smile grew as he mockingly repeated, "This is what I came into the Marines for!"

Dan glared at him with no effect on Randy.

"How 'bout you Craig?" Sean asked.

Craig swallowed and started to speak, but stopped. He shook his head abruptly. "Don't know." He blinked four times and set his fork down, then picked it up again and resumed eating.

The other three stared at him like he'd grown another head.

***

It was pouring down rain as the group did sit-ups with telephone poles, pull-ups on a slippery bar, took rifles apart with rain dripping from their eyelashes. Sean stood watching as the guy in front of him dragged a dummy through the surf. They ran in fatigues with backpacks on. Took guns apart outside in the dark... with the wind whistling through their helmets. One handed push-ups, scaling a rock wall in the dark. Seemingly endless challenges.

Sean stood with legs spread, arms crossed, and shoulders relaxed while watching Dan and Craig circling each other in the boxing ring. Dan towered over Craig by at least four inches. Randy leaned eagerly against the ropes next to Sean.

"Five bucks on Craig," Sean said.

Randy kept his eyes on the contestants. "You got it! Dan'll squash him."

"He won't be able to catch him... he looks pissed."

"Which one?" Randy asked.

"Craig, but he always looks-- " Sean started.

Craig dropped to the mat and started spinning around like a break-dancer.

Randy leaned back in surprise, "Holy shit! What's he doing?"

Craig suddenly stopped and arched his entire body up with head and elbows still on the ground and twisted his body like a corkscrew with legs. He kicked Dan several times before Dan was even aware of it. Then Craig was on his feet again... after another couple of spins on top of his head.

Dan sounded curious and pissed off at the same time as he demanded, "What the frick was that?"

Randy handed five bucks to Sean and ducked under the rope to enter the ring. Sean followed him.

"Yeah, dude, what was that?" Randy asked. "Can you teach me that crazy shit?"

Craig tried to hide his pleasure at their attention. "Break-fighting. When I was a kid I did a lot of break-dancing and did martial arts too. Then I started combining them."

Shaking his head, Dan said, "Thanks for not breaking my knees, man."

***

The greenery of the Costa Rican jungle foliage was beautiful. Sun beams lit the busy movements of the insects. The sharp cry of a Macaw reverberated through the quiet. The giant leaves of a fern moved. Slowly the fern parted and blue eyes scanned the horizon from beneath a green leaf plastered helmet. The helmet sank down again. The foliage moved as the helmet began to move forward. Three other plants moved in unison with the fern.

A whisper was heard amongst the plants. At first it was unintelligible. The front man stopped and then resumed his slow trek. A voice toward the back whispered, "Shut up!"

Suddenly the leader stood up, revealing Sean. He was furious. The other greenery-covered helmets rose to reveal Craig, Randy and Dan.

Sean growled, "Craig! If you blow one more op talking to yourself, I swear…" Sean suddenly had Craig by the throat.

Craig hung docilely before Sean's blazing anger.

"I swear, I'll kill you myself!" Sean whispered fiercely.

Dan and Randy wisely remained silent *and* out of reach.

Sean abruptly let go of Craig. "What's your frigging problem? This is the third training op you've blown."

Craig stayed silent.

"Do you want to be Recon or not?" They all stood looking at each other. Suddenly the jungle seemed oppressive. Sean continued calmer, "What's your problem man?"

Craig was clearly struggling with his emotions and voices in his head. "I'm schizo."

"You? Seriously? How in the hell did you get past the recruiters?" Dan joined in.

"They knew and said crazy is good." Craig shrugged. "That's the reason I joined the Marines. I wanted to learn to control it."

Sean jabbed a finger in Craig's sternum. "This is not a therapy group! Control your tongue or I will remove it. I don't care if you have the armies of Hell shouting in your head. Ignore them or get a desk job!"

"Yes sir," Craig answered.

The jungle parted and a Recon training sergeant stepped through. "What's going on?" he asked Sean.

"Team meeting sir," Sean answered with a calmness he didn't feel.

The sergeant seemed to consider this a moment. "Okay... tomorrow is test day. We'll give you a map to the flag. You have to get past us to get it. Are you ready?"

"Sir, yes sir!" the four responded in unison.

***

Randy stood rigidly at attention as an officer stopped before him. Sean, Craig, and Dan were at his side... all at attention. They were receiving their commission to Recon, the highest honor for a Marine cadet. Sean felt his eyes burning and wondered at it. The only other time he felt that way was when rage was pouring over him. Maybe his sister was right... men have the same burning sensation girls have, but perceive it as anger. He resisted a smile, as he looked at her in the audience remembering his retort back then, "Guys don't cry when they're mad, they make other guys cry!"

The rest of the ceremony was a blur. Afterwards he proudly received a hug from his father. His mother hovered next to him, waiting her turn. Each one of his sisters clung to him and cried with pride at their strong little brother.

That night, in the dim light, the four new Recon Marines clanked beer bottles together in a rough salute. The sound of music and talking was almost deafening in the rowdy civilian bar. They were the only four Marines, the bald ones.

"We did it!" Sean shouted over the noise. They all took a deep drink.

Randy leaned in to add, "Who would'a guessed that Crazy Craig would be the one who steered us clear of the trap?" Randy lifted his beer to Craig and the others join him.

"I guess your paranoia finally paid off," Sean said. "What made you suspect that waterfall?"

Craig shrugged, "I suspect everything."

Dan lifted his mug and looked thoughtfully at the amber liquid. "What's your weakness?" he asked no one in particular. "What makes you so mad you see red?"

They sat pondering this for a few moments before Randy responded. "My weakness is my country. It pisses me off when someone burns a flag."

They all nodded.

"I know this sounds stupid, but I love animals. Hate it when a pet is abused," Craig answered.

"Women," Sean started. When the other three laughed, he retorted, "Not like that! It makes me want to tear a dude apart when he hurts a woman."

"Hmm, you guys covered most of my triggers," Dan answered thoughtfully. "But honestly, I hate to see elderly people disrespected... especially if they're helpless."

"Well, I'd say we're pretty normal," Sean commented.

Four women in skimpy dresses sauntered up to the table. The mood shifted as the guys grinned.

***

The Recon team lay in a fan position on the floor of the jungle. A monkey screamed like a pissed off dinosaur. The darkness pressed down on the four men.

"Déjà vu... here we are again creeping around on the floor of the jungle in Costa Rica," Randy whispered sarcastically.

No one spoke for a moment.

Dan whispered, "Yeah, but this time it's for real."

"We'll be in and out by the end of the week. Grab the kid, deliver him to his daddy and get out," Sean reminded them.

The next day they watched as a six year-old boy played with a stick next to a large two-story home nestled in the jungle. An armed guard slowly followed him. The little guy squatted down and dug a hole in the garden with his stick. Presently a bright blue butterfly caught his attention. The guard followed.

At a signal from Sean, Randy tossed a chunk of bark about thirty feet away into the dense underbrush defining the property lines. The guard spun toward the sound with his gun aimed at the noise. He looked calm and capable of picking off an attacker.

The team watched the mansion for the rest of the day. They were as patient as the jungle predators around them. As the sun set, they ate their odorless rations. The darkness became oppressive with dense clouds pressing down. The house showed some movement behind curtains, seen as silhouettes from the yard. Lights were slowly being turned off throughout the house.

Outside, the four men were barely visible in their camouflage. Like shadows, they moved closer to the house. A back door opened. The guard from earlier stood in the doorframe, barely discernible because there was no light behind him. The team stopped moving. The guard retreated back into the house and shut the door. The sharp click of latches could be heard in the stillness. The team resumed their approach. One rose out of the shrubs and ascended the wall to the second story window.

Sean could see the six-year old boy sitting cross-legged in the center of his bed looking at a magazine. His tousled brown hair hung forward into his face as he turned the pages. A small lamp near the bed put off a feeble light. A bruise along his cheekbone added to his dejected look. The door opened abruptly and a Latina woman walked in. The boy cringed as he watched her approach.

"Turn off light!" she commanded harshly. She walked over to the lamp, turned it off and marched out of the room.

The boy curled up on his side in the fetal position, squeezing his eyes shut in the dim light. A slight sound made his eyes pop open. He searched the room, but seeing nothing closed his eyes again. A hand slid over his mouth, muffling his scream.

Sean raised a finger to his own lips in the universal sign of silence. He held up a white piece of paper with the word HELP written in black ink for the boy to see and pointed to himself.

The boy nodded.

Sean slowly removed his hand to see if the boy would scream. They stared into each other's eyes. With slight pressure Sean guided the child to get out of bed and follow him. They both silently crept across the room, until the boy bumped into the dresser and a figurine fell over. Out in the hall the woman heard the sound and rushed to the room. She flipped on the overhead light to see the boy sitting on the bed where she'd left him. His eyes were big as he waited to see what she'd do.

She looked across the room and saw the figurine on its side. She walked over to it and set it upright. Glaring a warning to the boy, she left the room again.

***

The next day Randy tapped on a hotel door. The four men were wearing basic Marine Corp uniforms. The door opened and a maid stepped aside to let them in. In the luxury hotel-suite were an elegant couple and the little boy. He hopped off his father's lap and trotted over to Sean. Sean knelt down to get a hug from the little guy. Senator Stone and his wife both rose to their feet to greet Randy, Sean, Dan, and Craig.

Senator Stone approached the team with hand extended. "Thank you for coming."

Sean shook his hand saying, "You're welcome sir." Each of the other three silently stepped forward to shake his hand.

The mother stood with her hand on her son's shoulder… tears sliding down her cheeks. "Thank you for rescuing our son. I… we…" She faltered as she choked down the sob welling up in her throat.

"We don't know how to thank you," the senator finished for his wife.

"You're welcome. It was our pleasure," Randy assured the distraught couple.

"If you ever need anything, let me know," Stone added.

Mrs. Stone nodded in agreement gratefully. The boy watched all of this in wonder, being at that age when the outside world was beginning to creep into his thoughts. His safe little bubble had been forever burst.

Later, as they stepped from the elevator into the lobby, Sean held the door for a small Costa Rican family.

"Gracias," the man said.

In Spanish, Sean responded, "No problem, at your service. Have a good day."

"Are you a policeman?" one of the children asked.

"No son, I'm a soldier from America," Sean replied.

When the door slid shut Craig turned to Sean. "I didn't know you spoke Spanish so well. Where'd ya learn it?"

Sean gave a lopsided smile, "I was raised on a farm with migrant workers. I learned pretty young... especially when I had a crush on a pretty little senorita."

CHAPTER TWO

Sean, Randy, Craig, and Dan were at yet another bar. The music was blaring hip-hop. The crowd was a mix in their twenties and thirties. It was five years later, and the guys looked a little more serious and mature.

Dan raised his beer for a toast. "To our future!"

"The future!" They repeated in unison. They tapped the bottle necks and took a swig.

Sean tilted his bottle towards Dan and Randy. "So when do you start with the Secret Service?"

"Next month," Randy answered. "We'll go through training together."

Dan added, "Thanks to Senator Stone we'll be assigned to the presidential team within the year."

Randy turned to Craig and asked, "How about you Craig?"

Craig looked inside his beer bottle as though the answer could be there. They waited patiently. "I'm going to move to Costa Rica," he answered finally.

Sean nodded, indicating he already knew this.

"Really?" Randy asked in surprise. "What made you decide to do that?"

"What will you do for work?" Dan asked.

Craig shrugged. "Not sure yet. My first job is to go with a tour guide I met while we were down there. She's got a celebrity who wants extra protection during his tour."

Randy laughed. "A bodyguard? That's genius, you'll be so good at that."

"Yeah, he'll be so paranoid he'll suspect everybody," Sean said with a laugh.

"How about you Sean?" Randy looked at Sean. "Still planning on joining the Sac PD?"

Sean nodded and took a drink.

Just then a man grabbed a woman roughly by the arm and yanked her to her feet. "You're coming home with me… now!" He barked at her. Red veins stood out on his forehead as he glared menacingly at the struggling woman.

"Get your hands off me!" she hissed in embarrassment. "It's over. Leave me alone."

Randy, Craig, and Dan swiveled their attention to Sean. A woman in distress. Sean stood so fast his chair toppled over backwards drawing the attention of the brute.

"Let 'er go," Sean growled as he approached the pair.

Brute turned on Sean as he put the still struggling woman behind him. "Back off, Jarhead," was the last thing he said before Sean's fist slammed into his chest. Brute staggered backwards gasping for breath, but he released the lady to her protective friends.

Randy laid a hand on Sean's arm. "Good shot buddy. Time to go."

Dan and Craig faced off with the wheezing man as Sean and Randy headed for the exit.

***

Sean entered the empty classroom at the academy and took a seat. Thirty minutes later the room was packed with people taking the Sacramento Police exam. He was one of the few who looked calm, relaxed. In his mid-twenties, he had the experience to stay focused. He finished and flipped his test over. He was the first one done.

Later that afternoon Sean raced across the blacktop and hit the wall at a full run. He scrambled over it and ran to the next obstacle. An hour later he was on a run… in the lead. Later, applicants watched Sean enviously as he scurried across a rocky path and tackled a dummy. After dragging a different dummy away from a car, Sean leaped over the finish-line. He was first overall.

Sean stood at the sidelines sweating and cheering his fellow applicants. A training officer stood watching Sean carefully. He approached Sean.

"You've got the best time so far," the officer commented.

"Yes sir," Sean responded without pride.

***

The police academy turned out to be exactly what Sean had hoped for. He wanted the challenge. Something intense enough to occupy his racing mind. His dad had told him it would get better with age. Sean hoped so. He was getting tired of the testosterone spikes.

An academy instructor stepped to Sean's side as they both observed the last group working the obstacle course. The trainer glanced at Sean, soaked in sweat, and back to the cadets doing burpies.

"Well, let's see how you do on the gun range tomorrow."

Sean answered, "Yes sir. I plan to be the best." Still not prideful, but confident.

A smile tugged at the trainer's mouth. He nodded and walked away.

The next day the cadets were lined up at the firing range bench. They had their ear protection gear on, but the noise was still deafening. Sean was ready to start. He waited patiently for the amateurs to get ready. Then it was his turn to fire. He emptied his magazine into a bulls-eye pattern. He dropped the spent magazine on the shelf, lay down the gun and stepped back.

The trainer watched him intently… looking for any arrogance that should be squelched.

Later, in the cafeteria, Sean finished his tray-lunch and stood stretching his arms above his head. The test results should be in by now. He ambled across the parking lot and entered the classroom. He stood in front of a wall with a sheet of paper taped to it. With his finger he slid down to Sean McGee. His score for class, physical, and firing range was number one. Sean gave a little smile as he thought of his Recon buddies. They would've given him a bad time for his *low* scores.

Another cadet stepped next to Sean and scanned the list. He paused at Sean's name and continued to his own name. Sean stepped to the side and mingled easily with the other cadets.

Sam, a wiry Filipino guy, singled out Sean. "Number one so far. How'd you learn to shoot like that?" His shoulders were squared off, chest out.

Sean answered quietly, "Marines... Recon. How about you? You're a great shot."

Sam relaxed his stiff shoulders at this reciprocal compliment. "My dad was in the military and we were all raised around guns. I've been shooting since I was a kid."

"My dad took me hunting when I was a kid, but that was mostly rifles..." Sean tipped his head towards the scores. "I see you're in second."

Sam grinned as he answered, "Not for long, buddy, not for long. Let's see how you do on EVOC."

"Yeah, that's not my strength," Sean laughed. "I was raised on a farm. Give me a tractor and I'm good."

A sign stating EMERGENCY VEHICLE OPERATIONS COURSE (EVOC) with an arrow pointed the cadets to the vehicle training course. Sean walked along with the group, filing into a viewing area.

Sam was the first one up. He gripped the steering wheel as he stomped the gas, pulling the car out of a spin. His lips were compressed in concentration. Sean stood amongst his fellow cadets watching the cop car squealing around the track. Sam was very good.

The trainer glanced between Sean and Sam. Sean caught his eye and smiled.

Sam skidded to a stop and jumped out of the car. After receiving his time, he jogged over to Sean.

Sam looked stoked as he nudged Sean. "You're next buddy. Good luck."

"Thanks, any tips for me?" Sean asked the dynamo bouncing at his side.

"Drive fast," he laughed as he clapped Sean on the back.

Sean walked away muttering to himself, "Drive fast, just drive fast huh?" Sean drove fast, but he wasn't first.

Afterward he stood stoically on the tarmac watching each cadet. When they made a mistake his eyes would narrow, when they'd pull out of a spin he nodded. His attention didn't waver for a second. Then it was his turn again. He improved his time by not losing control on the treacherous third corner.

Sean went back to the scoreboard. His finger slid down to McGee. He was still first overall.

Sam walked up behind Sean and blew on the back of Sean's neck.

Sean spun around with brows raised.

"That's me breathing down your neck," Sam said with a cocky grin.

Pretending to dust off Sam's shirt, Sean asked innocently, "Is that dust?"

"Hah! You haven't left me in the dust yet," Sam warned with a laugh.

Sean grinned. He liked Sam. He was a straight forward competitor. "It's a matter of time Sam."

***

Sean entered the sergeant's office. Standing at attention, he waited for the sergeant to finish what he was writing. The sergeant laid down his pen, took off his reading glasses, and leaned back in his chair. "Top gun, top of class, top physical, fifth on EVOC... top choice for placement."

"Thank you sir. I'd like to be here, in Downtown Sac, when there's an opening, sir," Sean asked politely.

The sergeant drummed his fingers on his desk for a moment. "We've got a couple of openings right now, but not Downtown. I'd like you to consider Midtown. I think it would be a good fit."

Sean relaxed his straight-forward gaze to glance at the sergeant. "Yes sir, I'm looking forward to it."

Leaning forward in his chair, the sergeant put his readers back on. Peering at Sean over the top of them he said, "Dismissed."

***

Sean was in the passenger seat of a SPD unit. His partner, Warrick was driving. Warrick was a tall broad-shouldered black man in his fifties. "Watch that little white car up there." Warrick pointed to the weaving car.

"Drunk?" Sean asked, as he watched the driver overcorrect back into his lane and almost hit a parked car.

Warrick shrugged slightly, "Dunno yet. Let's pull him over and see. Maybe he or she is on a cell phone... or high on something else."

"But the weaving is consistently going left and overcorrecting to the right. Looks drunk to me," Sean commented.

Warrick grinned in the dark interior, as he flipped the patrol lights on. "Okay rookie, let's check it out."

Sean watched Warrick administer the sobriety test moments later. Warrick was polite and soft spoken to the intoxicated driver. Sean nodded to himself and smiled slightly. He was impressed with Warrick. *The guy is a pro*, he thought as he watched Warrick lead the driver to the patrol car and gently tuck him into the back seat.

"That was well done," Sean said over the top of the car.

"Yeah? Why do you say that?" he asked.

"You were kind and calm. It showed me that it doesn't need to be done the hard way."

Warrick smiled wryly. "Usually... but sometimes that's the only way. I always try the nice way first." He started to duck into the car and came back up again. "Don't ever forget that you are here to take care of people and keep them safe."

Sean nodded and slid into the car. As they pulled out of the county jail parking lot, a call came in for a domestic fight. The address was around the corner, so within seconds they were parked out front of the four-plex. A chair flying through the window sent a shower of glass across the sidewalk. This was followed by a teen leaping out through the jagged frame.

"Bomb!" screamed the terrified boy.

Warrick and Sean stopped in their tracks.

"Is there anyone else in there?" Warrick demanded.

The boy nodded. "My big brother... he made it—the bomb."

Five minutes later, with the big brother in handcuffs in the back seat of the police car, they stood in the house looking at the jumble of wires and what looked like clay.

"How much time do we have?" asked another rookie as he looked over Sean's shoulder.

His training officer rolled her eyes and shook her head. "Get out front, and wait for the bomb squad. Or better yet, help Warrick make sure the apartments are cleared." As the young man trotted out the door, Officer Callen continued, "What do they teach them in the academy these days? They act like they got their training from the movies... What does he think?... the bomb's going to have a digital clock counting backwards?"

"Well there's no point in us getting blown up," Sean commented as he indicated the door. "Let the pros do it. We've got the area cleared."

"Yeah," Callen agreed as they trotted out the front door. They'd reached the bottom step when it detonated.

A short bark of noise hit Sean and then it seemed as though he was flying through silence, as the percussion lifted him and flung him across the hood of the patrol car. A warbled sound combined with the most intense dizziness he'd ever felt. It took three tries to get up to standing. Callen was already on her feet looking at the smoldering building. The front of the apartment was blown away exposing the destruction within.

Sean caught the smile on the bomber's face, and lost his temper. Yanking the scrawny guy out of the unit, he raised him up in the air, feet dangling. Before he could plant his fist in the guy's face, Warrick was there.

"Stop! Don't do it." Warrick's voice sounded as though it were coming from a great distance. He put a giant hand over Sean's fist. "He's not worth it. This is your adrenaline talking."

The kid's smirk had turned to terror.

"Put him down," Warrick ordered.

A couple of seconds ticked by, and then Sean abruptly let go. The guy crumpled to the ground. Warrick blocked Callen from getting at the pile of cowering humanity.

"Back off you two!" Warrick barked.

A medic cautiously approached Sean, only to be swatted away. "But sir, you're ear is bleeding."

Sean reached up and touched his ear. He drew away a finger covered with blood.

CHAPTER THREE

A year later, Sean stood talking to Warrick and Sam in the briefing room. Captain Grant came up to them.

"McGee, I've assigned you a trainee," the captain informed him in his usual abrupt way.

Sean and Warrick threw a quick glance at each other before Sean responded, "Thank you, Captain. To what do I owe this honor?"

"You seem to have a level head on your shoulders and you're a natural mentor. Usually I wait a little longer, but your past experience sped things up a bit," the captain answered as a female officer stepped up to the trio. She was tall, blonde and muscular. Her hair was pulled back in a ponytail. The captain turned towards her. "This is Kim Stevens," Grant said as he turned toward her. "Kim, this is Sean McGee. He'll be your training officer."

Sean and Kim shook hands.

"Well, Kim... let's get to work," Sean suggested with a lopsided grin. Sean paused and called out to the retreating captain. "Hey Cap, which unit do I take?"

"Ask Jones in the garage," Grant answered over his shoulder. The captain had another rookie to place.

An hour later Sean slowly cruised down Capital Avenue in a black SUV, past an immensely popular grouping of restaurants, pubs, wine bars, and bakeries. The Mexican restaurant on the corner of Capital and 18th Street dominated the scene. Hundreds of people milled about on the sidewalks. It was a typical warm Sacramento summer night. Sean nodded to the crowd, "Booze, men, and women spells trouble."

"Since the beginning of time," Kim answered cynically. "Check that out. See those two men? They just exchanged money and now the woman is on the other guys arm."

The thirty-something white male stepped up to the valet podium and handed the valet his ticket. The couple, white female—black male, sauntered down the street. She was pressing herself against his arm and looking up into his face.

"Good eye," Sean complimented. They circled around the block and drove up as the valet brought the first man's car around, a Mercedes. Kim held her phone up, hoping to get a frontal of the guys face, but he didn't turn toward them. Sean followed the car.

"Aren't you going to follow the buyer?" Kim asked in surprise.

"Nope, there's a million of them. I want the pimp. This isn't the first time I've seen this guy. He's dealing high-end sex slaves and I'm itching to take him down." Sean glanced at Kim. "Did you get a facial recognition on him?"

Kim shook her head no as she stared out the window at the Mercedes. "Don't you think it's bizarre that Sacramento has one of the largest sex slave markets in the United States?"

"Yes and no. Sac is also one of the most ethnically diverse cities in the U.S. Every nationality on Earth is here."

"So? What's that got to do with anything?" Kim asked as she entered the license in the system.

Sean shrugged. "I just think when you blend that many ideologies, things can get pretty muddied. Anything goes."

"Car belongs to Filip Var... var... inski. –Varvarinski." Kim struggled with the pronunciation. "Is that Russian?"

"Don't know... could be. Maybe it's Polish or Ukranian." They followed the car to the city limits.

Later at the office, Kim was at one computer and Sean at another. They worked in silence.

Warrick came in and sat by Sean. "What's up?"

Sean leaned back from the computer. "Nothing. Slow night... Ran into that dirt-bag pimp again tonight... got his plates."

Warrick swished the mouse of his computer to wake it up as he asked, "Which dirt-bag pimp?"

Sean turned toward his mentor. "That clean-cut white dude with the European look. The car's registered to Varvarinski."

Warrick taps the desk rhythmically with his long fingers. "Why does that sound familiar?"

"There's no hit on N-C-I-C," Sean commented.

"That CIA guy is here today. He's in Grant's office right now. You should see if you can get a word with him now that we have a possible name."

Sean turned back to his screen and continued typing. "Let me finish this report real quick." They all typed in silence for twenty minutes before Sean rolled back his chair and told Kim he'd see her tomorrow.

Sean stood in the hall… he could see Captain Grant through the glass window of the office door. A CIA agent was seated across from him. The agent was leaning back in his chair with legs crossed, European style.

The captain spotted Sean and waved him in. "What's up McGee?"

Sean entered and waved a hand toward the CIA agent. "Actually I was hoping to be able to speak to this agent."

Agent Becker stood up and faced Sean in a smooth movement. He was an average height man in his late fifties, early sixties. Reaching out a hand to Sean he introduced himself in a deep raspy voice, "Becker… what can I do for you?"

"McGee." Sean gripped his hand in a firm handshake. "I've been coming across the same pimp for awhile now, but tonight I may have gotten a lead. The Mercedes he was driving is registered to a Filip Varvarinksi. Do you know that name?"

Becker indicated the other office chair and answered as Sean sat down, "Russian. It's a grandpa who lives in Rancho Cordova. Lots of these cars are registered to him. He lets family and friends… *borrow* them."

Sean grunted, "So it's another dead-end?"

"Yes and no. Would you recognize him in a photo gallery?" Becker asked.

"I think so."

"Good, come by the agency tomorrow around… what time do you start?"

"Six."

"Come around five o'clock. Ask for me. I'll get you set up. Should only take about thirty minutes," Becker said.

Sean stood to shake his hand before leaving.

***

Sean entered the CIA office the next morning. He was disappointed with how mundane and dated the building looked. After passing through what Sean assumed was an x-ray scan, he was led to the elevators and told to get off on the second floor. Standing, Becker approached Sean from across a large room full of computers and agents.

"McGee… glad you could make it. Pantell will help you get started," Becker said, indicating a middle-aged barrel-chested man. "Pantell, this is Sean McGee, Sac PD. Can you get him going on a search for a pimp he's been trying to hunt down?"

Pantell stood to shake Sean's hand. He indicated a seat in front of a computer screen, saying, "Have a seat. I'll log you in." They sat down next to each other. Pantell typed rapidly on Sean's keyboard. "Narrow your search using key descriptors like; tall, light skin, tattoo. Here's a list to choose from," he said as he toggled down.

"Just click these buttons?"

Pantell nodded.

"That's easy," Sean said, moving the mouse and clicking. The screen showed an increasingly narrow search. He stopped and looked to Pantell.

Pantell glanced over, "Now click *show*."

Sean clicked the button and the screen filled with similar faces.

"Have fun," Pantell grinned and went back to work on his own computer.

The screen lit up Sean's face as his eyes searched for his suspect. His expression showed recognition. The screen was filled with a photo of the pimp Sean and Kim had seen yesterday. "This is him."

Pantell whistled, "Are you sure?"

Sean glanced at Pantell and nodded.

"Well, you're either one lucky, or unlucky S.O.B. That's one slippery dude right there," Pantell commented with a shake of his head.

Sean read out loud, "Boris Petrov, Mordovia-Russia... hmm... associated with the AP-13. Heads up a gang called SL02."

"Let me know if you corner that rat," Pantell requested. "We want a piece of him too."

"Is he a boss?"

"Yes, but not the *pakhan*. He's probably just an enforcer, which is powerful enough to run a prostitution ring for a pakhan."

"Do you know who the pakhan is?" Sean asked.

"No way," Pantell answered. "They have a complex system protecting their identity. If you I-D'ed a pakhan it would be the last thing you saw."

Sean nodded as he wrote the name down and then slid his chair back. "I gotta get to work. Thanks for helping me."

Pantell stood and shook Sean's hand again. He watched Sean leave with a thoughtful expression on his rugged face.

***

Sean and Kim walked across the strip-mall parking lot to their unit. "You went to the CIA station? That's cool,"

Kim commented as they walked. She had one hand pulling at the neck of her bullet-proof vest, trying to get some air to her suffocating skin.

"I admit it *was* pretty cool," Sean grinned sideways at her. "I've always had a secret fascination with CIA and FBI."

Kim laughed. "I won't tell anyone." The radio on their belts chirped simultaneously.

"Dispatch 9-1-1 hang up cellular. Closest locator is 26th and Victorian Alley. Unable to verify emergency," the radio squawked. They hopped in the SUV. Kim radioed dispatch. "Unit 528 responding. Current location Broadway and 25th."

Sean punched it out of the parking lot and headed towards the call. They turned east on X Street.

Kim asked Sean, "Where's Victorian Alley?"

"First alley south of V Street," Sean explained. "T Street -- Tomato Alley, U Street -- Uptown Alley, V Street -- Victorian."

"Oh! I didn't know that," Kim sounded surprised.

"Neither did I. Warrick taught me." They drove the rest of the way in silence. As they coasted down the quiet alley, they looked curiously at the lack of activity. A few cars were parked along an adjacent street in front of a couple of two-story apartments. They sat for a moment with the engine running in the fading sunlight contemplating the quiet scene.

"Well, let's check it out." Sean put the SUV in park.

Kim unfastened her seatbelt as she commented, "Got nothing better to do."

Sean stepped out and scanned the nearby homes. His gaze was razor sharp and piercing. He pointed to the closest door. "What've we got here?"

A woman was frantically, yet silently, waving them over to her front door.

Sean and Kim glanced at each other before they walked across the lawn to see what the lady wanted.

She pointed into her living room and whispered harshly, "She's in here!"

"Who?" Sean asked as he stepped to the door and peered in. A teenage female was laying in a pool of blood on the floor. She lifted her head and feebly answered, "He's killing my mom... her boyfriend... he's killing her. My little brother and sister are still up there." She pointed up at the ceiling.

"He's got a gun," the woman warned them as tears of terror streamed down her cheeks.

Sean nodded. He'd already noted the girl's jeans were riddled with bullet holes.

As Kim stepped out front to look up at the second floor windows, she held her radio to her mouth, "We need an ambulance here. Multiple GSW's, vic is a teen female." Framed in the window was a terrified face. Kim barely had time to catch the little seven-year old girl who leaped out the window into her arms, almost knocking her down. A younger boy poked his head out the window and shouted, "He's killen' her!"

Kim ordered in a low voice, "Jump!" The little boy glanced back over his shoulder into the interior. With a terrified scream he leaped out the window. Kim had to change her position to catch this second child.

Sean went down on one knee holding the little girl's shoulders. "Who else is up there?"

Her eyes were round and her lips quivered, but she managed to answer, "My mom and him."

Kim ushered the children into the relative safety of the lower duplex and told the woman to tie a towel or pillow case around the teen's upper thighs. She turned to follow Sean, but Sean had already disappeared through the open front door leading up a flight of stairs.

Sean glanced back at Kim and continued up the stairs, gun drawn. Finger next to the trigger. He stopped before he could see over the top of the highest step to the landing. Slowly he raised his baton above the rim and lowered it. Nothing. A slight scuffing sound of a shoe could be heard from the back of the house. Sean peeked over the top step to see a woman prostrate three feet away. He slithered to her side and felt for a pulse without looking at her. His eyes were scanning the hallway, counting doors. Laying sideways against the wall of the living room, Sean looked down his abdomen at Kim. With hand signals he told her there was an open space in front of him and three doors down the hall.

Pointing, Kim indicated she would clear the common space.

He folded around the corner to look into the living room. It was empty. Sean scurried down the hall.

Kim shouted, "Police! You're surrounded. Put your weapon down and step out into the hall with your hands above your head!" Silence.

Sean shouted as he passed the empty front room, "Clear!" He stopped at the first room, gun alongside his face. He looked eerily calm compared to Kim. He entered the room swiftly, ready to kill or be killed. "Clear one!" Sean entered the next room in the same manner. "Clear two!"

Kim's voice could be heard at the other end of the home, "Clear kitchen!" She entered the hallway in time to see Sean disappear into the last room. When she followed him into the room, gun panning the perimeter, Sean was halfway out the open window.

"I'm going after him. Call for back-up," he ordered.

"I already did."

Sean reached sideways and grabbed the nearby drain pipe and shimmied down. Kim looked to the school yard beyond the house and spotted an adult male dart behind a building. Sean was already at a dead run in that direction. Sirens drew closer. Kim pulled back in the window and ran down the stairs to the group below. They were huddled together in the puddle of blood from the teen. Kim ran around the building in the direction of Sean.

Darkness had settled around the school ground. Lights were warming up and spreading weak circles. Sean stood against a school wall. All was quiet except a dog barking in the distance. Kim approached from the house. She pointed to where she saw the guy run. Sean turned on his heel and ran the opposite direction around the school room. He signaled for Kim to go to the spot he'd just vacated.

Kim approached silently and picked up some gravel. Waiting a minute, she flicked the gravel to create a diversion.

Distracted by the clatter, the killer leveled his gun at the area the gravel had landed. Sean shimmied along the wall to the corner. He was just steps away from the killer. After a second to focus his energy for the coming battle, Sean leaped toward the man as he spun around. Sean tackled him.

Kim ran up, aiming her gun at the man's head. In one expert move Sean rolled the guy and snatched his gun away. After shoving it several feet away, Sean handcuffed him while reading him his Miranda rights. "You have the right to remain silent. Anything you say can…" The guy tried to get away from Sean. He regained control by putting a knee in the guys back. "and will be used against you in a court of law. You have the right to an attorney. If you cannot afford an attorney, one will be provided for you."

***

In a local 24-7 coffee shop, Warrick, Kim, Sam, and Sean stood around a couple of barstool-height tables. They were weighted down with their usual twenty-five or thirty pounds of police gear.

"How 'bout you? You have kids?" Kim asked Warrick, as she swirled her chai tea latte.

Warrick nodded as he answered, "I have one daughter, nine years-old. She's a hand-full, that one. All she can think about is sports. Matter-of-fact that's her nickname, Sport. Drives my wife crazy."

"Why?" Kim asked. It seemed to her that sports would be a good thing.

"Sadayo wants her to focus on academics. Sport wants to play softball and do martial arts."

Sam asked, "Sadayo? Isn't that Japanese?"

"It is," Warrick answered. "Met her while in Japan back in my Air Force days."

They all sipped their various coffee concoctions while watching a group of rowdy young guys sporting the *gangsta* look. Their pants were down below their butts. As they walked out of the shop they tried to strut manfully while keeping their pants up. Sean smiled as he

remarked, "I used to hate that style, but now I love it."
All four turned to look at Sean with surprise.

"Why do you like it now?" Sam asked.

"Can't run... easier to catch." Sean responded with a chuckle.

"True, but watch 'em when they go down. That's when they shoot. From the ground," Warrick commented dryly. This was met with silence while they watched the guys saunter down the street. "I heard you were thinking about becoming a CIA agent?" he asked Sean.

Sam swiveled his head abruptly to Sean with a look of disgust on his face. "A Spook? Why the hell would you do that?"

"I haven't committed yet... just thinking about it," Sean answered casually.

"A lot," Kim commented.

Sean gave her a warning look, but she just raised a brow, as she stared back at him.

"But why you wanna get off the streets that fast?" Sam asked, clearly confused. Everyone knew that Sean was an intensely dedicated cop.

Sean sighed abruptly, "Look -- I started off as Recon. My first mission was Costa Rica. And now I'm feeling the city limits. This Boris Petrov is running a sex trafficking business in my town. If I get close, he'll just disappear and someone else from his..." Sean made quote marks in the air, "family... will take over. I want the whole operation." Sean shoved away from the table, stabbing the air emphatically. "Bastards are selling those little girls!" Sean took a deep calming breath. "If I'm a Spook, I can work internationally."

Warrick gave a slight smile at Sean's enthusiasm.

Sam shook his head in disappointment.

Kim turned up the dial to the radio and listened through her ear-buds. Without a word they all headed out the door.

The radio in the SUV chirped as Sean started the engine. "We have what appears to be a 926 lying in the bushes at Fremont Park, east side. Unknown circumstances." Sean waved goodbye to Warrick and Sam as he turned the unit in the opposite direction. Kim and Sean drove silently along the dark, quiet streets. It was about four in the morning. As they turned left on 15th St., they could see a black male in his thirties standing on the sidewalk with a cell phone in his hand. He was wearing jogging attire and had a forehead flashlight. He turned toward the police car, his light flashing at the cop car windshield. The guy reached up and turned it off as the unit rolled up next to him.

Sean and Kim stepped out simultaneously and approached the jogger. He was clearly upset and rattled as he stood there shifting from foot to foot.

"Thank God you're here! She's dead," his voice quivered. "I tripped over her." He pointed to the park.

"Can you show us?" Sean asked in a calm cop-voice.

Nodding the man turned on his light and led them into the park. Their flashlight beams swept weirdly through the shrubs and trees as they followed the jogger. The jogger's forehead light riveted to a prone body in the path and then whipped up to Sean's face and back again to the body. "See? She's dead."

Kim squatted down and checked for a pulse. She looked up quickly. "Gotta a pulse here... weak." Kim rolled the victim on her back as the ambulance sirens grew louder. Kim sucked in her breath through her teeth,

"Wow! She sure took a beating!" The Caucasian female's face was beaten beyond recognition. She wore a skimpy spandex dress. One high-heeled shoe was missing. No identification.

The girl's eyelids fluttered and her mouth moved. "Help..." she whispered. Her head lolled to the side as she lost consciousness again. Kim's fingers went back to her throat to check her pulse.

Sean circled the scene taking hundreds of photos. "I'll lead the E-M-Ts in," he said as he turned away and headed back to the car."

"Can I leave?" the jogger asked.

"Nope," Kim answered without looking up. "I need to talk to you. Stick around."

He looked nervous and anxious to leave. He stayed.

Sean and the medics came trotting through the park with a gurney and medic bag. They swarmed the victim.

Kim, Sean, and the jogger stood to one side observing for a moment. Sean motioned to be followed. Kim fell into step behind Jogger. They stopped beside the cop car with its flashing lights.

Sean turned to the car and said, "Lights off." The lights stopped flashing.

Kim turned to Jogger, "So can you tell us what happened?"

As the jogger answered his eyes kept going back to park. "I was just doing my normal run. I always cut through this park... I tripped over something." He waved his arms around as he spoke. "I think it was her foot maybe. Anyway I looked down and like, you know, she was like laying there. I ran away, but then turned around and came back."

Kim looked up from her notepad. "Why'd you run away?"

He gave a harsh laugh. "Because it scared the shit out of me! But I realized she, like, might not be dead, so I came back. I didn't feel no pulse."

Sean interrupted, "Did you touch her? Other than tripping?"

The man frowned as he glanced at Sean. "Yeah, like I told this lady... I took her pulse." His gaze swiveled back to Kim. "I guess I don't really know how. I shoulda rolled her over."

Sean could tell the guy was more comfortable with Kim, but he needed to do his job. "Hold your hands out for me... please. I need to take a photo." The jogger mutely held out his bloody hands. After Sean took the photo with the police cell phone, he aimed it at the guy's face and took another photo. Sean typed the data into an app. The guys face appeared and a note ran across the screen, *Searching for match*. Sean turned his attention back to the curious jogger, "Turn your hands over."

He complied silently. Sean snapped more photos. He zoomed in on the man's shirt and down to his knees which were dirty.

"I'm going to need a saliva sample sir," Kim told him, as she held out a q-tip in a container. "Open up."

Jogger shook his head and backed up a step. "Why?"

In her most calming voice she answered, "Because we want to rule you out of the DNA samples we will be collecting from her body."

"Oh... okay." He opened his mouth for Kim to take a little swipe of his cheek. "Are you guys like, C-S-I or something?"

"No, we're police officers, but we collect evidence too, so in a way we are. We are investigating a crime scene right?"

The jogger nodded.

Kim continued, "I need your contact info."

Glancing at his cell phone, Sean said, "No record."

***

Sean stood in the hall next to the nurse's station. He could see Tasha's profile. She was laying on a hospital bed with crisp white sheets across her body. A nurse busily checked monitors and unnecessarily smoothed the sheets before leaving.

As she walked out Sean stopped her. "Is she conscious yet?" The nurse glanced at his badge and nodded before continuing down the hall. Sean stood in her doorway for a moment gazing at the black and blue, swollen face surrounded by pristine white bedding. Stepping to her side, he pulled up a chair. The sound startled her awake. Turning her head she saw Sean in his uniform and shrank back into the bed in fear.

"Hello," Sean greeted her gently as he sat down. "My name is Sean McGee. I was the officer who found you in the park. Can you tell me what happened?" She shook her head. "No, because you don't remember, or are you scared?"

No answer.

"What's your name?"

Tasha whispered, "Please leave me alone."

Sean stood slowly and turned away from her bed, then he stopped and turned back. "If you change your mind call me. Any time, okay?"

Tasha nodded silently and accepted the business card he handed her.

***

Sean and Kim leaned against the patrol car watching the crowd meander past as they exited a Kings' basketball game. Sean nudged Kim and pointed to a man walking towards them. "That's our pimp, Boris Petrov."

Boris continued to approach Sean and Kim. He stopped directly in front of them. Sean didn't move.

"I hear you are asking questions about me?" Boris asked with a slight Russian accent. "Making me sound like a bad guy." With his chin up slightly, hands spread out, "Well, here I am. Ask me whatever you want. I am no criminal."

Sean raised a brow. "That's not what Mother Russia says."

"In Russia I was bad... a criminal. But here, I am an American citizen. I work at a car dealership -- you can ask," Boris replied.

Sean allowed a ghost of a smile to show, "I'm not concerned about your day job Boris. I want to know what you do at night. I know you are a pimp."

Again Boris raised his hands. "You have the wrong man."

"I saw you last week exchange a woman for money. Right at the corner of Eighteenth and Capital."

Boris looked astonished. "With my cousin Tetyana? I set her up on a date with a buddy from work."

"Why the money?" Sean interrogated.

"He forgot his wallet the other day and I bought his lunch. He was paying me back. Is that a crime? No, I don't think so." Boris shrugged and started to turn away.

"I'm watching you," Sean assured him.

Boris turned back. "Oh yes, now I'm frightened," he responded sarcastically and spun off, disappearing in the crowd.

He and Kim glanced at each other. Sean shrugged, as he said, "I really scared him, huh?"

Kim laughed.

At the end of shift, they stood talking to a couple of the day-shift officers coming on. An office clerk stepped into the room and told Sean that the captain wanted to see him.

Sean knuckle-bumped Kim, "See ya tomorrow." He stepped into the doorway of the Captain Grant's office. "What's up Cap? You wanted to talk to me?"

The Captain looked up from the pile of paperwork strewn across his desk. He looked irritated. "I just got a complaint that you are harassing a guy…" He glanced at a piece of paper and read, "Boris Petrov. Care to explain yourself?"

Sean sat down. "He's the suspect I found over at the CIA headquarters. I wouldn't be surprised if he was the one who beat our vic from yesterday, Tasha Antipova."

Captain Grant raised his eyebrows and asked, "So you interrogate him on the sidewalk?"

Sean shook his head with a slight laugh. "He approached me. I didn't even leave my perch on the unit's hood."

"Yeah, well he lives in Rancho, so let their PD know what you've got so far."

"Yes, sir. Is that all?"

The captain leaned back in his swivel chair and looked at Sean over the top of his reading glasses. "Captain Becker was in here yesterday asking about you. He seems to think you're interested in becoming a Spook."

"What gave him that idea?" Sean asked.

Grant leveled a stare at Sean as he answered, "You searched jobs on the CIA website."

Sean raised both brows in surprise. "Oh..." They eyed each other in silence for a moment.

"I think you're overqualified myself," Captain Grant finally commented. "You are fast and fearless... I think that's a little overkill for the CIA. It's mostly investigative."

Sean had the grace to squirm in his seat before he answered, "You're right. I'd probably be bored... but, well, I find myself wanting to follow things to completion. It's driving me crazy that this sex slave industry in Sacramento isn't even run by Americans. They act like they're off limits! And for me as Sac P-D, it *is* off limits."

The captain sat contemplating Sean for a moment. "How's the vic from the park doing?"

"Tasha? She's recovering slowly. I've asked the doctor to keep her there as long as possible, otherwise she'll be back on the streets the second they let her out."

"Boris deals in high end prostitution. He's not going to have much use for her until she looks pretty again," Grant commented.

"I think he's responsible for this," Sean responded. "Boris'll finish the job when she steps out on that sidewalk."

The Captain nodded his head in agreement. "By-the-way, *if* you decide to do this CIA thing, don't tell a soul, or they won't be able to put you undercover. You'll need to come up with a front, but they'll walk you through it."

***

Boris sat in an easy chair looking at his phone. A polite tapping at the door preceded his secretary's entrance. "Sir, your man is here."

Boris barely tipped his head to indicate he wanted the man shown in.

A slender male with a tightly trimmed goatee and slicked back brown hair stepped into the room. After an assessing glance around the office, he stepped up to take Boris' outstretched hand. Without a word they sat facing each other in the leather chairs.

"I need you to do a job for me," Boris told him in Russian.

"Okay, yes... my fee is the same," the assassin stated calmly.

Boris nodded curtly. "It's a double-job." He handed the man a file.

"Then it's a double fee," he replied laconically as he flipped open the file. After a quick glance, he looked up at Boris. "For a police officer it's twice my usual fee."

"Understood," Boris answered simply.

***

Sean and Kim cruised through the quiet neighborhoods at the outskirts of Midtown Sacramento. Kim was driving. The lights from the dashboard lit up her face. They were silent, both lost in their own thoughts. As she left the neighborhood Sean pointed to a billboard for a cruise ship.

Sean leaned forward as he looked up at the sign. "Ever been on a cruise ship?" he asked.

"Once, when I was a teen. My parents took my sister and me on a Caribbean cruise.

"Did you like it?"

Kim didn't answer as they both listened to the dispatcher describe a 911. When another unit chirped in that they would respond, she answered, "I liked the Caribbean, but as a teen I was a little bored being stuck on the ship. The islands we stopped at were fun though." Kim glanced at Sean's profile. "How about you?"

"I've never been anywhere on vacation. Scurrying across the jungle floor in fatigues isn't exactly a vacay," Sean answered with a chuckle. "I'd like to go back to Central America." They were silent again, as they watched a couple of teenage boys walking down the sidewalk. "I thought of opening a travel agency."

Kim laughed. "People still use travel agencies?"

"It depends. I'd have one that specialized in off the beaten path trips with things like off-road tours of rivers and stuff." He tried to keep his voice light and casual. "Basically tying all the loose ends together for a seamless vacation. That's hard to do online, but the rest would be online."

Kim asked in disbelief, "You don't want to be a cop?"

"Not forever," Sean lied.

Kim shook her head in silence. They were both scanning the streets. Finally Kim said, "I just can't picture you as anything but a cop."

CHAPTER FOUR

"Sean stood inspecting the over-head menu at the coffee shop. A chunky teenager with jet black hair, of indeterminate gender, waited at the register. Sean watched a car pull up in the mirror behind the teen.

Pantell got out and came in. Sean turned to greet him. "Pantell."

Reaching out to shake Sean's hand, he responded, "McGee."

They both turned back to the bored teen. Sean stepped up to the register. "Iced mocha with whipped cream, extra ice." The kid rang him up and Sean ran his debit.

Pantell took his place as Sean walked away looking for a table. Pantell stood staring at the menu.

The teen prompted, "What can I get for you?

"Cup of coffee... black." He put cash down and walked away to join Sean at a corner table. "So what's up?" he asked as he sat down.

"Just curious about your job."

"Curious huh?" Pantell eyed Sean.

They leaned back as the teen placed their cups in front of them. The kid went back to the register, out of hearing.

Pantell smiled as he crossed his legs American style. "It's boring and the pay sucks, but otherwise it's great. How 'bout yours?"

"It's never boring and the pays good," Sean answered with a grin. They sat there casually looking at each other as they sipped.

"If you're not bored, then why're you asking about my job?"

"I feel held back by the city limits," Sean answered. He drew a line with his fingertip on the table. "I can work crime up to that city limits line."

"My job is right here in Sac. I'm investigative, but more on the research side. I'm not a field officer, though occasionally I get pulled out. I think you would hate my job."

Sean eyed him as he sipped mocha. "If you hate it then why do you do it?"

"I didn't say I hate it... I said *you'd* hate it. I think it's interesting to follow the evidence."

Sean lifted both hands questioningly. "Thought you said it's boring, does that mean the pay doesn't really suck too?"

Pantell laughed and lifted his cup of coffee in a toast. "Touché."

***

The hospital room was well lit, but the open curtain revealed the pitch black sky. Sean sat at Tasha's bedside. Her bruises were grayish green now and the swelling was gone. Several butterfly stitches pulled her cuts together on her forehead and chin. Sean and Tasha were in the middle of a quiet conversation. Kim stood at the door watching the halls.

Tasha picked at her bed sheets. "I have no family here. No friends."

Sean leaned his head forward and peeked up into her eyes. "Why'd you come all the way from the Ukraine to Sacramento if you don't know anyone?"

She looked down at her fidgeting hands.

Sean waited patiently.

Tasha whispered, "I'm stupid. He told me he had friends in California and he showed them a photograph of me and, and he said they wanted me to be a model for them."

Sean leaned forward and put his elbows on his knees. Looking at the floor he asked quietly, "Who told you that?"

Tasha shrugged. "A guy in my town. I've known him forever from a distance. Nobody special."

"Do you know his name?"

"I don't remember… it seems so long ago. My parents were so proud of me—I was going to be a model in America," she ended sadly.

"What's the name of your town?" Sean asked.

Suddenly vehement, Tasha lashed out, "What does it matter? That life is over. Gone! That girl is dead." She closed her eyes and turned her head away.

Sean stood slowly. "Okay Tasha, okay. Let me know if you remember." He looked sadly down at the battered girl, before turning to Kim.

Kim and Sean walked silently across the dark hospital parking lot toward the SUV with 'police' emblazoned across the side. When they reached its side, Kim glanced back at the hospital. A sudden pop of a gun shattered the night. Sean spun towards Kim in time to see her crumple to the ground. A red hole on her forehead and her eyes wide open... staring. Sean dove to the ground and scrambled to her side. After a quick glance at her face, he turned away to scan his surroundings. All was quiet for a moment. Then the hospital doors slammed open and a team of security guards burst out. They stopped as Sean threw up a warning hand. He shouted, "Back! I don't know where the shooter is. Cover me." Sean scurried to the police unit and opening the door, grabbed the radio.

Within minutes sirens were screaming from every direction.

***

The hospital staff wheeled Kim down the hall on a gurney. A sheet was pulled politely over her face. Sean didn't bother following. He just stood there in the hallway with a shocked look on his face. The nurse who attended to Tasha came out of the elevator. Seeing Sean, she came directly up to him.

"Officer McGee." The nurse laid her hand on his arm urgently. "You need to see this."

Sean mutely followed her into the elevator. The scratchy elevator music seemed surreal and intrusive. On the fourth floor Sean followed the nurse to Tasha's room. She stepped to the side. The room was full of doctors and nurses.

Sean could see past the busy staff. Tasha was laying there staring straight ahead... with a bullet hole through her forehead. Everything else went out of focus to Sean.

***

A crowd of uniforms blocked the view of the burial. The sun was brilliant. Several grey umbrellas drooped over the mourners, shielding them from the blazing heat. Sean stood alone. His face was chiseled stone. He stared straight ahead and appeared to be far away in his thoughts... memories of the day before—he'd been wearing street clothes, standing at a freshly dug grave. He had been the only one present at a very different funeral. The cemetery staff had lowered Tasha's narrow coffin into the ground. Sean knelt down next to the gaping hole and bowed his head. After a few seconds he'd made the sign of the cross and placed a fist upon his chest. When he'd stood up he noted a solitary figure in the distance leaning against a tree... watching him. Sean felt a flicker of recognition, but couldn't quite bring it into focus—Sean snapped back to present with a flinch at the sound of a woman crying. His eyes swiveled to Kim's mother as she clutched the folded flag to her heart and crumpled against Kim's father who clutched Kim's badge.

In that moment he knew who the man had been at Tasha's graveside—Boris Petrov. *The only reason he would've been at Tasha's funeral would be if he if he knew her.* Boris. A thirst for revenge coursed through Sean's veins.

***

Warrick and Sam were sitting at the table with Sean. Sam looked pissed, Warrick looked thoughtful. Sean's mouth was lifted in a slight one-sided smile.

"I can't believe you're quitting!" Sam spat.

Sean's smile grew slightly. "Believe it. I'm done."

Sam leaned back in his chair with a huff.

"What'er'ya gonna do now?" Warrick asked. He was intently watching Sean, as though trying to determine what Sean was *really* saying.

Sean met Warrick's eyes steadily. "I'm going to open a travel agency."

"Bullshit!" Sam slapped the table impatiently. "A travel agency? I don't believe you man... I thought I knew you. I thought you were going to do the CIA?"

"Changed my mind... Kim knew about the agency—the *travel* agency. We talked about it. It's something I've always wanted to do. I don't want to be stuck here in Sac Town." Sean shrugged.

Sam stood abruptly, shoving his chair back noisily. "Then go vacation!" Sam stomped out of the room. Several cops turned to watch.

"When's your last day?" Warrick asked calmly.

"Tuesday, after Monday graveyard."

"Where's your new travel agency going to be?" Warrick asked. "I might want to take the missus and my girl on a vacation."

Sean looked at Warrick for a moment. "Thanks Walter. I'm looking at small shops over in the Pavilions on Fair Oaks."

Warrick let out a soft whistle. "That'll cost ya."

"Do you think I'm making a mistake?"

Warrick smiled slightly and shook his head. "You've gotta follow your heart." He paused, "If you want to travel, then do it. I think *working* internationally will be good for you." Warrick winked as he stood up.

***

A subtle sign for "McGee Travel Agency" hung above a glass door nestled in the back corner of the high-end outdoor shopping mall. Two large plate-glass windows flanked the door. The window was barren at the moment. Sean backed up in his 4-Runner to the front parking spot and grabbed a box off the passenger seat. Getting out, he juggled the box as he fitted a key in the glass-door lock. Sean stood inside for a moment looking at the small space. Boxes were stacked everywhere. He passed them and opened an office door. A large desk occupied much of the room.

His phone beeped. Pulling it out of his pocket, he glanced at it and shoved it back in his pocket. After depositing the box on the desk, Sean walked back to the front door and waved at his sister getting out of a car. Sharice waved back as she walked toward him. Sean wrapped her in a bear hug. "Hi Sis. Thanks for helping."

Sharice leaned back and looked up at him with loving eyes. "I'm glad to get away from the boys. Mom's babysitting for me." They walked with arms around each other to the agency door. Standing to one side, Sean dramatically held the door for her.

"Welcome to McGee Travel Agency... where we make your travel dreams come true."

With the stereo tuned to country music they got to work. Sean opened a box and unloaded pamphlets onto a desk. Sharice opened more boxes and removed various travel magazines and pamphlets. Sean put together the magazine rack. She held up a stack of aluminum foil boxes questioningly. Sean pointed to his office. Sharice put posters in floating glass frames. Sean hung them in the window. They both sat with their feet up on the desk and ate pizza. Finally, Sharice unloaded desk paraphernalia onto the front-desk, arranging it.

Sean and Sharice both stood surveying their work. She stretched her arms high above her head and cracked her back with a quick twist.

"You better get home to those little monsters."

She nodded and shouldered her purse. Sean watched her get in her car before turning back to the agency. He locked the door and walked back to the office. Shutting the door behind him, he picked up a box and set it on the desk. He pulled out a large laptop and plugged it into the charger. Next he picked up a staple gun and one of the boxes of foil. Going over to the wall, he set the foil on the floor parallel to the wall. He opened a step ladder next to the foil box. Taking the edges of the foil he pulled it out slowly and climbed onto the ladder. He proceeded to staple the foil to the wall at the juncture of the ceiling.

Sean worked his way around the room, wallpapering it with foil. He finished with the ceiling.

The next day Sean was seated at his desk looking at the laptop screen, one hand on the mouse. One of his cell phones rang. Picking it up, he said, "McGee Travel, how can I help you start your adventure?"

A masculine laugh greeted Sean, "Dude... you sound so serious."

Sean smiled. "Hey Sam, good to hear your voice. I've been thinking about you lately." Sean leaned back in his tilting office chair and put his bare feet on the desk. "I need a running buddy. You still run? Or are you sitting around eating donuts?"

"I'll run you into the ground," Sam claimed. "When do'ya want to meet? You doing anything this afternoon?"

Sean glanced at his laptop. "I can do this afternoon. Want to meet up at the hatchery?"

"Sure... four o'clock good?"

"Yep, see ya there," Sean answered sliding his feet into his flip-flops.

***

Sean sat on the bumper of his 4-Runner in the shade. Sam pulled into the spot next to him in a Corvette. Sean let out a long slow whistle as Sam got out. Walking around the sports car, Sean commented, "Nice wheels."

Sam tried to hold back a grin of pride. He looked like a sixteen-year old with his first car. "I got it from my uncle. He collects cars and this one just needed a new engine. So all I had to do was buy the engine and pay to have it put in. I splurged on the paint job." Sam looked lovingly at the candy-apple red paint.

"You've always been a thrifty SOB." They laughed and shook hands, giving each other a manly shoulder hug.

"You ready old man, or do you need to stretch?" Sam teased.

Sean laughed as they trotted off towards the trail. By the time they ran up a steep dirt trail, thirty minutes later, they were both drenched in sweat and panting. When they reached the top they walked in circles for a couple of minutes before speaking.

Sean grunted, "Good run!"

Sam bent over trying to catch his breath. "Yeah, well we're only halfway."

"But the return is downhill." Sean leaned against a tree trunk to stretch his calves. "You still dating Mary?"

"Yeah... actually we're engaged now. Wedding's in the fall," Sam answered.

Sean turned a surprised face to Sam. "Engaged? Wow... that's awesome. She's done with her nursing degree yet?"

"Not yet, but she will by the time we get married." Sam looked nervous as he asked, "I was wondering if you'd be one of the groomsmen? My brother's going to be the best man."

Sean walked up to Sam and pounded him on the back affectionately. "Absolutely man. Thanks."

"It'll be at the Catholic Church. You cool with that?"

"Sure. I was raised Catholic."

Sam grinned. "So, how's the travel business?" he asked.

"I haven't officially opened the doors yet. I need to do some traveling to the places I'll be recommending. I plan to offer extreme vacations. You know -- off-roading through canyons, zip-lining in jungles, scuba diving. That kind of stuff."

They started back down the trail, jogging carefully on the steep dirt path. Sam commented, "Not exactly honeymoon vacations, huh?"

"I can hook you up—don't worry." Sean skidded and caught himself. "I'm heading off to England in a couple of weeks to check out the inland canal boats. You can rent one and then you and your group have to manage the locks as you go through the countryside."

***

A week later Sean answered his cell phone while scanning his computer at the travel agency.

"Hey buddy, you gotta minute?" Sam asked.

"Always for you. What's up?"

"I've got really bad news. Warrick was shot and killed this morning."

"What?" Sean asked in disbelief as he sank back into the office chair.

"I'm sorry man. I know you were tight."

"He's got a wife and kid," Sean said absently as the room spun crazily around him. He couldn't believe Warrick was dead. "Did they catch the bastard who shot him?"

"Yeah, he tried to get away, but we cornered him in a house. After a forty-five minute stand-off he shot himself. So he's dead," Sam answered matter-of-factly.

"Let me know when the funeral service will be."

"Absolutely... I'm sorry dude."

"Thanks for telling me. Talk to ya later." Sean sat cradling his head in his hands, as tears welled up and slipped down his rough cheeks.

CHAPTER FIVE

Sean sat next to Pantell on the airplane. They were both awake though the majority of the passengers were asleep. Sleeping is forbidden when armed. Pantell tilted his phone toward Sean. The screen read, *"This is a good way to communicate without a trace."* Then Pantell erased the message with the back button. He typed, *"Just be sure you don't accidently push send! :)"*

Sean took the phone, erased the message and typed, *"What about when we're not together?"*

Pantell read it and nodded. "I use various games like word games. They usually have PM capabilities." Pantell proceeded to download a game app onto Sean's phone. He went to settings turned off location permission. Then he typed into Sean's phone, *"Can still be located, but it's a lot harder."*

Sean nodded as he put the phone back in his pocket.

"What languages do you speak?" Pantell asked.

"Spanish, but they just started me on my Russian, then I guess we'll move on to German. I tell ya, Russian is a lot different than Spanish.

"Well at least we don't have to write it. For us *tour guides* it's all about the spoken languages," Pantell commented.

Sean leaned his head back on the seat. He rolled his head to look at Pantell. "How 'bout you? What do you speak?"

"Spanish, French, Russian, German, a little Chinese and of course… Pig-Latin."

Sean raised both brows. "Pig-Latin? Seriously?"

Pantell whispered, "Ep-yay. Most non-Americans don't know it. If English is your second language it's too difficult to follow even if you understand the concept behind it."

Sean laughed as he answered, "At-thay is-ay azy-cray!"

They both chuckled.

***

It was late afternoon and the restaurant was already full. The design made it noisy and hard to hear conversations. Pantell and Sean wound through the cafeteria style tables towards an older gentleman, Frank Goldschmidt, who stood up when he saw them. They shook hands and took the seats indicated.

Frank had a small briefcase on the table, which he patted as he talked. "I own a jewelry store in Sacramento, Goldschmidt Fine Jewelry."

Sean nodded, "Yeah, I've heard of it. What do you hope to offer my clientele Mr. Goldschmidt?"

"I understand you are designing tours that show a different aspect of a culture. I deal in antiquities and estate jewelry."

Sean leaned back as a waitress set his cup of coffee in front of him.

Frank continued, "I could lead a tour of some of the better establishments that sell antiquities. Maybe even set up a couple of estate sales at mansions."

Sean nodded and glanced at Pantell.

Pantell asked, "Can we see some examples of your purchases?"

Frank opened the briefcase to reveal several jewelry boxes. Lifting one out Frank opened it and tilted it toward Sean and Pantell. A necklace sparkled in the slanting light from the sun sitting low on the horizon. "Beautiful yes? This necklace tells an amazing story... mysteries only this necklace knows."

Pantell reached for the box and ran his fingers over the sparkling stones. Reaching into his coat pocket, Pantell pulled out a slim flat billfold. He pulled out several bills and handed them to Frank. He snapped the jewelry box shut with a sharp click. "Thank you Frank, my wife will love it," he said as he slid it into his pocket. "When will you be back in Sacramento?"

"In a couple of months. I have some leads I want to follow up on first."

When they got back to the hotel room, Pantell set up a device on the little hotel coffee table. Sean watched the procedure from an armchair. Pantell opened the jewelry case and dumped the necklace on the table. Lifting out the fake bottom, he pulled out a thumb-drive. Leaning sideways to see better, he stuck the USB into the port. The miniature screen lit up. They both leaned in to watch. A bubble view of a room showed a deluxe hotel suite with several men standing or sitting around. A door opened and a woman entered. The men stood. Pantell nodded happily, "Excellent..." He pulled out the jump drive. "We'll get this to the station here in Moscow and do some sightseeing before we head home."

Sean felt frustrated as he watched his partner. Finally working up the nerve, he asked, "I want to see it before we hand it off."

Pantell glanced at Sean with surprise.

"Can we make a copy for ourselves?" Sean asked.

"We're not supposed to," Pantell replied as he leaned back in his chair to stare at Sean. "What's gotten in to you?"

"Dunno, it's just a hunch." Sean shrugged. "I'd feel better if I could study this a little more. I want to learn this woman's tells."

Pantell looked intently at Sean for a moment. Sean maintained eye-contact. "This better not be about your obsession with Petrov."

"Everything is about Petrov," Sean answered succinctly.

Finally Pantell shook his head and answered. "Okay, but I hope this doesn't come back to bite us."

***

Sean approached Lieutenant Becker's office. Becker was seated at his desk working on his computer. Sean tapped on the door-frame. Looking up, Becker waved him in and half stood. "McGee, have a seat," he directed.

Sean sat in the chair directly opposite Becker. Sean looked cautious, and a little nervous, as he asked, "What's up boss?"

Becker tapped his pen lightly on the metal desktop. "Did you make a copy of the jump drive we got from Goldschmidt?"

Sean squirmed in his seat. "Yes, sir."

"Why?" Becker asked, looking calm and curious. "I told you to leave it at the station in Moscow."

"I did."

Becker began tapping his pen again. "*Why'd* you make a copy?"

Sean decided to be blunt. "It's my first evidential hard copy I've received and I wanted to study it." Becker just sat there looking at Sean. Sean said nothing.

"Okay, but next time you decide to do something like that, tell me. I don't like seeing one of my agents' names pop up on my national security breach app." Becker paused, as he studied Sean intently. "You're not a rogue maverick McGee... we work as a team, or you can work elsewhere."

"Yes sir," Sean said as he stood and started toward the door.

"When you see Pantell, tell him I want to talk to him," Becker ordered.

Sean paused with one hand on the door handle. *Oh man, this wasn't good!* "Pantell had nothing to do with this. It was --."

Becker held up a finger to silence Sean. "It has every-thing to do with Pantell. He's your training officer and knew what you were going to do... *and* he helped you make the copy. Send him in."

Sean left the office with a knot in his stomach. The hallway to the computer room seemed incredibly long. Pantell was at a computer reading the screen. Sean went over and sat next to him. Pantell swiveled his chair and smiled slightly. "Boss wants to see you," Sean told him remorsefully.

"Gee, thanks," Pantell said sarcastically.

"Sorry man."

Standing up, Pantell answered, "Don't worry about it... I'm a big boy. I knew what I was getting into when I let you make a copy of that drive." Pantell walked out, leaving Sean with head hanging.

Swiveling around to his computer, Sean noticed that Pantell hadn't logged out of his screen. Leaning over he moused over to the exit button. He didn't click though, he read the page first. It was a list of Russian names laid out like a family tree. One name stood out—Boris Petrov. Sean glanced around and snapped a photo with his cell phone.

***

A crowd of uniforms blocked Sean's view of the coffin as he shuffled forward at the funeral home. It was an open coffin. Sean felt like running the other direction, but forced himself to step up to the edge and look at his mentor and friend. Warrick was a handsome man, especially in his dress uniform. A sniffle caught his attention as he turned. A tiny Japanese woman sat in the front row with her eyes glued on the coffin bearing her husband. A pretty girl sat by her side with tears streaming down her face. *This must be Warrick's daughter.* She had mocha-brown skin and up tilted almond shaped eyes. Her full lips quivered as she tried to suppress her emotions, but she held her chin up defiantly.

***

A couple of nights later Sean was seated at the front desk of McGee Travel Agency with a computer lit up in front of him. He had an office phone cradled on his shoulder, nodding as he typed. He looked much different than he used to look as a cop. His hair was longer and he wore a Hawaiian shirt and flip-flops. "Okay Susan, I've got you booked for two weeks. Scuba package included and one excursion for three to go zip-lining. Let me know if you want anything else added to your itinerary." Sean jotted a note on the pad next to the keyboard. "Gotcha, thanks again. Bye now." Sean hung up and continued typing.

The door bell jingled. Sean glanced up and his hands froze above the keyboard.

Boris Petrov stepped into the air-conditioned office.

"Can I help you?" Sean asked, wondering what Boris was doing there, wondering how much trouble he'd get into if he killed him.

Boris looked around the office, seeming to study the various destination posters. "Yes, I wonder if you can tell me about my Mother-Russia? It's been many years and I miss it." Boris sat in the chair across from Sean. "I understand you were there recently, yes?

Sean leaned forward in his chair. His free hand gripped the SIG Velcroed to the underside of the desk. "Yes, I was there to look for ideas for tours. It's an interesting country," Sean commented flatly.

Boris glanced at Sean's forearm were it disappeared under the desk. He turned his gaze back to Sean. "As you know, Moscow is a beautiful place, but dangerous."

Sean tensed, but otherwise didn't move or speak.

"Did you enjoy Moscow?" he asked softly in a sing-song voice as he ran a slender finger across Sean's desk.

"It's a city," Sean answered dryly. "Nice, but a city. I wasn't there long. Is that where you are from—Moscow?"

Boris reached into his jacket pocket.

Sean slid his finger onto the trigger.

Pulling out a business card, Boris answered, "Yes, but I'm an American now." He stood. "Well... good luck with your new career."

Sean didn't stand up, but he reached for the card. He looked at it before he replied. "It was a pleasure meeting you... Boris. If I want you, I'll find you."

Boris paused for a moment and gave Sean a cold hard stare. Shaking his head slightly he turned and walked out of the travel agency.

Sean got up, locked the front door and went into his office. Shutting the office door behind him, he grabbed a light-weight chair and smashed it against his desk. Panting, he flung the remainder of the chair across the room. Scenes of revenge flashed through his mind. Taking a calming breath, he pulled out a cell phone. He dialed as he paced in the small space. Like a caged tiger. Sitting down in his rolling chair he stared at his foil lined walls while listening to the ringtone.

Pantell answered, "Hey McGee, what's up?"

"You in a secure area?" Sean asked.

Pantell glanced around the CIA office, "Yup."

"Boris was just here," Sean growled.

Pantell leaned forward abruptly, "Where?"

"At my agency."

"No shit?" Pantell grinned. "He just waltzed through your door? Did he recognize you?"

Sean propped his bare feet on the desk edge, leaving his flip-flops on the floor. "Oh, he recognized me all right and he knew I'd just been in Moscow. It was all a veiled threat."

"How'd he know you were in Moscow? Either he's watching you, or he has an inside contact," Pantell said, answering his own question.

Sean looked at the ceiling. "No shit Sherlock. Now what do I do?"

"Wait 'n see... nothing you can do but watch your back." Pantell paused before adding, "Don't drop your cover. Remember... you're an ex-cop turned travel agent... period!"

***

Sean stood at the hostess stand in a restaurant. He'd decided to try internet dating. Being lonely wasn't something he'd factored into becoming an undercover CIA agent. All the women he knew were off limits because they always asked too many questions. One of the guys at work said he just went on dates from a dating site. He'd refined his responses to make the girl comfortable and hopefully they would go out for a week or two. That wasn't what Sean was after, but maybe it would work. First he'd try going on this blind-date his sister had set up with one of her co-workers.

Sean watched as a twenty-something woman walked down the ramp onto the restaurant barge and approached the hostess stand. She fit the description his sister had given.

Sarah was an attractive, nondescript brunette. About five-foot-five, thin. She looked at Sean curiously.

Sean smiled, stepping forward. "Sarah?"

She nodded as she smiled nervously.

"You're Sean?" she asked. At his nod she reached out a delicate hand. After they shook hands, the hostess signaled them to follow her to a table next to the rail.

Sarah continued, "I've never been here before. I didn't even know it existed."

Sean held her chair out for her and pushed the seat in for her. Very old-fashioned and proper. He sat opposite her. "The Virgin Sturgeon has been here forever. It's burned and even sank, but it's still here."

Sean relaxed as they chatted, getting to know each other. The sun was beginning to shift, ricocheting off the river. As they finished their drinks and ordered dinner, Sean knew this was their first and last date. As she talked, he faded out and imagined the perfect girl for him. Athletic, smart, feisty, and ornery... and good looking as an afterthought. He started guiltily when he realized he wasn't paying attention to Sarah. Her tone had shifted.

Looking at her plate of food, Sarah asked in a quiet voice, "So your sister says you're a travel agent. That's not something you see every day."

Sean shifted uncomfortably. "Yeah well, my folks had one as I was growing up, so..."

Sarah glanced up to look at his face. "So you decided to follow in their footsteps. Didn't you used to be a policeman?"

Sean cleared his throat. "Yeah, for couple of years. It wasn't for me. I enjoy this more," he ended lamely.

Sarah looked at Sean inquisitively.

***

The next day Sean walked down the hall toward Pantell who was talking to another agent.

Pantell glanced towards Sean. Turning away from the other agent, he greeted Sean, "Hey Rookie, how's it going?"

"It's going. Not much happening with the Medicare fraud case. Seems they've gone underground again." They fell in step as they walked to the computer room. Sean glanced sideways at his mentor. "You're married... how do you make that work?"

Pantell looked curiously at Sean as they took a couple of seats in the corner. "You getting married?" At Sean's look, he decided to be serious. "She's a homicide detective for the Berkley PD. She knows what I do, but no questions. Otherwise you have to lie about it."

"Yeah," Sean said. "I'm not real good at that... at least not in a relationship. I don't think I can have a relationship with someone if I'm lying about my career."

Pantell leaned back and waited until Sean made eye-contact. "Then you can't have a relationship."

Sean nodded slowly as he fiddled with a pen.

CHAPTER SIX

Standing in front of his travel agency, Sean balanced on a curb while talking on a cell phone. He was wearing shorts and a loose button-up shirt. To the observant eye he had a gun attached to his belt, hidden under his shirt. As he twisted to maintain his balance the outline of the gun was slightly visible. "I want to check out a scuba club called Bon Temp in the Bahamas. Wanna go?" Sean asked.

"Absolutely," Randy answered in his cheerful loud voice. "I need a break. Do they have diving?"

Sean grinned, "Yep. You want me to see if Dapper Dan and Crazy Craig can make it?"

"I'll ask Dan today. You ask Craig," Randy answered.

"Text me your vacation dates."

"Gotcha. Hasta Luego." Randy hung up.

Sean's thumbs flew as he texted Craig, "Can you take a vacay? Dan, Randy and I want to go to the Bahamas together. Can you find time in your busy schedule?" Sean went back in the agency and re-arranged the rack with the cruise brochures. The phone rang, and he went back to work making reservations for one of his sister's best friends. After hanging up he checked his cell.

Sean looked at Craig's response; "When?"

Sean typed back, "I'll let you know when I get the dates from the boys."

***

Dan, Randy, Craig and Sean floated in the water behind the boat, waiting to climb the ladder. Waves splashed them in the face just enough to make it easier to keep their regulators in their mouths. The boat in front of them had GOSCUBA emblazoned across the back. When the diver in front of him was completely out of the water, Sean kicked forward and made a grab at the ladder. The boat bobbing up and down made it difficult. A wave yanked Sean sideways as he was removing his fins, and he lost his footing. He scrambled back onto the step in time to be lifted by a wave clear out of the water... still on the ladder.

Randy yelled up to the dive master, "Hey! Can you help the lady get on board?" The dive master chuckled at the masculine banter, as he reached down for Sean's fins. Once on board Sean checked his gauges and read off his depth and time before trudging back to his bench, trying not to trip over other divers. The dialogue blended with the sound of metal clanking and water slapping the boat. Everyone was talking at once as they sat on the benches and removed their vests with the tanks. The new divers nervously changed their tanks for fresh ones under the watchful eye of their instructors. The old timers teased each other about how they saw a bigger, better fish than the others.

"Did you see that Moray eel?" Dan asked as he plopped down next to Sean. "It was half way out of its den!"

"I was too busy watching that reef shark swimming around checking you out," Craig commented dryly.

"The sharks aren't shy here, that's for sure," Randy commented as he rinsed the salt water off. He shook his head like a dog sending water spraying every direction. "I'm heading top-deck," he said as he dodged teetering divers coming in out of the water with weight-belts, wet BCDs and tanks.

The surface interval was spent in silence sprawled out in the sun. After an hour they geared up and headed back in the water at the new site the captain had navigated to. They dove as a team in perfect unison, giving testimony to their years of working together.

***

That night Dan and Randy leaned against the crowded bar sipping beers. They stopped talking as Sean and Craig walk up. Craig's eyes narrowed suspiciously. His blonde hair was shoulder-blade long and dread-locked.

"Who're you talking about?" Craig demanded.

Randy laughed. "Not you! You're not interesting enough to talk about."

Craig relaxed.

"Can you imagine being so vain?" Sean asked in disbelief. "-- think'n everyone's talking about you!"

Dan smiled a slow smile and said with his slight southern drawl, "If you were as good-looking as Craig you'd understand it." He lifted his glass in salute to Craig.

Sean snorted and retorted, "Good looking? I've seen better looking sheep-dogs on my parent's ranch!" Sean got the bartender's attention and ordered two beers and a shot of whiskey.

Craig held the shot glass up in a toast. "Cheers!" They said in unison as the glasses clanked. Craig downed the shot and took a sip of his beer. All four men scanned the rowdy crowd as they relaxed against the counter.

Several women watched them. Giggling they turned back to each other. A woman standing near them smiled and angled her head toward Sean. Her eyes invited him to follow her and she pushed off the bar and sauntered away in her two-inch heels and slinky red dress. Sean grinned at his buddies and followed her to the pool table nearby. The three guys watched him flirting with the blonde bombshell.

"How does he do that?" Randy wanted to know.

"He looks trustworthy," Dan answered.

"And fun," Craig added enviously.

Smiling at each other they lifted their glasses in another salute.

Randy said, "To Sean."

"To Sean," Craig and Dan repeated.

***

The four went running on the beach along the surf in the early morning. The sun glinted sideways off the calm sea. As they came to the end of the beach they scrambled up and over the promontory point. Another powder pink beach stretched out ahead of them. They continued running, each lost in his own thoughts.

Sean slowed as he looked up on the grassy area. A bungalow with a broken front porch was nestled amongst the shrubs. "Hey, check this out." They all stopped running and looked at the dilapidated little place.

Randy started walking up the sand. "Let's check it out."

Pushing open the door they enter one-by-one. An iguana stared at them from the center of the large room.

"This is sweet," Sean said. "Can you imagine having a bungalow here? Someplace we can escape to?"

"I already have a place like this," Craig commented. The other three turned to look at him. "What? I live in Costa Rica... in the jungle... on the beach. But I'll come visit you."

Sean laughed. "Gee thanks."

***

It was a cold still day in Sacramento, but that didn't stop the traditional Second-Saturday-Art-walk. The mellow crowd wandered along the streets, in and out of stores, galleries, and restaurants. Sean had his hands wrapped around a cup of spiced apple cider. He was bundled up in a thick canvas rancher's style coat, a cowboy hat and a black scarf. As always, he had his own unique style. The men smiled, and the women smiled for a different reason. Sean was the embodiment of masculinity.

A prostitute approached him. She wore spiked heels, tights, and a skin-tight dress under her puffy down jacket. "Hello handsome," she purred.

Sean grinned. He remembered her, Elsa, from a bust a couple of years ago. He'd been impressed with her spunk back then. "Hi Elsa," he answered.

Her grey eyes narrowed at the use of her name. This guy looked familiar, but she couldn't place him. Maybe he was one of her regular Johns, yet she didn't think so. He didn't have that look as he watched her. "I know you?" she asked sweetly.

Sean gave a short laugh. "Well I guess you could say that... I had you in the back of my car."

Elsa immediately understood he was teasing her. She grinned. Her natural inclination was toward humor. At twenty-five she'd seen much to dampen that, but the smile crinkles persisted. "The back of your car, huh? Hmmm... was I good?"

"Good? Well you behaved yourself, but the hand-cuffs may have contributed to that," Sean lifted his cup, "Can I buy you a cider?"

She looked from him to the crowd. After surveying the artsy crowd, she seemed to come to grips with the lack of potential income. Fear of abuse from her pimp loomed in the back of her mind as she nodded and took his proffered arm. She could see Boris in the shadows, so she pressed her breast against Sean's arm and looked up at him with a flirtatious smile.

Sean caught the not-so-subtle change and guessed the cause. "I take it your pimp is in sight," he commented as he held the door for her.

Elsa's face paled at his words, and her step faltered.

"Come on. I'm not a cop anymore. You're safe." Sean led her to a table in the back and sat across from her. "So how've you been?"

"I've been fine up until now... I'll get a beat'n for this for sure," Elsa whispered. As she looked down her multi-colored hair drooped into her face.

Sean slid a hundred dollar bill across the table. "I play fair." He smiled gently at her swift glance. "I will pay for your time."

They sat for an hour talking about life, family, animals, anything but her work. When she stood, she held out her hand. "Thank you Sean. That's the most fun I've had since... I don't remember. Thanks."

Sean stood and shook her hand. "Until next time?"

"Sure," she replied with another grin.

***

The next month he encountered Elsa again on the busy Sacramento Art Walk.

She watched Sean carefully as he sauntered amongst the crowd. She prayed that another man wouldn't get to her before Sean saw her, but she couldn't bring herself to purposefully get his attention. She felt lodged between her job and a desire to have a friend.

Sean scanned the crowd, as always. He spotted Elsa watching him. Crossing the street he held out his hand in greeting. "Elsa! What a pleasure. How are you?"

It took her a moment to figure out what he said. It almost seemed a foreign language. Here she was dressed in a skin-tight velvet mini skirt, a cropped top, and fishnet nylons. He looked so wholesome in his jeans, tennies and fleece jacket. "It's great seeing you too." She couldn't bring herself to tell him how she was. She was coming off a meth binge and felt horrible.

Sean invited her into the same café. She stepped past him as he held the door for her. Glancing around self-consciously, she followed Sean to the same table.

He slid a hundred dollar bill across the little table and folded his hands on the table top. "So you didn't answer me... how are you doing?" He could tell she was coming off a high. Deep circles under her eyes and pale skin.

"I've had the flu for a couple of days, but I'm better now," she lied.

"Bullshit," Sean responded with a disarming grin. "Meth or Heroin?" he asked.

She just stared at him with distrust.

"Okay, it's not important. I'm glad you're over your *flu*." Sean leaned back to order from the waiter. "What do you want?" He asked Elsa.

She ordered a hot tea with lemon and honey.

After six more months of meeting, they greeted each other like old friends. She'd started dressing a little more conservatively on the night of the Art Walk. She also made a point of recovering from her binges before that night. She told him about how hard it was to see the new girls. They were so young.

"It must break your heart," Sean commented, trying not to show his bitter anger at their plight. This was the opportunity he'd been waiting for. His patience was about to pay off.

She nodded as her eyes welled with tears. "I know it sounds stupid, but I hate it. Once you're in, ain't no way out."

"That's not true," Sean interrupted softly.

Elsa stared at the tabletop, tears running down her cheeks. An intense heaviness pressed down on her chest, stifling her breath. She could hear her heart pounding. "Maybe they have a chance, but I don't," she whispered.

"That's not true either," Sean said gently. "I have an idea. I'd like your opinion."

***

Several months later Sean, Dan and Randy went back to the island, to their bungalow. As they climbed out of the borrowed truck, they looked at the shack with buyer's remorse. Trying to salvage his pride, Sean said, "Well boys, let's get to work. It's not going to fix itself!"

They carried boxes and buckets from the truck to the porch until the truck bed was emptied and set to work. Sean went around to the beach side and started ripping apart the deck and tossing the boards in a pile on the beach. They'd have a bonfire later.

Randy brushed the exterior walls with a stiff broom. He jumped back with a yelp when a bug fell toward him, making Sean laugh. But then Sean yelled and ran backwards. Dan and Randy trotted over to look at a giant tarantula between Sean and the bungalow.

Dan went back inside to continue patching the inner walls with spackle. Then he started in the front room painting it white. Randy painted the exterior with white paint.

Sean could be heard hammering and cussing as he built the deck. After an especially vile list of expletives and the sound of the hammer ricocheting off the deck, Randy suggested it was time for a swim and lunch. Sean answered by tearing off his shoes and running into the ocean. Afterwards they walked over to the resort and showing their bracelets, went into the restaurant.

"This was a great idea Sean," Randy commented looking at the burger buffet.

"I figured it would be much easier if we stayed here and had food... food we didn't have to try to prepare." Sean held his plate out for the cook to deposit his hamburger patty.

"That looks like it hurts," Randy pointed to Sean's cut and swollen knuckle.

"It's not too bad, but it always sucks to have a knuckle wound," Sean said as he flexed and straightened his hand. "At least I didn't get bit by the tarantula!"

"No doubt." Randy nodded his head toward the table Dan had picked. "Dan doesn't get to choose tables anymore," he said sarcastically as they approached the table with a small family.

Sean laughed at his friend. "They're probably a lot more interesting than the vacant girls you usually find."

"Ouch," Randy complained.

A couple of hours later, after sitting at the table talking and laughing with the family, they headed back down the beach to their little bungalow. They stopped to admire it. The white paint made it look classic Caribbean. "The trim needs to be turquoise or coral," Dan decided.

"Okay Picasso," Sean teased as they all went back to work.

That evening Randy and Sean wrestled a couch through the front door and collapsed on it. Dan plopped down between them and handed them a couple of beers. They sat silently staring out the dirty bay window at the ocean. After a twelve-pack of beer all three were asleep... Sean stretched out on the floor, Dan slouched back with his feet on coffee table. Randy curled up in the other corner of the couch.

When they woke up it was dark and they were hungry. "Let's go eat and then it's time for a bonfire."

***

Early the next morning the ocean was calm. The air was fresh and clean. The three men sat silently drinking coffee and staring at the rhythmic waves washing the beach.

Sean propped his feet up on the new railing. "I needed this."

Randy turned to survey Sean. "Running a travel agency is stressful huh?" he asked sarcastically.

Dan grunted a laugh, but Sean remained serious.

Randy continued, "Come on dude. We know you're not a *travel* agent... you're an agent, but I don't know with whom."

Sean continued to stare out to sea. "Who told you that?"

"What, I can't have my own opinion?"

Sean just turned a steely stare on him with a brow raised. Dan watched with interest. As much as they'd all become friends, they still regarded Sean as their leader.

"Okay, okay... Craig told me."

Sean barked out a laugh. "And you believed him? He's paranoid. He's always imagining things."

"So which agency do you work for?" Randy asked.

Sean looked seriously at his two friends before answering. "CIA."

Randy simply nodded and said, "Okay."

"What did-ya finally do about that pimp you hated so much... the one who threatened you?" Dan asked.

That closed look dropped across Sean's expressive face again. "I'm working on it," he replied laconically.

Randy and Dan exchanged knowing looks. Both were glad they weren't Boris Petrov.

CHAPTER SEVEN

Sean sat in his office chair with his feet up on the desk, a laptop open on his lap. He turned his attention to a note-pad to write something down and went back to the screen. His brows puckered as he mumbled, "What have we here?" He rapidly clicked through a website with scantily clad women.

An hour later, Sean sauntered down the Agency hall wearing his usual shorts and baggy button-up shirt. He turned into the computer room. Screens glowed and flickered as various agents worked. Sean spotted Pantell and took the computer next to him.

Pantell looked up. "Hey rookie, whatcha doing here?"

"Hey boss," Sean said. "I needed a more powerful search engine. I've got to follow up on something in the deep web."

"Still working on that pimp, Boris?"

"Yep. Think I've got a cyber-sex site with some connections to prostitution here in Sac-Town." Sean glanced sideways at Pantell. "I recognized one of Boris' girls from the photos."

Pantell shook his head as he answered, "I tell ya, investigations into cyber crimes just makes me tired."

"This isn't a cyber crime per se... Like stealing your bank PIN or something. It's a physical crime using the web to set it up," Sean paused as he typed. "But I can't follow the rabbit trail easily. This is a very sophisticated operation."

Pantell sighed as he turned back to his screen. "You make me feel old."

"You *are* old," Sean answered with a grin.

***

Several computer screens glowed in the semi-dark metal room. A female and two males worked at three of them. The light glowed bluish-green on Ryan's face, making his eyes glitter strangely. He tipped his head to one side inquisitively. "Boss, you need to see this."

Derik approached and leaned over Ryan's shoulder. He pulled a chair over and took Ryan's place in front of the keyboard. His fingers sped over the keys, making the other two computer techs take notice. It wasn't often Derik took over their computers.

"What's going on?" Ryan asked as he watched.

"I'm building a wall... someone at the CIA breached our system," he answered curtly. "Andrei, start building a new site. Completely new from the ground up. I can hold them off here for a couple of days."

Andrei spun around in his seat and began working. The girl, Megan, rolled over to watch her boss work. Derik was one of the greatest computer geeks of his time. He was well paid by Boris to make sure the prostitution site was impenetrable. Derik paused after a few minutes and said with fingers hovering over the keyboard, "Don't you two have something to do?"

They rolled back to the other computers in the tight space.

***

"This program must use a huge amount of space." Sean commented. "It seems to be non-stop activity."

"Probably is combining pornography with the prostitution services," Pantell commented as he leaned over to look at Sean's screen.

"Yeah, and the passwords needed to move deeper are equal to the CIA!" Sean grunted. Suddenly he leaned forward and said, "Whoa, check that out... it's slowing down fast!" as they watched it slowed down and completely stopped activity in a matter of minutes.

"They spotted you and bugged out, buddy," Pantell chuckled as he went back to his computer.

Sean sat with his mouth open staring at his screen. "Well crap! Now what do I do?"

"Start over." Pantell glanced sideways at Sean, "They'll build a new and improved platform."

***

A week later Sean stepped through the doors of his favorite café, Brindles. A quiet upscale place in the shopping center his travel agency was in. In the back was an excellent bar... quiet and calm with a great selection of beer. The bartender smiled at him and asked if he wanted to try the new stout they'd just gotten in. Sean sat down as she slid a taster size cup toward him and waited for his response.

He took a sip and sighed in appreciation as he closed his eyes dramatically.

The bartender giggled. "So you want a glass?"

"Yes, please," Sean answered with his grin.

A young lady came in and sat next to him. Sean turned his smile to her and said hello. She responded likewise. After she ordered an apple martini, she told Sean, "I've never been here before. It's kind of hidden away."

"It is. What brings you here?" Sean asked.

"I was over at the kitchen store and saw this little place." She took a dainty sip off her martini.

"So are you a great cook?" Sean clarified at her questioning look, "You were at a kitchen store. I was wondering if you are a gourmet cook or something."

"Oh good lord, no," She answered with a laugh. "No, I was buying a birthday present for a friend who *is* a very good cook. I'm a pro at heating up soup though!"

Sean laughed at her. "Well, I like to cook. Mostly barbequing. I love that store."

An hour later they were still talking, and Sean had his swivel barstool turned towards hers. It was getting crowded and harder to hear each other. Sean leaned toward her to be heard, and to smell her perfume, and asked, "You wanna sit out on the patio?"

She nodded and picked up her second martini and followed Sean to the garden patio. She chose a table and they both sat down with an increased awareness in the other. The move outside seemed to have turned it into a date. She suddenly seemed shy.

Sean didn't let the silence become awkward, "So, my name is Sean. I work in this complex."

"I'm Megan."

***

The property looked perfect. A three-bedroom house on a two acre lot nestled in the forest. Deer fencing surrounded the yard. Everett, the property manager stood quietly and watched Sean prowl around the home.

"If I commit for one year will you lower the rent?"

"I can do that." Everett eyed Sean suspiciously. "You know this is in a no-grow zone, right?"

Sean grinned. He hadn't thought of that. "That's even better. I don't want anything to do with growing pot plants, but I didn't know there were no-grow zones."

"The townsfolk of Lewiston decided to vote on it. And it passed. Some of the biggest growers live here, but they grow elsewhere," the man explained.

"Is meth a problem here?"

"Oh yeah, sure, can't really get away from it, even up here." Everett walked him to the back side of the property and pointed to the raised plant beds. "Here's the garden you were asking about."

"Do you get much snow here?"

"A little… usually just a couple of inches, but some years it can be a few feet."

"Okay, I'll take it," Sean said as he imagined the garden and a dog or two… maybe chickens.

"Will this be a vacation home?" Everett asked.

"Kind of." With his hands deep in his pockets, Sean looked pensively at the serious man. Trusting his instincts he said, "This will be a refuge for young ladies."

"How many?" he asked.

"Two or three girls and one permanent woman to watch over them."

"Are they in danger," Everett asked.

Sean paused for a moment weighing his words. He finally nodded and answered simply, "Yes."

A full minute passed as the two men contemplated each other. Finally Everett put out a hand and agreed. They shook on it and he led Sean back into the house to sign the papers. He paid an extra deposit for animals.

"There can be no men here, unless it's workmen scheduled in advance with Elsa," Sean told the landlord as he got into his SUV.

***

Sean's sister, Sharice walked around his office and tidied the magazine rack. "You keep this place very neat and clean Sean!"

Sean glanced up at her. "You sound surprised," he commented dryly.

"I *am* surprised. I was raised with you... your room was a pigsty."

"The Marines broke that pattern a long time ago sis." Sean watched her wandering around. "If I remember right, your room wasn't exactly clean either."

"That was Barb's fault, my side was neat," she argued. A couple of minutes later, "Are you dating anyone?"

"Not really," Sean leaned back and propped his feet up on his desk. Apparently his nosy sister wanted to talk. "I've met a girl for drinks a couple of times after work, but it's just because she goes to the same place."

Sharice flopped into the seat in front of his desk. Her feet joined his. "What's her name? What's she do?"

"Is this an interrogation?"

"Yup, it's the only way to get information out of you. You never talk about your life anymore." Sharice pouted prettily.

"It's not interesting," Sean answered. Sharice stuck her bottom lip out further. He hated it when she did that. "Okay her name is Megan. She is a computer geek. She works for a private company developing software. But, we're not dating. We happen to go to the same bar for a cocktail."

"Dost thou protest too much?" she teased.

Sean rolled his eyes. "Good grief! This is why I don't tell you anything!" She batted her eyes innocently, making him laugh. "No one could ever be as wonderful as you anyway, so why bother?" Sean added sweetly.

As he walked her out to her car later, he looked in the direction of the café. A dark sedan rolled past them. Sean instinctively watched the car. He couldn't make out the driver's face. Every nerve was on alert as he said goodbye to Sharice. As she drove away Sean stood at the curb staring after the sedan. It stopped in front of Brindles. The passenger door opened and Megan got out.

He felt as though he'd been punched in the solar plexus. All his instincts screamed that this was Boris, but how could that be? It wasn't the same car he'd come in before to intimidate him. *Besides, how could Megan be in Boris' car? Was she a spy?* The driver turned his head to an angle where Sean could see it wasn't Boris, though he was similar looking.

He went back into to the agency and ran the plates. It came up as a male with no priors. He finished up his work as quickly as possible. Half an hour later he sauntered through the doors to the bar. Megan saw him in the mirror behind the bar and turned on her stool. "Hello Sean," she greeted with a smile on her pretty face.

He went straight to her and sat down. "Hey there, how was your day?" he nodded to the bartender when she pointed to a draft beer handle.

"It started off bad. My car broke down yesterday, and I thought it would be done by now, but nooo. I'm so frustrated." She sipped her martini. "I had to ask for a ride here from my boss. My sister will pick me up when she gets off work in an hour and give me a ride home... what a pain."

"That was nice of your boss to give you a ride," Sean responded.

"Yeah, he wasn't too thrilled about it," she grimaced. "It's not like it's far... ten minutes tops!"

"Is he kind of a hard guy?"

"He's intense. He doesn't like change. Typical brilliant mind." Megan stared into her drink thoughtfully while Sean studied her face.

"How's he so brilliant?" Sean asked using a purposefully dismissive tone.

"How's he brilliant?" she countered. "He's like amazing with computers. He can build an entirely new program in a couple of hours. I mean design it from scratch... with impossible firewalls. We just had a breach in our system and he shut it down in a matter of minutes and built a new one. He's a genius."

"What kind of program is it?" Sean asked casually as he sipped his beer. He watched her face become shuttered.

"I'm not allowed to talk about it. I'd probably get in trouble for saying what I have." Her face flushed pink as he studied her. "Let's talk about something else. How was your day?"

It was Sean's turn to lie, as he told her half-truths about his schedule at the travel agency. For the first time he didn't feel so guilty about not being transparent. They were on equal footing.

***

A couple of days later Sean heard the front doorbell chime. He came out of his office, shutting the door behind him. Megan was standing near the front door looking at a travel poster. She turned to him with a smile. "Surprise!" She held both hands up and did a little dance.

"Well hello there. I *am* surprised," he said as he approached her. "What brings you here… looking for vacation advice?" he grinned.

She shook her head no as she looked curiously around. "I just wanted to see where you work."

Sean held his arms wide and said, "Well, this is it! Not very exciting, but it keeps me busy. I was just closing up for the day." He sat on the edge of his desk and watched her. Megan wandered around the agency like a girl with an agenda. Touching this, lifting that. He smiled. She finally made her way to him and sat next to him on the desk.

"I like it," she said simply, as she gazed up into his eyes.

He leaned into her slightly and said, "I'm glad you like it." Sean felt torn between genuinely enjoying her femininity and analyzing her motive.

She leaned into him.

"If you wait a minute, I'll close up and walk over to Brindles with you." Sean tipped his face close to hers as he talked.

Looking up at him inches away, she breathed, "Okay."

The phone ringing broke the spell. Sean leaned around her and picked up the receiver. "McGee Travel, can I help you?" Sean looked apologetic as he got up and circled around his desk to the computer. He sat down and tended to his customer while Megan resumed prowling about the agency like a restless lioness.

Sean hung up and shut down the computer. Grabbing his keys, he herded Megan out.

***

Pantell glanced up at Sean. "Hey," he said going back to his computer.

"Hey," Sean answered.

"We're meeting with Goldschmidt in the morning," Pantell told him as he typed.

Sean looked at his profile. "When were you planning on telling me?"

"Just now," Pantell grunted. "I just told you."

Sean turned his attention to the screen in front of him as he began the series of log-ins. "You don't have many friends do you?"

Pantell grinned but didn't answer.

"What time?" Sean asked.

"Nine, at his jewelry store," he answered. "He's got some new intel. He called me about ten minutes ago."

"You wanna meet there or drive out together?" Sean asked as he typed in the last security question.

"We can go together... Since you're my only friend," Pantell added sarcastically.

"True. I'll pick you up out front at eight-thirty."

Silence descended as they focused on their research. Sean had discovered a new pornography site similar in style to the one he associated with Boris' prostitution business. This time he moved slower as he unraveled the layers of encryption. "I'm gonna go to talk to Allen. This cyber stuff is a little over my head." Sean strode down the hall to the cyber crime lab.

Detective Allen was standing at a table with computer parts laid out in front of him. He was a slightly paunchy man in his late twenties with premature balding. He wore fashionable blue-rimmed glasses and a white lab coat. He glanced up when Sean entered. "Hey McGee, what can I do for you?"

"I need help breaking through a website. Its top layer is porn, but the next layer is high-end prostitution. The last time I got to the prostitution level, they detected me and shut the whole thing down."

Allen looked intrigued as he asked for the address. Sean watched over Allen's shoulder as he worked. "Hum... this is very well designed."

"Don't go too fast. I don't want them to block you."

"Okay, why don't you come back in about thirty minutes. I'll surf around the site while I do my other work, then I'll try to get to the next level," Allen told him as he clicked on a girl and returned his attention to the parts in front of him.

Sean came back as promised and Detective Allen glanced up. "Oh good you're back. This site's actually pretty limited. Maybe because it's new. Anyway I think the majority of the website is on the next level," Allen waved Sean closer. "I just got this…" Allen said as he pointed at the pop-up on the screen. It asked him if wanted to chat.

Sean rubbed his hands together eagerly. "Oh this is good."

***

Elsa was waiting for Sean in front of the café. She greeted him with a smile, but Sean noted the restraint. Something was on her mind.

"Hey there," Sean said as he leaned forward and placed a light brotherly kiss on her cheek.

She blushed profusely.

Sean made a note to himself to not do that again. Any touch would be misconstrued. Sean held the door for her as he considered his tactic this week. He noted again the lack of mirth around her thin lips. After sitting down, he asked, "Something's wrong?"

Elsa smiled ironically at this observation. "Everything in my life is wrong," she answered harshly. Seeing Sean's innocent face, she repented, "I'm sorry. It's not your fault."

"Don't be sorry," he assured her. "Something is on your mind… what's up?"

She sat silently for so long, Sean thought she'd decided to not speak when she said, "You know I've been doing this for a long time—eleven years. I hate it, but I'm used to it." She made designs on the table-top with a fingertip.

Sean waited.

"Anyway, we got a new girl yesterday. She's just a baby and so scared," Elsa's eyes welled with unshed tears.

"I remember that feeling like it was yesterday for me. It just breaks my heart."

"You wish you could help her but are powerless to do so?" Sean asked.

Elsa nodded as tears slid down her cheeks.

"Would you help her if you had the chance?"

She looked up suspiciously. "I can't help nobody… not even myself!"

"Would you let me help her through you?" Sean asked.

"Maybe… depends."

Sean leaned forward and began to describe his plan.

CHAPTER EIGHT

The next morning Sean pulled up in front of the non-descript high-rise building housing the CIA. No signs indicated this. Few knew it was there. Pantell hopped in and Sean pulled back into the morning traffic.

"Have you been to the jewelry store? Do you know where it is?" Pantell asked, as Sean wove through traffic.

"Yeah I know where it is, but I've never been in that mall, so I don't know where it is inside the mall," Sean answered.

They drove in silence, listening to a radio talk show. The mall parking lot was mostly empty. Pantell led the way down the quiet marble-tiled interior. Speed walkers went past them in little chattery groups. Most of the stores had open fronts, but Goldschmidt had thick glass doors in the midst of a wall of glass. The plush carpet absorbed the sounds giving the store a hushed-intimate quality. Glass display cases held rare jewelry and artifacts from around the world.

The soft bell alerted the young lady to their presence. As she approached, Pantell said, "Is Frank in?"

She nodded with a smile and pointing to the coffee counter said, "I'll let him know he has guests. Please have a cup of coffee if you'd like." She disappeared behind a wall.

Sean went straight to the coffee. He was stirring in a sugar cube when Frank came out moments later.

"Hello my friends," Frank greeted them with his slight Russian accent. "Come, come, we will be more comfortable in my office." He waved them to follow him. Once seated with the door shut Frank assured them they were able to speak without detection.

"What've you got for us?" Pantell asked as he sipped his black coffee.

"I'm not sure, honestly. A few times recently I've been close to getting some good intel... as you know camera placement is my specialty," Frank added. "I've placed some very good ones lately. But each time the location has yielded nothing. The room will have weeks of activity, but the day I place the camera, it stops." Frank snapped his fingers emphatically. "At first I thought it was a coincidence. However, after four different placements in the last couple of years being detected, I know." Frank tapped a forefinger to his temple.

"You know?" Pantell prompted.

"Somewhere there is a mole." Frank leaned forward eagerly. "I think it's someone in the Sacramento office!"

Pantell and Sean just stared at him in disbelief.

"Why the Sac office?" Pantell asked.

"Because each assignment was vetted through this office," Frank answered.

"Then why are you talking to us?" Sean asked.

"I trust Pantell, we've been working together for too long," Frank answered. "You are too new, so it can't be you."

They spent the next hour going over each case in detail. Sean's skin tingled with excitement. *This* was the spy business! And Goldschmidt was a veteran spy. When they got back in Sean's SUV, Pantell warned Sean, "I know this is obvious… but don't breath a word of this to anyone back at the station."

"Gotcha."

"I'll write up the report," Pantell said after a pause. "I hope he's wrong."

"I'll drop you off. I've got a good lead to follow with the Petrov case," Sean told him.

"So Allen was able to help you?"

"Yep, he got me past the first wall in the new website." Sean pulled up to the curb. "I'll see ya tomorrow."

"Yeah," Pantell got out and shut the door.

"You can't wait to see me, I know," Sean said to the empty space with a laugh. Once back at the travel agency Sean buried himself in research for several hours. He scheduled a *date* with one of the girls from the site. Pulling out his cell, he texted Sam to see if he wanted to go for a run.

"*Can't today… working a double.*" Sam replied. "*Tomorrow 2:00?*"

Sean grunted in frustration. Sitting for a minute he tried to decide if he should run by himself or wait until tomorrow. "*Tomorrow 2:00 at Nimbus Dam.*" Sean closed and locked his inner office and then the agency. He went straight home and got his swimsuit and duffle bag. He'd swim laps at the gym.

At the pool he dove into the cool water and went to the bottom. He glided gracefully along the lane stripe until his lungs begged for air. Surfacing, Sean began an hour-long routine. As he swam, he ran the prostitution case over and over in his mind. How could he actually trap Boris and his gang? The water rushing past his ears pulled him into a mesmerizing depth of thought. When he finished he sat dripping on the edge of the pool and gave a smile of satisfaction. He had a plan.

***

That same day, the eldest of his five sisters called him. Sean saw her name on the screen and sighed. Answering it he started with, "Hey Judy, what do you want me to do now?"

"What?" his indignant sister demanded. "I can't call you without a reason?"

"No, not usually," Sean smiled at this banter. "So… what is it?"

Judy chuckled, "Yeah, okay. I found a house for you."

Sean barked out a laugh. "You what? A house? Who said I wanted to buy a house?"

"I did. You want a house. Meet me there in thirty minutes. I'll text you the address, just tell the security guard you're with me," she retorted and hung up.

Sean stared in disbelief at the silent phone. He gave a little jump when the text alert beeped the address.

Thirty minutes later he drove slowly down the quiet street. Old trees reached out over the narrow road protectively. He pulled in behind his sister's car. She was on the porch waiting for him.

"I don't see one of your signs in the lawn," he commented as he tried to keep a disinterested look on his face.

"It's not listed yet. I just wrote it up today." She held the door open for him. "I wanted you to have the first shot at it. It's underpriced for a quick sale. The neighbor-hood is perfect."

Sean wandered into the kitchen which had a large window looking out on a pool.

"It needs work." Judy stepped up next to him. They stood looking out into the peaceful, medium sized yard.

He pushed away and cruised the kitchen. Opening a door he found the two-car garage. Back in the house he slowly worked his way through the house. Judy wisely stayed in the kitchen. The master bedroom had sliding doors to the yard. Sean stood at the window with arms folded. Deep in thought. Finally he opened the door and roamed around the yard. A dog could be heard barking a couple of houses down. A squirrel scolded him from a giant tree over the grassy area.

Judy watched him smugly from the kitchen.

When Sean came back in he groaned, "I want to say no just to wipe that little satisfied smile off your face."

She grinned.

"I'll take it," Sean said with a grunt of defeat.

"You don't even know how much it is, or how much the HOA fees are," she commented.

***

Megan sat perched on the edge of her barstool at Brindles. Sean went straight to her and sat down. She turned and gave him a hug. Within seconds he noted her furrowed brow and circles under her eyes. "What's up? You look stressed out."

She purposefully relaxed her forehead, as she an-swered, "Just tired."

"You hungry?"

"Not starving, but I could eat. Why?"

"I'm starving, let's go into the restaurant and have an early dinner," Sean pointed over his shoulder with his thumb.

"Okay, I'll get a salad," she commented as she picked up her cocktail and pivoted around.

Sean threw cash down and propelled Megan to the restaurant with a hand on the small of her back.

"Let's sit outside," she motioned to the patio. Sitting down, she crossed her legs and arranged her skirt across her knees.

Sean watched the intensely feminine action. It frustrated him to know she was linked to the Petrov case.

"Now it's my turn to ask you what's wrong. You suddenly looked very conflicted." She sipped her martini as she watched him.

"Just tired," he teased, using her words.

"Touché," she grinned as she lifted her glass.

"Long day at work?" he asked. The waitress set his beer in front of him. "Thanks," he said with a genuine smile. Turning back to Megan, he caught her smile. "What?"

"Nothing, I just think you are incredibly sweet. And yes it was a long day at work. I love my job, but being indoors all day can be boring. It's a small space and only four of us, so yeah… it gets old."

"Do you have other options?" Sean wondered if she could be extricated from this situation.

Her face clouded over. The furrowed brow reappeared. Slowly she shook her head. It was a hopeless gesture. Megan looked down.

Sean reached across the small table and tipped her chin up. Tears welled in her large eyes. Looking into each other's eyes they watched as the other built firewalls. Impenetrable walls. She gave a weak smile, as she turned her face a little to the side to break contact. Reaching a sad truce, they lifted their drinks in a toast. "To secrets." Sean lifted his beer.

She raised her glass. "Secrets."

They settled into talking about what they could. Sean told her he bought a house, and the conversation became animated as Sean described his pushy big sister.

***

Straightening his tie, Sean stepped back to assess this unusual attire. Suits weren't his normal look. But his *date* was at the Waterhouse. She was very expensive. The suit seemed the best choice. He snatched up the keys from the kitchen counter as he headed out to the old, dusty SUV. As he drove, he wondered how he was going to avoid having sex with this high-end prostitute without raising any red flags.

He'd already seen a picture of her from the website, so as he entered the exclusive restaurant he scanned the lobby for her. His main concern was if she would be handed off by Boris. Evangeline was sitting near the door, with an elegant calf length black dress on. A light shawl hung over one forearm. A small clutch rested on her lap. As she raised her eyes to his, he knew it would be easy to resist temptation. Her eyes were empty.

She smiled as she rose and reached out a delicate hand, all in one smooth motion. She must've seen his profile description from the website. Sean took her hand and introduced himself as John Smith, to which she smiled at the obviously fake name.

Throughout the meal, the conversation was shallow and somewhat boring to Sean. *Why did I waste this money? What was I hoping to discover?* He didn't have an answer, but he relaxed and allowed his mind to stay open to opportunity. Somehow this would pay off later.

"So you own a travel agency?" Evangeline sipped her red wine. The most expensive one on the menu.

"Yes," Sean answered as he watched her face for any emotion. "I am a retired cop." This seemed to spark a slight interest.

She swirled her glass expertly. "You're young to be retired."

"True, I found the inability to stop crime before it happened was too frustrating for me." Sean leaned back to allow the dessert to be set before him. After the server had moved away Sean noticed a fleeting look of disdain cross her face.

"Apparently not *all* crime is abhorrent to you," she commented sarcastically.

"We're consenting adults," Sean said arrogantly. He hoped this was a chink in her armor.

"Ah...," she murmured as she took another sip of her wine. "So are a lot of things that are illegal." She leaned back and crossed her long legs, and ran her fingers through her thick auburn hair.

"Are you consenting? Or are you being forced?" he asked.

Evangeline glanced down and sighed. Looking back up she answered, "Yes, of course I'm consenting."

"So what do you do for a living, besides going out on dates?" Sean asked before taking a bite of the cheesecake.

"I'm a full time student."

"Really? What are you studying?"

"US history," she answered.

"Where're you from? I detect a hint of an accent." Sean smiled innocently.

"I'm from Slovakia, but that was a long time ago." She glanced at her wrist watch. Leaning forward, she placed a hand over his. "You like women with accents?" she asked with a sensual smile.

Sean resisted the urge to shudder in revulsion, but she must have detected his feelings. She withdrew her hand and leaned back with a narrowed gaze.

"So you are a policeman-turned-agent?"

"Travel agent," Sean corrected.

"Yes, of course."

Sean suddenly wondered if she knew about him. If Boris had told her to get information from him. Thinking fast, he added, "I've always wanted to be a private detective though. Maybe an agent for the FBI or CIA, or something. I do some investigations on the side."

She leaned forward with the first real interest she'd shown all evening. "That's fascinating. What kind of things do you investigate?"

"Politicians and covert military operations. I'm intrigued by conspiracies."

"Me too," she commented as she rested her chin on her folded hands. Evangeline presented a picture of rapt attention.

Wow, she's good. He decided to see how far he could string her along. He described an elaborate conspiracy, half truth, half his imagination. "And I can prove it," he finished boldly.

***

"I fed her some cockamamie BS about how the US government is planning on overtaking Latvia to give us a better stronghold on the Northern European region." Sean sat facing Pantell in the break-room.

"Why'd you go on the date?" he wanted to know.

"I'm not sure… I guess I'm curious about the operation." Sean shrugged.

"We've got to go to Quantico to do some covert training. That's your old stomping grounds, right?" Pantell started gathering his lunch debris.

"Yeah, I spent some time there." Sean stood and added modestly, "I know some people."

"We leave on the thirteenth for a week."

"The change of scenery will do me good." They walked back to the computer room in silence. "I'm going to do my documentation at the travel agency. Catch ya tomorrow," Sean said with a wave.

As he drove through the capitol city, he marveled at the pervasive underground crime. Most people had no idea. Coming around a corner, he spotted Boris walking with a beautiful woman on his arm. Boris didn't notice him. The woman looked like his property.

Sean whipped up his phone and took a photo.

Back at his agency he copied the photo to his growing file of pictures associated with Boris. He sent a group text to Randy and Dan to see if anyone wanted to meet him at the bungalow in the Bahamas. Next he contacted Lewis at Quantico to let him know he was coming.

His cell phone buzzed. Sean glanced over at it and sat motionless for a moment. A slow smile crept up his face as he stared at the phone screen. It was a text from Judy. She had the keys to his new house. Suddenly he was a blur of activity, as he scooped up his car keys, phone, and briefcase. He paused to text Judy, and then he locked the agency door and trotted to his SUV. An unusual feeling of peace embraced him as he turned onto *his* street.

Sean grinned as he pulled into his driveway. Getting out he stood surveying his kingdom. A weed caught his eye. His sister pulled up as he was squatted down pulling the weed out. He straightened up and looked around for a garbage can.

"You're going to have to buy a can," Judy said with a laugh, as she watched Sean trying to decide what to do with the unfortunate plant. "Actually you'll need to sign up for three cans; garbage, green waste, recyclables."

"Really?" Sean looked surprised. They didn't have that at his parent's ranch, and they definitely didn't have it at the apartments he'd been living in.

"Really." She led him to the door and ceremoniously handed him the keys and a bottle of wine. "Congratulations little brother... you deserve it." She hugged him and turned away.

"Aren't you coming in?"

"Nope, this is your moment. Enjoy," she said as she opened the door to her Mercedes.

Sean watched her drive away, then he looked down at the keys in his hand. Taking a deep breath he unlocked the door and stepped in.

***

The next several days were spent shuffling his belongings from his apartment to the house. His siblings showed up in force, leaving their children with Grandma and Grandpa. The house was complete chaos. Boxes everywhere, the sofa in the middle of the room, the TV sitting on the floor, a brother-in-law on a ladder in the middle of the kitchen replacing an overhead fan. Judy busied herself putting the dishes and kitchen items away. Sharice and his other sister, Beth, took over the master suite.

"Sean?" a feminine voice called from the back of the house. Sean found a sister in a spare room. "Is this going to be your office?" Barb asked.

"Nope, no office," Sean answered. "It'll eventually be another guest room, for now it's storage." At her inquisitive look, he continued, "I don't want to mix work with home. I work enough hours as it is."

Barb leaned into the hall and yelled, "Bring boxes marked storage to the last room on the left!" She turned and immediately started organizing the room.

"Thanks Sis." Sean went back to the garage to help off-load the rental truck. When the pizza was delivered they all stopped to devour it along with soda, beer, and wine. He felt overflowing love for his sisters and their husbands. This was what life was supposed to be like, not the ugliness he dealt with every day.

That evening he herded them out with boxes of leftover pizza.

"Don't you want to keep it bachelor?" Sharice asked with sisterly concern.

"I'm sick of pizza. That's all I've eaten for three days. I'll go grocery shopping when I get back from my trip." Sean stood on the porch watching his big family prepare to leave.

"Where are you going?" Beth asked.

"Sharice and I are going up north to check out the old gold mining towns," he answered.

Sharice avoided eye-contact and flushed slightly.

"Take lots of pictures this time," Beth admonished.

"Okay little Miss Bossy-Pants." Sean kissed her affectionately on the top of her head.

When he'd waved the last car away, he stood in the fading light and breathed a sigh of contentment. Spying another weed, he yanked it out and walked around to the side-yard and dropped it into his brand new green-waste bin.

Back in the house he eyed his suitcase sitting on the bed. He burrowed through his boxes and found his swim trunks. Five minutes later he was standing in his pool with a beer in his hand. *Being single was going to work out fine,* he thought smugly.

***

Sean drove up Interstate 5 with two passengers; Elsa and his sister Sharice. Sean had decided to recruit Sharice to be a chaperone and to stay with Elsa for the first week. His mother volunteered to watch her grandsons for a week. She thought it was sweet that her two youngest children were going on vacation together. Sean had sworn his sister to secrecy.

Elsa sat next to him, alternating between talking non-stop and stony silence. Sean hoped she would be able to recover enough of her true personality to function as a house-leader.

She'd been stunned at Sean's idea. She had worked up until the last moment, even though Sean told her she didn't have to. Elsa knew Boris and his pimps. They would never let her quit. Never. She was determined to give no hint to her friends as to where she was going. She even made a point of chatting about random places in the opposite direction.

"You're terrified," Sean broke into one of her brooding moments.

She started crying... again. Muttering a foul word, she swiped the tears away. "I've been terrified for my entire life. I was passed from foster home to foster home. I was beaten and tortured and then pampered and loved. Now... now," she choked back a sob. "Now I'm going to be on my own. Running a household... Yeah, I'm terrified."

"You'll survive," Sean answered firmly. "You will step up and learn what you have learn and we will save little girls from prostitution. No one is more qualified than you to do it."

She bit her bottom lip and nodded.

Sharice listened in awe from the back seat. She hadn't known her brother had it in him to pull this off.

When they arrived in the little mountain town Elsa practically pressed her face to the window. She was breathless with excitement. "I've never been to the mountains before. Look! A horse," she swiveled her head to stare at this phenomena. When Sean abruptly slowed down she turned to see several deer crossing the road. Elsa squealed and covered her mouth. "Bambi!"

Sean and Sharice laughed at her childish excitement. The gravel road Sean turned onto brought fresh oohs and aahs. Sean stopped at a gate and got out to open it, then he drove up the driveway to the ranch-style house. A small beat-up car was parked under a lean-to awning.

"Someone's here?" Elsa asked in alarm.

"No, that's your car." He parked next to it and got out.

She got out and walked over to the ancient car. "Really? It's mine?" her hand hovered above the grey hood. When Sean nodded, she laid her hand gently on the car and started crying again.

"Crybaby," Sean teased. "Do you have a license?"

"No, I barely know how to drive."

"Sharice will teach you," Sean assured her. "Come on, let's get you two settled. I have to check into the hotel."

"You're not staying the night?" Elsa asked.

"For the fourth time, no. No men allowed over night. Period."

Sharice hooked her arm through Elsa's arm and said, "Come on. Let's check it out. Inside first or outside?"

Elsa giggled. "You choose."

Sharice guided her steps to the yard. A half an hour later they came in to find their luggage already in their rooms and Sean sitting on the kitchen counter drinking a cup of coffee. "Wanna a cup?" he asked pointing to the steaming coffee pot.

Sharice grinned and grabbed a cup out of a box. Standing next to her brother sipping from a cup with kitties on it, she watched Elsa inspect every corner of the little home.

"I'll be back in a couple of hours with dinner and groceries." Sean scooted off his perch and gave his sister a peck on the cheek. He smiled at Elsa and said, "See ya in a bit crybaby."

Elsa stuck out her tongue at him.

"Elsa, where do want your dishes?" Sharice asked as she looked at the limited cupboards.

"Gosh, I don't know. I've never had a kitchen or cooked a meal in my life." She looked panicked as she looked at the stove. Pointing at the microwave, she said, "I know how to heat up packaged food."

Sharice forced herself to hide her emotions as she answered, "You still have to decide where to put your dishes, silly. And I'll teach you to cook. You can always look up instructions on the internet... you know, videos and stuff." When this was met with silence, Sharice turned to Elsa. Her bottom lip was quivering. "What's wrong?"

Elsa swallowed hard, swiped angrily at her eyes, and lifted her chin. "I don't know how to read big words," she replied staring out the window at the yard. "This is so stupid. I can't do this."

"I can't read French," Sharice responded simply.

"So..." Elsa glanced at her to see if she was being mocked. "What does that have to do with anything?"

Sharice shrugged and said, "I can't read French because I was never taught how. I'm not stupid just because I wasn't taught something. You can read well enough to go on-line and take lessons on reading and writing. That's how I learned Spanish. I'll show you how." She lifted up the box and rattled it suggestively. "Point to a cabinet, so I can get started getting this put away."

Elsa turned in circle. She finally pointed to a cabinet. Peering into another box, she found glassware. She set that box under another cabinet. Her organization skills showed as she placed each box where it would be unloaded.

When Sean returned, the kitchen was done and the girls were in the bathrooms organizing towels and shampoo. "I'm back," he yelled as he set the bags down on the counter.

"It's about time! I'm starving," Sharice called from the back bathroom.

"Well get out here then… it's not going to cook it-self."

"What?" Sharice demanded as she came around the corner. "You got something we have to prepare?"

Elsa looked curiously in the bags. Reaching in, she pulled out a container of pre-made soup.

"Where'd ya put the pots and pans?" Sharice asked.

"Can't we microwave it?" Elsa asked.

"Nope. Dump it in a pot on the stove." Sharice pulled out the fixings for sandwiches. She purposefully didn't look in Elsa's direction. Sean followed her lead and pulled out plates. He set the table with the new round placemats and pulled the napkins out of a bag.

Elsa looked at all the knobs on the stove in puzzle-ment. She turned one dial and held her hand over the burner. Feeling the heat she decided she'd gotten it right and put the pan on it. Then she began the battle of peel-ing off the plastic soup lid.

Sharice reached around her and moved the empty pan off the burner. "Wait until you get the soup in the pot first, *then* put it on the burner."

"Oh, okay," Elsa felt the color rising in her cheeks, but the other two ignored her embarrassment as they busied themselves. She dumped the soup in the pot and put it back on the burner. "What number should it be on?"

"Two is barely warm, ten is super hot. I would put it on five or six," Sharice answered from the other side of the kitchen as she filled the refrigerator.

"Call me when it's ready. I want to look over the property and make sure everything is okay," Sean said as he went out the front door. Going around the corner out of sight, he stopped and looked up to Heaven. "Am I doing this right? I hope so, because I feel like I'm in over my head." A squirrel stopped on a branch near him and chirped loudly as its tail flipped back and forth. "Are you God?" Sean asked with a laugh. The squirrel stopped abruptly and contemplated Sean.

CHAPTER NINE

The Agency jet landed with a skip and hop at the Quantico airstrip. Sean, Pantell, and several other Sacramento agents stepped out into the sticky heat. As they crossed the tarmac, Sean spotted Lewis. "See you later," Sean said over his shoulder to Pantell as he cut away towards Lewis, who stood with feet apart, squinting as usual.

Not caring about what anyone thought, Sean saluted his old Recon leader, and then embraced him with a bear hug. "It's good to see you! Jeez, you're a skinny runt," Sean said with a laugh, as they crossed the road to a jeep.

"No, you're fat," Lewis retorted, as he backed the jeep up. "You've gained at least twenty pounds."

"Pure muscle, my friend... pure muscle." Sean patted his flat stomach. Looking at Lewis' chiseled profile, Sean asked, "So it's Major Lewis now, huh?"

Lewis grunted an affirmative, as he pulled into the barracks. "So, are you still Recon?"

Sean dramatically placed a fist on his chest and answered with the final part of the Recon motto; "Never shall I forget the principles I accepted to become a Recon Marine. Honor, Perseverance, Spirit and Heart. A Recon

Marine can speak without saying a word and achieve what others can only imagine... Celer, Silens, Mortalis."

"Big words for a CIA agent," Lewis teased.

"Don't be jealous little fella," Sean answered with a thump on Lewis' back.

"Harting wants to see you for dinner tonight, if you're available."

Sean glanced at Lewis with raised brows. "Dinner? Okay, where?"

Lewis stopped and faced Sean. "At his house. You can bring your partner. It's a non-uniform gathering. You know you've always been his favorite, and now his granddaughters are of an eligible age," Lewis added meaningfully.

"Oh boy," Sean groaned. "Not the Harting girls!" The last time he'd seen the two girls in question, they were pimply, pudgy teenagers. Sean paused and texted Pantell to let him know about dinner. The rest of the afternoon was spent wandering the grounds.

He stopped by Commandant Harting's office to check in. The secretary ushered him into the office. Harting stood as Sean entered. Sean executed a perfect salute and stood at attention before the most powerful man in the Marine Corp.

"At ease Marine," Harting came around his desk to shake Sean's hand. "Have a seat." He ordered in his infamous gruff voice.

Sean obediently sat down. "How are you, sir?"

"Excellent, excellent. You're coming tonight for dinner?"

Sean wasn't sure if that was a question or a command, but he answered, "I'd be honored, but I don't have formal wear."

"Not a problem, very informal," Harting assured him.

"Lewis told me I can invite my partner, Pantell. Is that correct?"

"Of course, Edna will be happy to put out another place setting." Harting eyed him across the expanse of the mahogany desk. "So you are a CIA agent now? You like it?"

"I do. My background with Recon and then the police force has helped me look at cases differently than other agents. I was getting too frustrated with the confines of the city limits. Now I can pursue a criminal trail anywhere on Earth."

Harting looked genuinely interested as they chatted for the next half hour. "So, I'll see you tonight. Rebecca and Hannah are looking forward to seeing you again. They have grown into young ladies since you've seen them last," Harting commented as he walked Sean to the door.

"I'm looking forward to seeing them as well," Sean responded politely.

He went to the dorms where he'd managed to get a two person room. Pantell was stretched out on the bed. He woke when Sean entered.

"That looks good," Sean commented as he flopped on his little bed. Within minutes they were both snoring.

That evening, Sean and Pantell dressed as formally as their wardrobe would allow.

"How is it we're having dinner at the Commandant's house?" Pantell asked as he shrugged into his sports coat.

"I told you I have friends here," Sean said as he pushed his tie into place.

"I didn't know you meant the Commandant of the friggen Marine Corp!" Pantell patted his thinning hair into place.

"It's nice to have all the information up front isn't it?" Sean grinned good-naturedly at Pantell. "Come on, don't get all flustered. He's a nice guy."

Pantell responded with a grunt and followed Sean out the door. A jeep was waiting for them in front of their barracks with a driver standing at its side. He saluted Sean and held the door for them.

"You were Army, right?" Sean asked Pantell.

"Yep, Gulf War."

"I've never been in war combat," Sean shot an admiring look at Pantell.

"Me either. I just ate a lot of sand, got sunburned, and worked on gunked up truck engines," he answered. "I know you've seen some action."

"Not really, my team did a lot of extractions… sort of our specialty. We prided ourselves in not being seen."

The driver pulled up in front of a military mansion. The lights from a crystal chandelier spilled out onto the perfectly groomed front lawn. Pantell took a deep breath.

A Marine butler stood at attention to admit them into the house. An elderly lady with fluffy white hair bustled out into the hallway to greet them.

Sean took her proffered hand, and lifted her fingers to his lips. "Mrs. Harting, you look lovely as usual."

She gave him a sweet smile. "You're such a flirt Sean."

He swept an arm and introduced Pantell, who'd never kissed a lady's fingers in his life. He shook her hand lightly. "Thank you so much for inviting me, ma'am."

Two ladies in their twenties hovered behind their grandmother. Both were attractive girls in the Southern debutante way... tailored flowery dresses with perfectly styled hair. The younger was fair-skinned with a vivid blush on her round cheeks, the older sister gracefully approached Sean and gave a slight curtsy before offering her hand.

Sean held her finger tips and made a show of inspecting her. "Is this little Rebecca?"

"Yes it is," she drawled with a grin.

"And who is this young lady?" Sean peered around Rebecca's shoulders. "Surely not the little girl who used to run wild with twigs in her curly hair?"

Hannah came forward with her eyes glued to the marble floor, and sank into a curtsy.

Sean tipped her chin up and grinned into her eyes. "Yep, this is the rug-rat I know!"

Hannah's cheeks bunched up as she smiled back.

Sean turned to Pantell, and said, "Miss Rebecca, Miss Hannah."

Pantell bowed, and the girls curtsied.

"Come in for a cocktail, men," Harting commanded from the door of the library.

***

Sean was bored after a long day of training... mostly classroom lectures. Nothing new. He hoped tomorrow would be better. He needed to get off the base. "Pantell," he hollered through the bathroom door, "Let's go to town and grab a bite to eat."

"Sounds good," came the muffled reply.

"I'll meet you in the parking lot. I'll go see if I can find a ride."

Twenty minutes later, Pantell found Sean in a jeep in front of the barracks. As he slid into the passenger's seat, he commented, "You *do* know how to acquire things don't you?"

Sean just grinned. "What sounds good?" he asked as they passed the guarded gates.

"Do they have a restaurant with good burgers and fries, preferably one with good beer?"

"Oh yeah, I know just the place." Sean pulled into a space ten minutes later. As they waited to be seated, he asked Pantell if he wanted to go over to DC before they headed back to Sacramento.

"Sure, tomorrow night… if we get done this early again."

They spent the meal chatting about the covert training they'd received that day. It was more about the rules and politics of undercover work than on technique and skills. The next day was supposed to be more practical with some field work using new weapons.

***

The second day ended early and that meant Washington DC was a go. They donned their nice clothes they'd worn to Harting's dinner party. This time Pantell drove. He'd spent time in DC and knew the area. "You'll like this pub I'm taking you to. They've got ten drafts on tap, and great food. It's not cheap, but nothing here is," Pantell added.

"Check that out!" Sean pulled his phone out and took a picture of a couple sauntering down the sidewalk. "That's the date I had from Boris' prostitution site."

"That's a CIA station chief with her. He and I worked together back in Houston."

"Don't get his attention," Sean warned. "I think it's fishy that she is with him. She had a serious interest in the story I told her about wanting to be an agent." Sean watched them from his rearview mirror. "I can imagine the stories she's getting from him."

"He's not stupid."

"Neither is she," Sean retorted dryly. "They went into that restaurant."

"I'll park," Pantell said as he pulled into a parking garage.

Back up on the street, they walked past the restaurant. It had a long bar perpendicular to the street. "So what should we do?" Sean asked his partner.

"I say we go in and have a drink and see what happens," Pantell turned back. They entered the bar and took two seats where they could see the couple in the giant mirror behind the bar.

"If he approaches us, I need to make sure she doesn't associate us with him and the CIA." Sean whispered.

Pantell rolled his eyes. "No kidding, really? I was planning to strike up a conversation about the CIA and covert operations!"

"Sorry, I forget you know more about this than I do. What is your cover?"

"I'm a state worker. I work in the Department of Labor analyzing unemployment trends.

"Good lord, how'd you come up with something that mundane?"

Pantell laughed. "It wasn't easy."

"Why are we here?" Sean asked.

"I'm your uncle. We're on vacation."

"I'm checking out the area for my travel agency." Sean nodded.

"Do you think she'll recognize you?" Pantell asked as he watched the couple leaning into each other at their little table for two.

"Well, I hope so. She cost me a fortune in food and cocktails," Sean answered dryly. "Besides, I'm unforgettable."

"And humble too," Pantell laughed as he held up his beer for a toast. "Cagle doesn't have a cover identity because he's management, not undercover." As Pantell said this, he caught Chief Cagle's eye. A look of understanding passed between them. Pantell looked at Evangeline and back to Cagle then gave a slight shake of his head in warning.

Evangeline was daintily swirling her wine and missed the exchange. She smiled up to his face and said something. Cagle's attention appeared to be completely on her, but Pantell knew otherwise. Cagle's attention was divided. They would be contacted that night by the chief, of that Pantell was sure.

Sean's mind kept tugging him to resolve a mystery regarding this woman. Even on their *date*, he'd felt something nagging in the back of his mind about her. "For some reason she looks familiar to me... I mean other than our date."

Pantell inspected Evangeline's face. Suddenly he sucked in a breath and turned to Sean. "Is that the lady in the video from Moscow?"

"Oh Jeez, how'd I miss that?"

"She looks different, but I'm sure it's her."

***

Sean and Pantell were leaning back patting their bellies when Cagle texted Pantell. They directed Cagle to the pub and waited. When the chief came in ten minutes later, they both stood and flagged him to their table. He was a tall elegant man with short black hair and a silver goatee.

After being introduced to Sean, Cagle sat down and asked, "Pantell, you old dog, how are you? We haven't seen each other in, what ten years? And here you are invading my privacy on a date." He had a smile combined with a raised brow as he leaned back in his wooden seat.

"Date? Since when are you so hard up you need to pay for a date?" Pantell teased.

"Pay?" Cagle's brow furrowed in confusion. "I met her at the gym. She's new in town."

Both Sean and Pantell were silent, neither wanting to burst his bubble. Cagle's brow drew together as he realized they had something serious to tell him. He'd been in the spy business long enough to know that dangers lurked in every new acquaintance.

He leaned forward abruptly. "Spit it out Pantell! What's up?"

Pantell nodded to Sean, who looked uncomfortable. Sean reached for his phone and clicked to the dating site he had open and ready for this question. He handed the phone to Cagle.

Looking at Evangeline's face on the screen, Cagle glanced up. He looked back at the screen and swiping, he read the description.

"Is this the same woman you just had dinner with?" Sean asked quietly.

"Yes, there's no doubt about it unless she has an identical twin sister."

"In my investigations back in Sacramento I paid to go out to dinner with her."

"What, may I ask were you investigating?" Cagle asked.

Sean paused uncomfortably before responding, "A Russian prostitution ring."

"Prostitution?"

"Yes sir," Sean answered.

"Maybe she left that life behind her when she moved here, huh?" Cagle responded somewhat belligerently.

"Sure," Sean nodded. "I can't say what her current motives are. I just wanted you to be aware she is part of an ongoing investigation. Is the name Boris Petrov familiar to you?"

Cagle shook his head. Taking a deep breath, he seemed to be getting a hold of his wounded pride. "Okay, so what is it you suspect her of, and why do you feel a need to warn me. Trust me, I did not pay her for that date. This is the fourth time we've gone out."

"Only a hunch, sir... but I suspect she is high up in the ranks with Petrov." Sean paused as he worked up the courage to say what he truly suspected. He knew he could slip considerably in their esteem. Taking a deep breath, he said, "I think she may be a spy for the Russians."

Cagle grinned. "A spy?" his smile faded when he noted Pantell was serious. "Really? Pantell, you believe this?"

"No reason not to." Pantell responded. Tipping his head toward Sean he continued, "He's a pretty smart kid."

"Maybe I'm wrong, she could be a spy for the Russian Mafia or the government... not that there's much difference since part of all mafia moneys go to the Russian president. We haven't compared intel yet, but she looks like a spy we saw on a different Russia-based case." Sean said. "I'm just asking you to be cautious and to help us by gathering intel if you suspect her actions. This could be a major break-through in this case... to have an inside mole, so-to-speak."

After several minutes of thought, Cagle nodded. "Fair enough. I've been warned. If anything suspicious comes up, I will investigate and report my findings to you."

Sean reached across the table and shook his hand in relief. "Thank you."

"When are you heading back?" he asked Pantell.

"Tomorrow. We're at Quantico for some training," Pantell answered.

Sean pardoned himself to go pay the bill.

"Too bad we don't have more time to catch up." Pantell commented.

"You really think there may be something to this?" Cagle asked.

"Yeah, I do. I'm glad we have you giving us the inside scoop. Try to find out where her loyalties lay. Does she know what you do for a living?"

"Not completely. She knows I work for the government as a manager."

"Well, don't lie too much. If she's doing what we think she's doing, she already knows exactly what you do. If you lie, she'll know you're onto her," Pantell advised. "Remember the name Boris Petrov. He's our man, a real slimeball."

***

"Hey Pantell," Sean started, "I've gotta go up to my property in Nor Cal. Is that gonna be a problem?" He held the cell phone between his shoulder and ear as he paced his small office at the travel agency.

"That'll work. We got nothing going on right now. Be back on Monday."

"Okay boss." Sean hung up and called Elsa.

"Hello," Elsa answered on the second ring. "What's up?"

"Are you ready for a roommate?"

She was silent for a moment, though he could hear her breathing in quick little puffs. "I think so. When?"

"Tonight. If everything goes as planned I should get her out this evening. It'll take three or four hours to get there, so I'll text you when we leave," he answered. "I'll try to get some food in her on the way, but she may not be able, depending on how high she is."

"Is it Latisha?" Elsa asked, holding her breath as she waited for his answer.

"No… I'm sorry Elsa. I tried, but she is too paranoid and defensive right now. They're watching her like a hawk. But I'll try again… I promise." Sean pinched the bridge of his nose.

"It's okay Sean. I know you're trying your hardest," she answered firmly. "Is she one of my sisters?"

"Yeah, you probably know her… goes by *Candy*."

"Candy is a good girl, but she's a handful. She was Boris' personal slave for her first year."

Sean didn't tell her he knew that and it was his reason for choosing her.

***

Sean followed the sleek black teenager into the motel room he'd pre-booked. She tossed a sassy look over her shoulder after she surveyed the room. She walked directly to the bed and sat down. Crossing her long bare legs, she patted the bed invitingly.

Sean locked and bolted the door behind him, to which she grinned. It wasn't the first time she'd been locked in with a customer.

"Would you like to be set free?" Sean asked. He'd rehearsed this a million times and knew immediately that he'd started off on an awkward note.

Candy looked at him in confusion for a second and regaining her composure, she answered, "Sure... Are you going to set me free?" Standing up, she slowly walked towards him as she pulled the thin straps of her dress off her shoulders. Usually the guys didn't want to set her free, they wanted to bind her or cuff her.

Sean looked at her seriously as he reached out and replaced the straps on her ebony shoulders.

The teenager stood undecided for a moment. She wasn't sure what tactic to use on this guy. It seemed he wanted to be in the *rescuer role*.

"I understand this is a shock, but I'm serious," Sean stated slowly. "If you would like to be free from this... job, I can make it happen. Right now."

She took a step back. Her eyes widened as she tried to understand.

"All you have to do is say yes, and I will take you far-far away from here." Reading the look of sudden disappointed comprehension on her face, he hurried on, "Not for me... not with me. I mean free from prostitution."

Candy stood rooted to the dingy carpet.

"You have to answer quickly. Will you take the risk? Are you willing to trust me?" Sean looked at her with all the compassion flowing through his heart.

The sounds of the cheap hotel were muffled through the thin walls. Finally she asked, "Where?"

"I can't tell you that, but I will if you come with me." Sean held his breath as he watched her emotions flash across her face. He breathed a sigh of relief when Candy nodded her head slightly. Holding a finger to his lips he set the TV to a loud show and going to an adjoining door, he opened it and waved her to follow him. Sean shut the door and dead-bolted it. Putting a hand on her elbow he guided her to the bathroom. "Change your appearance," Sean ordered as he pointed to the bags in the bathroom. "I'll wait out here."

Ten minutes later a laughing, obviously stoned couple walked down the street away from the hotel. He wore baggy clothes and a snow-boarder-style beanie. She had equally mismatched and baggy clothes on. A mass of dreadlocks draped down her back. They entered the light-rail and exited at the end of the line in Folsom.

Sean guided her to his SUV and they were on the highway five minutes later.

"Hi, my name is Sean," he said as he glanced at the grinning girl next to him.

"My name is Candy... no it's not. My name is Jazmine," she answered.

"Nice to meet you Jazmine. What kind of music do you like?" Sean asked pointing to the dial.

She turned it to a hip-hop station and spent the next two hours looking out the window into the dark night. She hadn't been this far from Sacramento since her abduction. When she was a kid her mom used to take them on annual trips to Disneyland, and sometimes they'd go to the ocean. That seemed a long time ago. Turning to look at him, she asked quietly, "Why me?"

"Why not you?" Sean asked in return.

She didn't answer and returned her attention to the road. Her head bobbed a couple of times and finally settled back on the headrest. Little delicate snores followed.

Sean smiled in the dark as he drove north.

***

Jazmine awoke when the door opened. She jolted upright in momentary terror.

Sean walked to the gate. Unhooking it, he pushed it to the fence. Coming back, he drove through the gate and got back out to close and lock the gate. Climbing back in he grinned and said, "Welcome to your new home."

She watched in rapt attention as he drove up the driveway and the house came into view. Every light was on, making it glow invitingly. A woman was waiting on the step. A white woman. Jazmine cringed on the inside at the thought of meeting this woman, knowing what she did every night.

Sean parked and got out. Before Jazmine could get her seatbelt off, he was at her door. Opening it he gallantly waited for her to get out. Then taking her elbow again he guided her up the wide steps.

Elsa came forward with both hands extended and tears flowing freely down her face. "Candy," she whispered as she enveloped the teen in her arms.

"Oh my God... Elsa?" Jazmine asked before she burst into her first series of tears that would last months, if not years.

Sean quietly carried Jazmine's little bag into the house as the two stood rocking in a bear hug embrace on the porch. "Well Jazmine, I'm exhausted. I'm going to head to my hotel. I'll see you guys in the morning."

They waved good bye from the porch as he backed up and turned down the driveway.

"Jazmine?" Elsa asked looking sideways at the tall lanky teenager next to her.

"Yeah, my name's Jazmine," she answered and turned to look curiously at the house.

Elsa hooked her arm and guided her into the home. It was lightly furnished now. It turned out Elsa liked simplistic décor. Instead of a couch, she'd chosen three overstuffed easy-chairs and a loveseat. These girls would need their space. "Are you hungry?"

Jazmine shook her head. "Nope, we done stopped at fast food back a couple hours ago."

"How 'bout some popcorn?"

"Yeah, sure," Jazmine suddenly felt out of place as she surveyed the cozy little home. "Is this your place?"

"No, it's our place," Elsa answered. "Come on. Let me show you your room."

Jazmine trailed after her in a daze. Elsa had to gently push her to get her through the bedroom door. Fresh tears coursed down her cheeks as she slowly turned in a circle. The little twin bed was covered with a fluffy comforter. An area rug took up most of the floor. A bean-bag chair and a small dresser completed the furnishings. Jazmine sank to the soft rug and flopped to her side. Pulling her knees up to her chest, her small frame shook with sobs.

Elsa slipped out of the room to let her cry in private. Throwing a bag of popcorn in the microwave, she hummed happily as she pulled out a big bowl. Next she filled a cup with water and ice. Then she went into the front-room and stoked the fire. It was going to be a long night, but she felt happier than she'd felt in years.

CHAPTER TEN

"Are we still on for the bungalow on the eleventh?" Sean asked Randy as he stood in front of his agency watching for Megan's arrival.

"I am, I'll confirm with Dan. I'll shoot you a text in a bit."

"Okay, do you mind if I invite Crazy Craig?" Sean asked.

"Nope, that'd be great to see him."

Sean texted Craig and pocketing his phone, locked the door of the agency. Megan smiled from across the lot as she stood in the shade of a crepe myrtle. They gave each other a hug that was somewhere between friendship and dating.

An hour later Sean got simultaneous texts from Craig and Randy confirming the dates. "Excellent, I'm going to get some vacation time with three of my buddies," he answered to Megan's enquiring look.

"Where?"

"Cabo," he lied.

"Good for you. Sounds fun." She laid a twenty down as she told him it was her turn to pay.

A week later Sean, Randy, Dan and Craig met at the airport check-in for the island flight. As always they drew a bit of attention… four good looking, muscular men. Craig's dreadlocks had reached mid back now. He kept it all back with a bandana. Dan looked exactly as he had in basic training—tall, skinny, and a clean shaven face. Randy had filled out across the chest and had salon-bleached streaks in his hair. They each carried a duffle bag, Recon-style.

As they crossed the tarmac on the island, Randy asked, "Where're we gonna get food? The resort is closed for the summer."

"They have a skeleton crew. Pierre, the village chief, will be there." Sean took the lead on the path leading off the road. A couple of minutes later they stepped into the clearing. The pretty little white bungalow was such a contrast to the four rugged men, they stopped and looked at it in wonder. "Well, let's get settled and hop in the ocean," Sean said as he unlocked the door. "Craig, you get the couch."

Craig crossed over the glistening painted wood floor to the over-sized couch and tossed his bag on the floor next to it.

Randy pulled out three coins and handed one each to Dan and Sean. "Odd coin gets the room alone."

They flipped the coins and Dan won. He laughed at the other two as he went to the room with one bed. Sean and Randy got the room with two beds. Minutes later they were all trotting down the sandy beach into the crashing waves.

"Who's running the travel agency while you're gone? Did you just close the doors for a couple of weeks?" Randy asked as he bobbed up and down in the surf.

"Nah, I hired a lady who only wants part time work."

Randy was on the verge of responding when a wave crashed over him. He came up sputtering. "Thanks for the warning!" he accused as he splashed water in Sean's laughing face.

***

Walking down the beach that evening, Craig asked why the resort was closed for summer.

"Hurricane season," Sean answered.

"Oh great! We're here during hurricane season?" Craig complained as he looked to the overcast sky with concern.

"I hear one is heading this way... Lucy, I think. She's just a category two now," Randy commented as the first raindrop prophetically dropped.

They walked up onto the empty Bon Temp grounds. As they approached the dock, Craig commented, "Whoa, look at that! The dock is gone."

"It's just taken apart whenever a storm is coming in. It's been taken apart a couple of times while we've been here before because the ocean was too rough." Sean paused to explain, "There's a little protected marina around the point that they use for divers."

They skirted around the resort to Pierre's house. Sean rapped on his door but got no answer, so they circled around to the restaurant. A small group of employees were sitting around several tables chatting. An elegant Frenchman rose to greet them. Bright blue eyes sparkled as he shook their hands and invited them to the table. Sean placed a bottle of wine from California on the table.

"Have you had dinner yet?" Pierre asked.

"No, we were hoping we could buy a meal here, until we can get groceries."

"Of course, of course," Pierre signaled the kitchen staff to add four to the meal. "Maybe we can ask you to work for your food, yes?"

"Work?" Randy asked as they all sat down.

"Yes," Pierre waved a tanned hand out to sea. "We have a storm coming, no? We need to prepare. There isn't much to do because the guest rooms are all boarded up for the season."

"I noticed the dock was dismantled already."

"Oh yes, we don't use it when we have no guests. But there is still much to do and four strong men would make the work easier," Pierre answered as he opened the bottle of wine.

Sean glanced around at the guys, who all shrugged and nodded agreement. "Sure we'll help out. When does Lucy arrive?"

"Tomorrow night at six o'clock. Do you have a safe place to stay?" Pierre asked with concern.

"Yeah, the bungalow is hurricane proofed. Is it going to hit us dead-on?" Sean asked. At Pierre's puzzled look he clarified, "Is the hurricane coming straight at the island?"

"No, that way…" Pierre swept his finger left to right over the ocean. "We will get the edge of her, but she has already upgraded to a category three, so that will be strong winds."

They passed the rest of the meal in planning for the work to be done the next day.

That night they sat out on the deck of the bungalow, each nursing a beer with their feet propped up on the rail.

The sun was peeking under the blanket of clouds swirling above. Their faces glowed orange with the fiery sunset, the wind whipped their clothes.

"Thanks for having a fourth chair for me," Craig said quietly.

"Who said it was for you?" Randy teased.

"It's for me." Craig took a sip of beer, then asked, "It is, right?"

The other three chuckled at his vacillating confidence.

"Yeah, it's for you."

***

The next day was busy as they all carted wooden storm shutters to the restaurant, bar, and the library.

"You guys come with me," ordered Stephan, the chief of maintenance. "We're going to go out to the beach bar and secure it. It's old, so it'll take a little more work."

They followed him along the beach boardwalk to the small bar jutting out over the sandy beach. The wind whipped viciously at them in protest.

"This is only a category three?" Randy yelled over the howling storm.

Stephan shook his head and shouted back, "She's a four now. ETA six o'clock. That means we need to have this battened down by two o'clock." He pointed to Sean. "Hand me that drill."

At two that afternoon they were struggling up the beach against a solid one-directional wind. Though the sun was nowhere to be seen, they wore their sunglasses to protect their eyes from the flying sand. No conversation was possible. The last thirty feet to their porch was the most difficult as the sand was powder fine here.

Sean waited until they were all next to the back door before he opened it, and they hurried in amidst a cloud of sand. The bungalow was dark and gloomy with the panoramic windows shuttered. They'd left the front bedroom window un-shuttered, so they went in to look out at the ocean in awe.

"Holy shit!" Dan muttered.

"It looks like a hot tub with all the jets on." Sean sat on the edge of the bed.

"What's that?" Dan pointed to a large object far out in the turmoil. "Is that a tanker?"

"No, I don't think so. That would be crazy."

They stared silently at the slowly moving object.

"Is that an island?"

The electricity flickered and went out.

"I think that's a wave," Craig commented uneasily.

"Good lord, I'm glad that's going the other way." Randy commented. "Who wants a beer?" They followed Randy into the dark kitchen. "Better drink them now while they're cold," he said with a laugh.

They held their beer bottles up in a cheer. Sean said, "To Lucy!"

"To Lucy!" they rejoined and took a gulp. Without saying a word they returned to the window to watch the drama unfold.

Sean went back to the kitchen and returned with several paper bags full of food from Pierre's chef. He spread it out on the bed. Dan and Craig pulled in a couple of chairs from the front-room and they all sat facing the window. Randy turned on his playlist of island music and plugged it into a little battery powered speaker.

Craig went to his duffle and pulled out a bottle of whiskey. He took a swig and passed it around. They all sighed in manful happiness as the fire went down their throats.

By seven o'clock the palm trees were laying sideways and the island-sized waves were rolling past the horizon. They struggled against the hundred mile an hour winds to place the shutters over the bedroom window. Moving to the front-room, they sprawled on the overstuffed furniture. Randy turned on an electric lamp. Placing that on the table, he dumped a deck of cards into his hand and shuffled.

Sean got up and ambled over to the table. Craig and Dan eyed each other from their comfortable chairs. With a grunt Dan got up and Craig followed.

"Five Card draw?" Randy asked. They all tapped the table in agreement. "It's nice having a secret hideaway," Randy commented as he dealt the cards.

"Nothing's secret," Craig grunted as he picked up his cards and organized them.

"Well, it's kinda secret," Randy amended with a laugh.

"It needs an escape route." Craig laid a card down and reached for the replacement Randy flipped his way.

Randy pointed to the door. "You can escape that-a-way."

"Escape from what?" Dan wanted to know.

"Hurricanes, people."

Sean laughed. "What do you suggest Crazy Craig?"

Craig glanced around the room. His eyes came to rest on the wood floor. "You should put a tunnel there."

Sean looked quizzically at Craig, "And where would it go?"

"Inland. That way it won't fill with water... well it would right here, but not as it ascended."

Laying his hand down, Dan said, "Fold. It's not a bad idea actually."

"He doesn't have to dig it!" Randy pointed to Craig.

Changing the subject, Sean asked, "So how do you guys like working for President Stone?"

"He's great... calm." Randy slid a little stack of poker chips to up the ante. "It's a nice break from the drama king we just had."

"I bet," Sean laughed. "It surprised me that he let you go on vacation at the same time."

"He gives us special treatment because of rescuing his son." Dan sat back down with another beer.

They all jumped as something crashed against the bungalow. Sean got up and went into the bedroom where the sound had come. Returning, he shrugged and said, "Didn't seem to do much damage. We'll see in the morning."

"So Craig, how's the bodyguard business?" Randy asked.

Craig looked bashful at the attention. "It's good."

They all looked expectantly at him, causing him to clear his throat.

"Who's the most interesting person you've protected? Who was the most difficult?"

"Umm, well... the most interesting one was a politician, but I can't tell you who. But you know him. The most difficult is the super rich businessmen and women. They're accustomed to doing whatever they want...

don't like taking orders and want to do whatever interests them. It's like guarding kids. Spoiled kids." Craig laid his winning hand down, causing the others to groan and slap their cards down.

"How about you Sean? Are you enjoying the CIA?" Craig asked mischievously.

Sean cringed. "Can't talk about it, but yes. I'm learning a lot and traveling a lot. But I'd like to settle down. I didn't think of that when I took the job."

"Jeez, we've got women constantly trying to reel us in because we're Secret Service! It's crazy." Randy commented. Dan nodded.

"How 'bout you Craig? Any girlfriends?"

"Lots of girls, no girlfriends. Montezuma is a hotbed of sex, drugs, and rock'n roll. There's not a whole lot of real women... you know... ladies." He missed the exchanged looks of amusement as he was looking down at his cards. "But it's fun."

"The only girl I've liked is a suspect in the case I'm working on," Sean commented wryly.

"Bummer," Craig said.

"Yeah, but I bought a house, so that's been cool."

***

Boris sat in what he considered his private office, though in reality it was a bar. A karaoke bar with private party rooms. Shortly after this bar had opened his gang had recognized the value to themselves and took it over. The Vietnamese owner tried to stop the take-over, but after an intense conversation with Boris and several of his bodyguards, he realized the futility of fighting Boris. They paid for the drinks and rooms, but they were the only customers. It didn't take long for American customers to see the danger of hanging out with a bunch of criminals, though Boris didn't see it that way. To him it was a pleasant place to do business, and get high, without the pesky office rent.

When one of his men rapped on the door of the room and entered, Boris glanced up from the line of cocaine he was sniffing, old-school. He snapped his fingers and the two young girls left. Boris waved a hand to the now vacant couch. "What is it Alec?"

"We have a problem sir," Alec said as he sat on the edge of the couch. "Candy has disappeared."

Boris just stared at Alec. Finally he asked when.

"Last week," Alec held up a hand in defense as he saw the rage building in his boss's eyes. "I've searched and questioned everyone I could think of... she's gone."

"Like Elsa?" Boris leaned back in the soft couch and crossed his legs casually, in complete opposition to the wicked-angry look in his eyes. "Now I know it's personal."

"But who?" Alec asked.

"I have a suspicion. Leave it to me."

***

Pierre had told them it would be safe to come out of the bungalow at eight a.m., so Craig was the first one to get out the door. He prowled back and forth like a released tiger. The ocean still heaved like a giant agitator, but the sky was starting to clear to the south. The wind whipped at their hair as the four men stood on the porch sipping their coffee.

"No more storms in the forecast. You wanna take up Capt'n Dibo on scuba diving tomorrow. He wants to get the boat out for a trial run before the club opens. This is the catamaran from their other resort. They transferred it here last week."

"Sounds good. Is it in the marina?" Randy asked.

"Yeah, hopefully it's not damaged from Lucy."

"That's the first time I've been in a hurricane," Dan commented.

They all nodded agreement. Sean pulled a porch chair out and sat down. "My back's killing me today," he complained as he sank into the low chair.

"You're always injured!" Randy mocked. "Now I, on the other hand, am like a rock."

"Yeah... intellectually maybe." Sean retorted. The other two toasted him with coffee mugs in the air.

Craig peered around the corner from the deck to see what had crashed into the wall. "Doesn't look bad from here."

They crowded around him to look at the tree branch leaning against the wall.

An hour later they were back at the resort helping restore the grounds, clean out the pool, eat lunch, stack shutters, drink more beer, and sweep water out of rooms.

They scheduled a dive for the next day as they ate dinner that night. The captain was a big laughing man from St. Lucia. His smile and teasing was infectious as he warned them the dive would be poor visibility.

***

The next day dawned clear and calm, but as Dibo had warned them the churned up water decreased visibility.

"It's better than the quarry we trained in," Dan commented as they stood on the rocking catamaran.

Craig helped by catching the anchor line. They dangled the back-up air regulator over the side. "Do we need the safety stop bar?" he asked as Dibo lifted it from its place.

"No, but we'll do it for test run of equipment," he answered in his pidgin English. "Can't assume anytang." He lowered the long horizontal bar over the side with Craig's help. "Okay, we sit and I tell you 'bout this site, yeah?"

They obediently sat on the benches in front of their tanks. Captain Dibo held a map for them to look at as he explained the topography they'd expect to see. He spoke too loud and waved his hands constantly in his description. Country music blared from the helm.

This is the coolest moment right now, Sean thought with suppressed emotion. He loved his friends and would do anything for them. Randy caught his eye and winked. Sean grinned.

"I go with you," Dibo ended.

"Who's going to stay with the boat?" Dan asked.

"Boat fine!" Dibo dismissively swept the air with one giant paw. "I dive with you as a team, yeah?"

"Let's do this," Craig said eagerly as he slipped into the BCD.

Minutes later they signaled the 'okay' sign to each other and descended. The waves rolling above them sent sunlit shadows dancing across the ocean floor. As one they turned toward the coral wall as they dropped forty feet. At the edge Dibo turned left and guided them to a deep crevice in the wall. Pointing down he indicated with hand signals they would be swept down with the current and would need to swim right to get out of the deep-water waterfall. He swam over to the current going down through the crevice and shot down like a rollercoaster. Sean shrugged at his friends and followed. His adrenaline spiked as he felt himself being pulled down. He saw where Dibo had escaped to the right and kicked hard to follow him. He left the current and got out of the way as Randy, Dan, and Craig kicked out of the vicious current. They high-fived each other and continued the dive at a much calmer pace.

The second dive was through a cavern. Dibo warned them ahead of time that two sharks guarded the entrance. "Don't worry, they're fine, no problems. You don't hurt them, they don't hurt you, yeah?"

"How do we get past them," Craig asked.

"They will move, no worry," Dibo nodded happily.

As they approached the cavern opening, the two silvery sharks hovered near the entrance as though fulfilling a job description. There was a momentary stand-off as the five divers hovered in front of the sharks. Dibo swam slowly forward and the sharks moved away from the divers. The exit to the cavern brought them out along a colorful wall at about sixty feet. They slowly ascended to the top of the wall to cruise amongst the little mounds of coral.

Dan tapping on his tank with a little metal stick drew their attention. He pointed to the giant manta ray soaring slowly past them in the deep. The five of them stopped kicking so as to not scare it away. They floated calmly, arms folded across their chests, watching this graceful creature. When it disappeared into the inky darkness of the deep water, they turned to each other with happy crinkled eyes showing their smiles. A round of okay signs went around the group and they worked their way back to the moored boat.

***

The middle-aged woman glanced up from the computer screen when the door bell chimed. This was only her second walk-in to McGee Travel Agency since she started a week and half ago. "Can I help you?" Carolyn asked as she swiveled her chair to face the clean-cut man wearing a ten-thousand dollar suit. She used to work for a high end men's clothing store… she knew her suits.

"Yes, is Sean McGee in?" he asked with a slight Russian accent.

"No, I'm sorry. Can I help you?" she asked as she wondered why warning bells were going off in her head.

"Oh dear, how unfortunate. I had hoped to catch him." Boris stood fingering the brochure rack. "When will Sean be back from…?"

"Cabo San Lucas," she supplied. "In a couple of days. He's been gone for a week and half. Are you sure I can't help you? Would you like me to relay a message?" Carolyn asked watching his face.

Boris stood looking around the agency, thinking. If it had been over a week then it was unlikely Sean was responsible for Candy's disappearance. Somehow, Boris was sure Sean was involved. "Tell him an old friend came by to talk. My name is Boris."

She pulled over a notepad and wrote the note down. She glanced up when the door chimed again. He was gone.

***

Exiting customs in Miami, they stood for a few minutes chatting.

"Hey, good luck with the new house Craig." Sean gave Craig a back thumping hug. "Let me know when I'm invited for a visit."

Craig tried to look un-moved as he assured Sean he'd invite him soon. They shook hands with each other and split off in separate directions; Costa Rica, Washington DC, Sacramento.

Back in Sacramento, Sean held the note in his hand. *Boris had been by, huh? That's interesting.*

***

A couple of nights later, Sean was staring up at the stars from his floatie. One hand trailed in the pool water while the other steadied a beer on his stomach. He slowly took stock of his life. He was a little lonely, but had an aversion to shallow relationships. He loved his job, but did he love it enough to stay single? Did he like Megan enough to try to date her?

His phone chirped a message. Sean paddled to the side and read a text from Pantell telling him to come into the station tomorrow. Sean typed a response and drifted across the pool wondering what Pantell had to tell him. It was interesting to peel back a layer on the dating site to reveal a prostitution ring. Staring at the Big Dipper, he wondered how many more layers there were. He instinctively felt there was some spy network involved. Someone bigger than Boris. Was it the Russian government? Maybe an American. Counterintelligence from within?

Was this related to the mole Frank Goldschmidt referred to?

A slow smile spread across his rough face as he thought of the aggravation he was causing Boris.

His phone chirped again. Rolling his eyes, Sean paddled back to the edge and pulled up a text from Sam.

"*I'm out front.*" Sam had written.

"*Okay, give me a sec.*" Sean grunted as he rolled off the float into the chilly water. A minute later he was opening the front door with a towel wrapped around his waist.

Sam laughed as he came in. "I brought my trunks. Dang it was hot today!"

"Hundred and six." Sean responded Sacramento style. Most conversations included the day's temperature, especially in the summer. "I keep waiting for that delta breeze to kick in." He led the way to the back yard and got back in the pool.

"I don't think it's going to happen today."

"Grab a beer from the fridge." Sean pointed to a small refrigerator on the porch.

Sam stripped off his clothes and changed into his swim trunks on the dark porch before grabbing two beers. Handing one to Sean, he sank into the water with a sigh of relief. "I hate wearing that f-ing vest on days like this. I just cannot cool off. I point the vents at my face… I even bought one of those hoses that hooks up to the air conditioner vent. I can insert it in my collar, but still it's so hot!"

Sean grinned at his friend. "Poor baby," he teased.

"Yeah, you sit in your little air-conditioned office wearing a Hawaiian shirt," Sam retorted before he sank under the water.

"Getting nervous about the wedding yet?" Sean asked when he resurfaced. It was only a month away. Hopefully Pantell wasn't going to drag him away on an op.

"Yeah, sure." Sam shrugged. "Mary's amazing though. She's so organized, it's scary. You got your tux ready?"

"Yup," Sean answered as he took a swig of his beer.

Sam looked uncomfortable for a moment, then asked, "You're gonna make it to the wedding, right?"

Sean's first reaction was to be defensive, but he stopped himself. This was a serious event for Sam, and he had the right to be inquisitive. "I'm ninety-nine percent sure. If I wake up with the flu, I'll let you know."

"Okay, I can accept that."

"Why do you ask?" Sean asked.

"Well, I know your job takes you away unexpectedly on occasion." They floated in the dark quietly for several minutes. Each lost in their own thoughts. Finally Sam added, "I know what you do for a living, dude. I know you're a Spook."

Sean wasn't willing to lie, nor was he willing to talk about it, so he said nothing. He lifted his beer in a toast, "To your wedding!"

Sam lifted his beer and answered, "To my wedding."

CHAPTER ELEVEN

The following morning found Sean circling the block for a parking space near the CIA Station. He parked next to an unconscious man cuddling a pile of belongings.

As he walked down the hallway he nodded to Becker. Becker nodded back and watched Sean saunter past with his usual laid-back style. Pantell was waiting for him in the computer lab. He stood and motioned Sean to a separate conference room.

Once in with the door shut, Pantell told Sean, "We leave at o-six-hundred tomorrow morning. I'll swing by and get you."

"Where are we going, why, and when are we getting back?" Sean asked.

"To Washington DC, then Moscow." Pantell pushed a folder across the table to Sean. "We need to follow up on a lead with Cagle, which will put us in Russia. We should be back by Thursday, but ya never know. Why do you ask… do you have plans?" Pantell asked teasingly.

"Not this week, but I'm in a wedding in a month. If I'm not coming back in time, I need to tell the groom as soon as possible." Sean opened the folder and began reading the report.

When Pantell came by his house the next morning, Sean was standing on the sidewalk with a duffle bag. "I filed the concealed carry for the flight," Pantell said as he made a u-turn.

That evening they were met at the airport in Washington DC by Chief Cagle. As they drove he told them they'd talk where they would be secure. Once settled at the DC Station, Sean commented admiringly, "Wow, nice digs here!"

"Compared to Sac it is," Cagle chuckled. "The Sacramento CIA definitely allocates its budget for technologies, not décor." He slid a photo across the desk. "Is this your man?"

Sean glanced at the photo of Boris. "Yep, that's the scumbag." He slid it sideways for Pantell who nodded in agreement. "So he's here?"

"He is, but not for long. I booked a Moscow flight for you two. I told Evangeline I had two agents going to Moscow today. Within the hour our darling Evangeline and Boris were booked for the same flight." Cagle slid a packet across the desk and leaned back. "You were right about her, kid. She's a spy. She pried every bit of *false* information out of me. Good insight, rookie."

Sean wasn't sure how to take the compliment sandwiched between the rookie references. He chose to be gracious. "Thanks sir, I've been on this guy's tail since I was on the police force. I hold him responsible for the murder of one of his girls and my partner."

"Sounds personal?"

"It is to him." Sean maintained eye contact. "He would like me to go away."

Cagle nodded and pointed to the packet. "I've listed the different false information I gave her. So far one has rebounded back to me. I told her I had a Russian diplomat staying here at a certain hotel, I had the hotel room tapped with cameras. A male entered and placed his own cameras… this guy." Cagle pointed to the photo of Boris.

"How'd you explain the empty room to Evangeline?" Sean wanted to know.

"Empty? Who said the room was empty? I had an agent who looks Russian stay there for the night," Cagle grinned. "He got pretty creative with his time. He even laid out a map and made up a fake scenario. I included his story for you to study on your flight."

"My concern is she'll recognize Romeo here," Pantell said, pointing at Sean with his thumb.

"You didn't use your real name did you?" Cagle asked.

"No, I used John Smith," Sean answered.

"Okay, you'll have to come up with a disguise. Down the hall, second door to the left."

Sean left Pantell with Cagle and went in search of his disguise. He lightly knocked as he entered the room. A middle-aged woman turned to him.

"Come on in," she invited with a wave of her hand. She looked him over toe to top. "Need a disguise?"

"Yes ma'am." Sean glanced curiously around the small workshop.

"First things first is your hair… wig or hair color?" she asked while inspecting his hair.

"I'd prefer a wig. I'm going to be in a wedding soon and dyed hair would be hard to explain," Sean answered.

She stared at him like an artist looking at a blank canvas. Nodding, she reached for a black wig.

Thirty minutes later he walked back into Cagle's office. Both men looked at him in surprise at the interruption before they realized it was Sean. Pantell whistled softly. "Damn, that old Hazel is good."

Cagle nodded in admiration at the transformation. Sean now had cropped jet black hair, an earring, sallow skin, a paunchy gut, a slight over-bite, and he wore dark rimmed glasses with beige tinted lenses.

"What an improvement," Pantell teased.

"Maybe you should go see if she can help you," Sean laughed. "Do we have a Hazel back in Sacto?"

"Yup, but it's a Fred," Pantell answered. "You chose a wig huh? Not a good idea. If you get in a scuffle and it comes off, you're screwed. It's better to do those wash out dies."

"She gave me some in case I changed my mind. I'll do it after the flight."

**

Sean and Pantell boarded the plane first, taking their seats in the last row. The seats didn't tilt back, but that was fine... they wouldn't be sleeping anyway. Evangeline and Boris took the seats four rows up. Boris looked directly at Sean but not a flicker of recognition showed on his face.

Ten hours later Sean and Pantell disembarked behind them.

"Now what?" Sean asked his partner.

"Now we go to our hotel and sleep," Pantell said wearily. "The spy business can wait until all the players are rested up." Flying from Sacramento to Washington and then to Moscow with no sleep was exhausting to the point of impaired judgment.

Sean nodded thankfully. His head was buzzing from all the caffeine he'd consumed. A limo driver stood at the exit from luggage claim with GRIFFON printed on a placard. "That's us," Sean pointed.

Once in the small limo, the driver introduced himself, "Welcome to Moscow boys. My name's Jake. I'm an agent and your tour guide while visiting this crazy city."

"Right now all I want is a comfortable bed," Pantell grunted.

"Yes sir," Jake answered good-naturedly as he wove through traffic. "I already checked and your room is bugged, so keep that in mind when you're snoring. Hopefully you don't talk in your sleep. There's no bug in the bathroom."

Sean leaned his head back on the headrest and closed his eyes trying to shut out Jake's cheerful chatting.

When they entered their hotel room thirty minutes later, they both went straight to the beds. Sitting on the edge, Sean tore off his shoes, and stripped down to his underwear. "I'm going to soak in the tub. You better use the bathroom first."

Pantell grunted again and headed in. When he came out Sean stood.

Grabbing his shaving bag, Sean bid him good night and went into the bathroom. Tearing off the wig he started filling the small bathtub with hot water. Next he pulled the temporary dye from his kit and smeared it into his hair. Sinking into the hot water, Sean sighed with joy. It took every ounce of self control to stay awake for the thirty minutes Hazel recommended. He rinsed off the dye and staggered to bed and fell into a deep sleep.

Sean's eyes popped open. The room was dark and silent. Rolling his head towards Pantell's bed he could
make out his outline. The digital clock barely illuminated
his face, but he could see Pantell's eyes… they were open
and looking his direction. A scuffing sound came from
behind Sean in the direction of the door. Pantell immediately closed his eyes to a squint. A soft snore emitted
from his still form.

The intruder must've had night-vision goggles on because he moved with ease straight to their suitcases. The
slight sound of a zipper being slowly opened indicated it
was Sean's duffle bag as Pantell had an old-fashioned suitcase with latches, which would make a loud clicking
sound if opened. Sean made a mental note to get a suitcase like Pantell's. Suddenly Pantell flipped the reading
light on and he and Sean spun towards the suitcases.
With two barrels trained on his head, the guy froze.

"Hands up!" Pantell ordered in perfect Russian.

His hands went up. "You won't shoot me," he commented quietly as he backed towards the door.

"*I* will," Sean responded as he rolled out of bed and
blocked his way. "Sit in that chair," Sean commanded
pointing to the desk chair with his Glock.

The Russian just stood there, not moving. Pantell circled around behind the guy. Suddenly the intruder
dropped to the floor and kicked Pantell's feet out from
under him. Pandemonium broke out as Pantell went
down. They fought from the floor, rolling wildly with
the Russian trying to escape. Pantell's gun bounced a few
feet away, and that became the object of their struggle.
Sean kept his gun trained on the two as he danced around
them to Pantell's gun. He kicked it under the bed thereby
changing the tone of the fight. Pantell was on top one

moment pummeling the guys face. A second later Pantell was being choked in an arm lock. Sean saw his opportunity and clocked the assailant with his gun.

The man went down. Panting, Sean and Pantell faced each other, Sean keeping his gun trained on the unconscious Russian, Pantell from the floor. "You okay?" Sean asked.

"Yeah," Pantell huffed.

The Russian sprang into action again. This time he swept Sean off his feet and bolted for the door. Before Sean could bring his weapon around the man was through the door.

"Let him go," Pantell ordered. "He's nothing and wouldn't talk anyway."

Sean looked across the carpet admiringly at Pantell. "Remind me to not get in a wrestling match with you!"

"What time is it?"

Sean lifted his head and looked at the clock. "Three o'nine."

Pantell rolled to his hands and knees and used the nearby chair to hoist himself up. "I'm going to wash up and go back to bed," he said as he limped to the bathroom.

Sean retrieved Pantell's gun from under the bed and crawled back between the sheets—after re-locking the door and balancing a water bottle on the door handle. Laying with eyes wide open, he wondered if sleep was possible. Pantell returned to bed and was snoring ten minutes later. Sean sighed in frustration. He decided to go over his Russian verb conjugations to calm his racing thoughts. An hour later he too was asleep.

***

The next morning Pantell glanced at Sean's black hair. "Good thing you did your hair last night, huh?"

"Yup, your face looks a little worse for wear," Sean commented as he assessed the black eye and cut lip as they stood in front of the elevators of a downtown skyscraper.

"Getting mugged in the street right in front of the hotel was a bit unexpected, but at least the other guy looks worse." Pantell touched his swollen lip.

Sean smiled at his cover story and nodded. "Streets are dangerous at night here."

Entering the elevator, Pantell pushed the button for the restaurant. "I've eaten here a couple of times. Good food," Pantell explained as they shot up twenty floors.

They got off the elevator and were greeted by a hostess. She told them they were expected. They looked at each other with raised brows and followed the petite blonde to a table next to the window. A pale middle-aged man stood and extended a hand in greeting.

"Hi, name's Greg Tandle," he stated with an American accent. "Cagle assigned me to help you guys out while here."

"I'm George Griffon, this here is Andy Gallagher," Pantell responded as he shook the man's slender hand.

Sean shook his hand silently. *Why are we using our cover names with a CIA agent?* As they sat, he let Pantell control the conversation, explaining the mugging and injuries. He couldn't decide if Pantell was just being overly cautious, or if it was normal to stick with an alias even when working with other agents. He covertly assessed his partner and decided Pantell was playing a part. So Tandle wasn't to be trusted. Fascinating.

"So you're interested in some unfinished business back in Sacramento?" Tandle was saying. "What've you discovered so far?" He leaned back casually and crossed his legs European-style.

"We know who the pakhan is," Pantell lied.

The man's eyes narrowed slightly. "Really? That's amazing."

Sean took over. "One of his top guys, Boris Petrov, is running a prostitution ring out of Sacramento, California. We busted him, twisted his arm—so to speak—and he gave us the name."

Pantell sipped his coffee. "That's why we're here... we followed Petrov and one of his women this far."

"What's this pakhan's name?" Tandle asked, as a slight smile lifted one corner of his soft lips.

Pantell shook his head and grinned. "Nope, no-can-do. I'll let you know when we catch him."

"I would like that very much," Tandle responded laconically.

"Absolutely! We want to keep you in the loop," Pantell assured him. "We really want to catch up with Petrov before he gets off'ed."

"If I find him first, you'll be the first to know." His grey eyes inspected Pantell's face carefully. "Do you have any ideas as to where this Petrov is?"

"Oh yeah," Pantell responded around a mouthful of biscuit. "Got him in my sights. Plan to corner him tonight."

"Wonderful, I'll read your report tomorrow." He stood. "Sorry to leave you so abruptly, but I've business to attend to back at the office," he said as he turned to the elevators.

"Catch you later," Pantell called out to his rigid back. Once the elevator doors swished shut, Pantell leaned back in his chair.

"These guys don't waste any time do they?" Sean commented.

"I guess not! This ought to be very interesting. You know you just signed Petrov's death certificate, right?" Pantell asked.

"That's the idea." Sean wiped the butter off his fingertips.

Pantell shook his head at his partner, "Let's get over to the station and see how things are progressing."

When they stepped out onto the busy sidewalk a half an hour later, Jake was magically waiting for them. "Did you tell him to come get us?" Sean asked his partner in Spanish.

Pantell shook his head and went straight to the waiting car. "Jake! How'd you know to come here to get us?"

"I've been watching you since you arrived," he answered simply.

"So you know we were attacked last night at the hotel," Pantell asked sarcastically.

"You had it handled by the time I got to your room." Jake held the door open like a chauffeur.

"And you know we just had breakfast with Tandle," Sean added from the back seat.

"Who's Tandle?" Jake asked the rearview mirror as he navigated the congested thoroughfare.

***

The Moscow station was a subtle building that in no way betrayed it's interior. Jake immediately escorted them to the station chief. The interview was brief and to the point. The chief seemed overworked and harassed.

"Do you need anything from me? Any support?" Chief Braun asked tersely, as he glanced up from a stack of papers on his desk.

"Not at this point. We will need you when we corner the leader of this gang."

The look Braun gave them was anything but friendly. "I'll loan you Jake. Make sure he knows what you're doing at all times."

"Do you have an agent named Greg Tandle?" Sean asked.

Braun stared at Sean with renewed interest. "Tandle?"

"Yeah, we just had breakfast with him. He claimed to be one of your agents," Pantell explained.

"Now *that's* interesting. He was brutally murdered a month ago in the Ukraine."

This was met with silence. All three men pondered the significance of using the name of a murdered agent.

"Undoubtedly it was a message to us, but what is the message?" Pantell asked.

"We'll be next if we don't back off," Sean answered sarcastically. "Unless we just had breakfast with Tandle's ghost."

"There's an extremely violent Russian-Ukranian gang here," Braun told them. "I'm going to send you over to the team working on this." He put a finger on the phone intercom and ordered his secretary to send Jake in. Seconds later Jake poked his head in the door.

"Yeah, boss? You need me?"

"Introduce these guys to Johnson and Tau. Tell them to work with 'em." Braun swiped the air like he was trying to get rid of a pesky fly.

They got the message and followed Jake out of the office.

"Well, he's not exactly the friendliest guy around, is he?" Pantell commented dryly.

"Yeah, he's not a favorite around here." Jake shrugged his skinny shoulders and added, "He needs to retire."

They were ushered into a large room full of computers like every other agency. Jake led them to a male and female agent sitting at a table with papers and photos strewn across the surface. They both looked up at the interruption.

"Hey Jake, what's up?" Karen Tau asked.

"I've got a couple of agents here from California. They're on the trail of a Russian cell. This morning some dude had breakfast with them and introduced himself as Tandle. Boss wants you to brief them and work with them while they're here." Jake waved a hand at the two agents who stood. "Pantell and McGee, this is Tau and Johnson."

Clark Johnson, a red-faced obese man, extended a hand. "Good to meet you."

Tau, tall, slender, and blonde invited them to sit down. "So this guy said he was Tandle huh? That's pretty ballsy--"

"And stupid," Johnson interrupted. "Now we know which gang it is."

"It's a fairly small operation but very well organized." Tau slid a piece of paper across the table. It had a grid of eight faces on it. "Any of these guys look familiar?" she asked hopefully.

Sean peered over Pantell's shoulder at the photos. None looked like their guy from the restaurant. Pantell shook his head and handed it back.

Tau and Johnson looked at each other significantly. Johnson slid another grouping of photos towards them. Sean scanned them and turned his attention to a photo at Tau's elbow. "That's the man." Sean pointed to the picture of the man who'd said he was Tandle.

"Yep," Pantell said, nodding.

The immediate silence was broken by a low whistle from Johnson.

"I hope you're ready to work? This is going to get ugly fast." Tau leaned back thoughtfully. "We're going to have to re-think our strategy."

"We are this close to pinning this guy." Johnson held up his fingers to indicate a miniscule amount.

"Is this the pakhan for this gang?" Sean asked eagerly.

"No, but it's his visible self... his spy-bodyguard-manager," Johnson answered.

"Getting to the pakhan is impossible. No one in the gang, except the top two managers, even knows who the pakhan is," Tau added.

"We told him we knew who the pakhan was," Pantell told them.

"How'd you get him to believe that?" Tau asked with a laugh.

"We told him we'd busted one of his goons, named Boris Petrov... squeezed the information out of him. That seemed to get his attention." Sean grinned. *There's more than one way to kill a snake.*

"There's no way this guy thought Petrov knew the name of the pakhan, but that still makes Petrov dirty," Johnson mused.

"So we need to find Petrov... or at least his body," Tau commented as she pulled her laptop close. "Let's get to work. We have a very short window of opportunity here."

***

Boris and Evangeline stood beside each other in the dark warehouse. Several men stood around them. Boris glared at his adversary. "Why would I tell them who my pakhan is if I don't know that myself?"

"Maybe you do know," replied Lev, the pale man who met Sean and Pantell for breakfast.

"I don't mean disrespect Lev," Boris demanded, "But why are you taking a CIA agent's word over mine?"

They stared at each other for a moment.

"Because you brought them here, to my country, and now they are asking questions and say you confessed." Lev pointed a slim finger at Evangeline who was silently observing them. "And why did you bring her?"

"I think she has potential. Evangeline has gotten intel directly from the CIA chief in Washington DC." Boris angled his head to her, "Tell them."

Evangeline maintained eye contact with Lev. He waited thirty seconds to see if she squirmed. She stood poised and emotionless. She'd worked as a Russian operative for many years. This scene wasn't new to her.

"Okay, tell me."

"Chief Cagle told me about the two men you met with this morning. He even gave me the flight they'd be on."

"Why would he tell you?" Lev asked curtly.

"Lover's say a lot when they're relaxed," she answered simply.

"I don't need you anymore," Lev said and signaled his guard to take her away. As she was dragged out of the area, Boris stood stoically, awaiting his fate. Lev circled him slowly. "I'm pleased with business back in Sacramento. You have your brother working with you, yes?"

Boris nodded.

"You love your brother." Lev stopped behind Boris, making the hair rise on the back of his neck. He continued his leisurely stroll around Boris. "Don't make me kill him too."

Boris kept his eyes fixed on a distant spot. Lev signaled his men and they silently withdrew behind Boris. Several minutes later, Boris turned to see he was alone.

***

Johnson's phone chirped a text. Glancing at it he grimaced. "They just found Evangeline's body. This is a message aimed at us."

"Why do you say that?" Sean asked, looking up from his computer.

"Because they found her," Tau answered. "Where?" she directed her question to Johnson.

He handed the phone to her, as he stood up. "Let's go."

They climbed into a compact car and swerved through traffic. The crowded streets disappeared as Johnson expertly cut off onto side-streets and alleys. When they arrived at the scene, the local city police were walking up the river embankment to their patrol cars. An ambulance slowly passed them as they pulled into the dock parking lot. Johnson waved them to stop and jumped out of the car to approach the van.

"You have the body?" he asked in Russian, showing a badge.

The driver nodded and stopped. Getting out he went around to the doors and opened them. Sean peered around Johnson's ample shoulders. "Yup, that's her."

She looked peaceful in death. Johnson pulled the sheet back to reveal an opening where her heart should have been. "This is the work of our guy, Lev."

CHAPTER TWELVE

When they landed at Sac airport, Sean and Pantell went straight to the CIA station to report to Becker. "You're back," Becker waved them into his office. "That was quick. Have a seat and tell me what happened."

They sat down. Sean leaned forward with his elbows on his knees to stretch out his back. Pantell explained their encounter with Lev.

Becker leaned forward with interest. "Lev? Are you sure?"

"Fairly sure," Pantell answered. "Directly after meeting him and telling him about Petrov and Evangeline, she was brutally murdered. According to the local agents on his trail, it was a signature murder."

"But you think you met with him at the restaurant. What did he look like?" Becker asked.

Pantell and Sean looked at each other and shrugged. "Honestly he looked kind of sickly," Pantell said.

"Tall, slim, effeminate, and pale." Sean knuckled his eyes.

"Can we follow-up more tomorrow?" Pantell asked. "We're about to drop dead from exhaustion here."

"Yeah, of course, of course." Becker stood and shook their hands. "We'll continue this tomorrow. "

"Thanks man." Sean glanced sideways at Pantell as they went down the hall.

Pantell grunted. "I thought he was never gonna shut-up. He doesn't usually want to know every detail like that."

"I heard he was on a similar case when he first came to this office," Sean remarked as he stood looking at Pantell over the top of his car.

"That was before my time. He's fluent in Russian, German, and Polish. I know he worked a lot of northern European cases before he became lieutenant and took a desk."

The ride to Sean's was in silence. As Pantell pulled into the driveway, Sean asked if they had to work the next day.

"You can if you want to," Pantell answered. "I plan on sleeping. I'm not used to all this flying around the world crap."

Sean laughed as he grabbed his duffle and waved goodbye.

His phone chirped a message as he turned the key in the front door. He ignored it. After fifteen minutes standing in a hot shower trying to rinse the temporary color out of his hair, he cracked open a beer and flopped onto his overstuffed couch. His phone chirped again. With a sigh he picked up the offensive device and read the text from Elsa.

"J is settling in. Hard first couple days… withdrawals, anger, tears… normal stuff. But we need to talk. She has another G for us."

Sean perked up. Another G? That must mean *girl*. His fatigue was swept away at the thought of another rescue. He dialed Elsa.

"Hi Sean. Is this line safe?" Elsa asked in her newly developed professional tone.

He sighed in disappointment. "No. I'll call you in about an hour okay?"

"Okay, until then." And the line went dead.

He smiled in satisfaction. He'd chosen wisely when he chose Elsa, he thought as he grabbed his car keys off the counter and set the alarm.

***

A week later, Sean followed a young prostitute down a dark alley. She glanced nervously over her shoulder at him. According to Jazmine, Sissy was only fifteen. She'd not adapted yet to her slavery and was still being beaten on a regular basis. Jazmine was concerned she would never adapt... some don't. Sissy was from the Ukraine. Another "come to America and be a model" bait and switch.

Sissy stopped abruptly and glared fiercely at Sean as he approached.

He hid a smile at this little wild-cat. He just hoped they could communicate past their language barriers. "Hello," Sean said when he was about ten feet away. He stopped and watched her.

She stared back, but seemed to feel less threatened. "Why you follow? I'm not working right now!"

Not sure how to approach the subject, Sean finally asked, "Do you like your work?"

Her eyes narrowed to slits. "Who are you?"

Sean didn't answer.

"What work you think I do?" she demanded belligerently tossing her purple hair over her skinny shoulder.

"You work for Boris."

Taking a step back she looked up and down the empty alley. Obviously terrified, she slid a hand subconsciously to her throat.

"I won't hurt you," Sean said quietly. "Do you like your work, Sissy?"

"No, of course I don't like." Her small pointed chin went up defiantly.

Sean was amazed at her bravery. "Do you want to stop this work? I can help you get away."

"How?" she demanded in a whisper, stepping closer for the first time. "How you do this? It's not possible."

"I can do it, but you have to want it."

They stood silently surveying each other for several minutes. Finally she lifted one slender shoulder and said, "Sure, okay."

"You have to do what I tell you right now… can you do that?"

She seemed to weigh her options and nodded firmly. "Yes."

Sean led her to a nearby motel and repeated his routine he'd used with Jazmine.

An hour and half later they were driving north through the night.

"Are you hungry?" Sean asked.

"Yes, but I have no money," she responded. "I left everything behind."

"No problem, we'll share something," Sean took the next exit and went through a drive-through fast food restaurant. She silently wolfed down the hamburger while Sean ate the fries. "Hey, where's my hamburger?" he teased.

"You took too long," Sissy answered, licking her fingers daintily. "What's your name?"

"I'm Sean. How about you? Is Sissy your real name?"

"No, my name is Alexia. I from the Ukraine," she answered with pride.

No wonder Jazmine wanted to rescue this girl... she wouldn't have lasted long with her rebellious personality.

"Okay Alexia, we'll be at your new home in about two hours. If you want to sleep, this would be a good time."

"I'm not tired. I was shot-up this afternoon," she pulled up the sleeve of the baggy sweatshirt Sean had given her and showed him the needle marks on her snowy-white forearm. "I'm still high. Later, tomorrow, I will be able to sleep." She stared straight ahead into the black night.

"Okay, no problem." He turned the radio up slightly and left her to her thoughts. He had a lot to think about too. Alexia was his last rescue until he could find homes for the two girls. He might need to dig into his funds to get Alexia back to the Ukraine, if that's what she wanted.

Sean was fairly certain he'd tracked down Jazmine's mother, Donna. She was the right age, had children the age Jazmine's siblings would be now. They lived in Las Vegas and Donna had plastered the city with missing daughter posters for the last couple of years. He'd found Donna's social-media page and thought the coincidence of the girl being named Jazmine too strong, plus she looked like her. It had to be her, but he didn't want to contact her until he'd spoken to Jazmine.

***

Elsa and Jazmine were standing in the porch light when Sean drove up the gravel driveway.

Alexia was watching the approach with extreme curiosity. Sean hadn't told her where, or to whom, she was being taken to. As far as she knew it was to another pimp. As soon as she made out the features of the two women waiting she gasped and grabbed the door handle. As soon as the tires came to a stop she'd leaped from the SUV and ran up the steps to embrace Jazmine. They both cried and laughed as they rocked back and forth.

Elsa smiled at Sean and nodded her head. He smiled back and came up the steps to shake her hand. This was the first time he'd seen Jazmine since he'd taken her. She looked fantastic in her skinny jeans and hooded college sweatshirt.

"Cup of coffee?" Elsa asked as she opened the front door in invitation to Sean.

He followed her in, leaving the teens to cry it out on the porch. "Decaf?" he asked as he stretched his arms overhead.

"Sure, I have decaf," Elsa said as she opened a cupboard door and pulled out a canister. She turned to a coffee maker and expertly prepared a pot. Pushing the button, she turned back to him and grinned.

"How're you doing Elsa?" Sean asked seriously.

"I've never been happier in my entire life than I am right now," she answered simply.

"No problems?"

"One time Jazzi got a hold of my cell phone. I figured it out and deleted the text she'd sent a friend before it sent."

Sean raised one brow. "Before it sent?"

"Yeah, we don't have service here and I keep the WiFi off, so it would've sent when I turned it on, or we went into Weaverville to get groceries." Elsa grinned as she picked out a cup for Sean and handed it to him. "Don't worry, we had a nice long talk. I think she got the message."

"I hadn't thought of that," Sean admitted.

"You can't think of everything," she gently chided him.

"What did she text?"

"Just that she was safe."

Sean looked at her over the top of his coffee. "How do you manage the WiFi now?" he asked.

"I have a password that only I know. That way if they want to take some online classes or research something, I can log in and sit by their side."

They both turned to the door as the girls came in. Alexia's eyes were red rimmed, but she was smiling.

"Hello Sissy," Elsa greeted the teen with a gentle smile.

"My name is Alexia," she replied with a glance at Jazzi.

"I'm Jazzi," Jazzi told Alexia with a grin.

"Well I'm Elsa. Let me show you to your room," Elsa guided Alexia down the hall, leaving Sean with Jazzi.

Sean took a sip of his coffee as they surveyed each other. "I need to talk to you," Sean started as he turned to the table and sat down. Looking back at Jazzi, he could see her frozen to the spot. Her eyes were wide and terror held her face rigid. "Oh no, I'm sorry Jazmine, nothing's wrong. You're okay... I just need your approval for something."

Her face relaxed slightly as she took the opposite seat. "What is it?"

"I think I may have found your mother," Sean started, but stopped at her expression. Jazmine's face contorted as fear, anxiety, and hope raced across it.

"Yes?" she squeaked out.

"Do you want me to contact her and re-unite you two? What do you want?"

"She doesn't want me, she never even tried to find me." Her tone was low and bitter.

"Well, if this is your mother..." Sean slid his phone over to her with a photograph of a woman showing. "She did try, very hard, to find you."

"Boris said she refused to come visit me and said I was dead to her."

"Boris said that huh?" Sean stared at her over the rim of his cup. "Boris? And you believe him over your own mother?"

Her eyes blanched as she blinked back the tears. She couldn't speak past her constricted throat, so she just nodded slightly.

"Hmm... well, anyway, do you want me to establish contact with her?" Sean prodded gently.

"What's going on here?" Elsa asked from the kitchen.

"I may have found Jazmine's mother. She lives in Las Vegas."

Elsa slid into the nearest chair. "It's too soon, Sean. We need at least another month or two. She has a lot of healing to do yet."

Sean turned his attention to Jazzi.

She looked completely overwhelmed, but nodded in agreement. "Not yet," she whispered.

"Okay, no problem. When you're ready, if ever, then let me know... okay?"

Her face relaxed immediately.

"So what've you been up to?" Sean asked, changing the subject.

"We planted a garden up above the shed," Elsa told him with pride. "We need more gardening supplies."

"Yes ma'am," Sean said with a mock salute. "Anything else?"

"They say it snows up here in the mountains. They say we'll need snow tires and a snow shovel," she said, making Sean laugh.

"Well, I'd better be going." Sean carried the cup to the sink. "I'll be back in the morning. Are you going to be all right tonight?"

"We got it handled, boss," Elsa teased as she ushered him out the door.

The next morning Sean stood in front of his cheap hotel and cradled a steaming cup of coffee as he surveyed the majestic mountains. He decided, the next time he came up, he'd take the girls on a drive to the lake. The marina had good ice cream. They'd like that.

***

A couple of hours later, Sean was driving south... deep in thought. There are lots of ways to destroy someone. Sean turned over all the possibilities in his mind as he ran his forefinger back and forth over his top lip... his favorite thinking pose. Financial, physical, and emotional. Stealing his girls covered both financial and emotional at the same time. He'd save physical for self-defense.

***

Boris flung his glass across the room. Alec flinched as the glass shattered. "How?" Boris shouted at his henchman. "How is this possible that *three* girls have disappeared?" he shouted. In a rage he pulled out his pistol and aimed it at Alec's head.

"I don't know," he answered as he squared his shoulders in preparation for his impending death.

Boris shot the giant flat screen T.V. behind Alec and swung the pistol sight back to Alec. "Find out!"

"You know I wouldn't have come to you with this news if I hadn't already tried everything in my power to find them."

The silence extended well beyond the comfortable limit as Boris tried to decide what to do. He didn't want to kill Alec.

"Maybe it's another gang?" Alec suggested.

This hadn't occurred to Boris. He lowered the weapon. "Which one?"

Alec shrugged. "I don't know who would dare steal your girls... Skarga hates your guts, as does Tang."

"Check it out," Boris ordered as he slid his pistol back into his holster. "Make sure it's not one of our brothers," he said quietly, referring to the other Russian based groups working under Lev. There was always an intense competition amongst them.

"Yes sir." Alec spun on his heel and escaped his boss's wrath.

Boris sat back down on the couch and stared moodily at the mural plastered on the wall. One by one he picked off the bosses in town... he could think of two who would do this to him.

A massive percussive blast startled Boris out of his thoughts. Jumping to his feet he flung open the door and ran into the hallway. The few people at the bar at this early hour were chattering excitedly as they stood at the front door and looked out. Boris muscled past them to see a ball of flames where his Mercedes had been parked. Anger and fear raced back and forth across his brain dimming his vision and making him feel dizzy.

"Whose car is that?" a barfly asked as he stared in fascination at the leaping flames.

The wail of sirens in the distance made Boris cringe. He marched back to the room and grabbed his jacket and strode out the back door. In minutes he was in the giant department store in the adjacent lot. Pulling out his cell he called Alec and told him to come get him.

**

The next day Sean strode into his agency, greeting Carolyn with a smile and a hug. "Good morning. What're you doing here? Did you miss me?" he teased.

"Oh sure," she shook her head at her boss's playfulness. "You were only gone a couple of days. It's when you're gone two weeks that I notice." She primly took her seat at the computer. "I've got to finalize the Campbell's trip to Panama. They keep adding excursions at the last minute! They're driving me crazy," she said calmly, making Sean smile at her serene profile. "Busy morning?" she asked.

"You might say that. You staying the whole day?" he asked as he unlocked his office.

"Nope, as soon as I'm done with this, I'm out." Carolyn's fingers tapped away at the keyboard as she talked. "I have lunch plans with my daughter."

"How old is your daughter?" Sean asked poking his head around the corner.

"Twenty-eight and *married*," she answered without looking at him.

"I was just curious," Sean said.

"Yeah, sure."

Laughing he went into his office and shut the door. He called Pantell to check in and then started a search on the Russian gangs in Sacramento. On a notepad he jotted down names and their respective territories. From a small TV he watched the news report about the car bombing in Rancho Cordova. The reporter spoke gravely as she pointed out this was most likely the work of a gang. The Flints use this particular bomb as a signature hit. The only curious thing was there had been no-one in the Mercedes.

Sean checked off the name Flint on his list. Suddenly Sean stopped what he was doing and rapidly tapped his pen on the desktop. An idea flashed into a plan. He called Elsa.

"Hey, it's Sean,"

"Hi, what's up?" Elsa asked as she stirred the soup on her stove. The girls were curled up in their chairs watching a movie.

"Do you know any of the girls working under the Flint gang?"

"Yeah, some of them used to work for Boris and he traded them during their last territory re-allocation. Boris wasn't happy about it... why?" She stepped out on the porch for privacy.

"I want a name of a girl from that gang to take," Sean stated simply.

"I don't have any room, Sean. Though the girls may be willing to share a room. I'll ask them and get back with you."

"Good, do that," Sean said and hung up. His thoughts were racing. A much bigger plan was coming together. Maybe he could kill two birds with one stone... so-to-speak.

He grabbed his keys and strode past Carolyn who glanced up in surprise.

"Lock up when you leave," he said over his shoulder.

Twenty-five minutes later he entered the CIA office and went straight to the computer room to find Pantell at his usual screen. He sat next to Pantell and waited for him to stop typing. "Hey big guy, I've got a question."

Pantell turned to him and crossed his legs. With one hand lightly drumming the desk, he said, "Okay, then I've got a question for you."

"You first," Sean suspected what the question would be, so wasn't surprised when Pantell asked if he'd heard about the car bombing. Sean nodded.

"Did you know it was Petrov's car?"

Sean nodded again.

Pantell gazed at his young partner. Finally he sighed and said, "I'm getting to old for this shit."

"Nah, you're in your prime, oh wise one." Sean laughed when Pantell rolled his eyes.

"So, my turn… who heads up prostitution gang investigations?"

"The police department," Pantell retorted.

"Okay, who heads up the foreign-based gangs?" Sean asked again. "I'm curious if this car bombing was a rival gang."

"Is this going to get me in trouble again?"

"Come on boss, I need your help on this," Sean dropped the playful act and looked seriously at Pantell.

Pantell sighed again and stood up. "Come on rookie, I'll introduce you myself."

Sean followed Pantell to a small meeting room where two men were working. A color-coded map took up one wall. A list of names with corresponding photos adorned another wall. They looked up at the intrusion.

Castle stepped around to shake Pantell's hand. "What's up?"

Pantell introduced Castle and his partner, Heckle.

Castle looked like a NFL linebacker. He had a twenty-inch thick neck and a jolly face.

Heckle was a black man with the build of a competition body-builder. His green eyes had that razor-sharp look of the highly intelligent risk taker. Sean liked him immediately. The two took each other's measure as they shook hands.

"McGee's interested in Russian gangs and prostitution rings." Pantell started on point.

"Well, you came to the right place. What do you want to know?" Castle asked as he indicated the available seats.

"I've got a report to write. I'll leave McGee with you," Pantell said and left.

Sean sat down and asked if they knew who was responsible for the car bombing from that morning.

Castle took off his glasses and polished them with a cloth. This was a habit when he was talking. It kept him from getting nervous. "It is typical of several gangs. The Flints are pretty proud of this trademark move, but I don't see the motive. They aren't enemy gangs."

"Do the SL02s have specific enemies. You know, which gangs would do this to Petrov?"

"How do you know it was Petrov's car?" Heckle asked.

"I looked up the plate and got the grandfather who fronts all of Petrov's cars. It was a navy blue Mercedes, which is what he always drives. Just a guess," Sean answered with a disarming smile.

Castle continued cleaning his glasses.

"What's your history with this gang," Heckle asked bluntly.

"He killed my partner and nearly beat to death a sixteen year old prostitute. He finished her off with a bullet between the eyes while she was lying in a hospital bed. He got my partner with the same pattern." Sean shrugged. "I guess I'd just like to know more about my enemies."

"What makes you so sure it was Petrov who killed 'em?" Castle asked over the top of his gleaming spectacles.

"Gut instinct," Sean shrugged again.

Making up his mind, Heckle said, "The Russians are their own worst enemies. The SL gangs compete with each other for territory, but side with each other against the other gangs. That's why they're so powerful. They are very diverse in their specialties. Everything from drugs, prostitution, fraud, car theft, murder, you name it."

"Unlike other gangs, they own car dealerships, medical supply companies, bars, even legitimate restaurants," Castle added. "I can't say conclusively, but they have some police officials and politicians in their back pockets."

Sean failed to hide the gleam of excitement in his eyes as he listened. So many possibilities. He stood and walked to the map. He knew they wouldn't let him take a photo, so he studied it carefully. "So this is Petrov's area?" Sean tapped the yellow area tagged SL02.

"Yes," Heckle answered. "His cousin is next door in green... SL96. He's been here since 1996, Petrov came in 2002."

Sean slid his finger slowly across the map, going from gang to gang. His finger stopped over another neighboring area colored red. "SL01? Who's this?"

"That's probably SL96's biggest rival. Slovanic arrived the year before Petrov and they've been bitter enemies ever since."

Sean traced the SL01 border. *Bitter enemies... excellent.*

"Are they related too?" Sean asked.

"Brother-in-law."

"Brother-in-law? How is that possible? It breaks the second law in the Vorovskoy Zakon!" Sean said, turning toward Heckle in surprise.

"The Thieves Code of conduct... you know your stuff McGee. Slovanic is widowed. He has no family other than the gang." Castle pointed to the pictures. "There he is, right there."

Sean turned his attention to the photos. Directly above Boris' picture was a lean man with a scar cut across his face and disappearing into his hairline. A list of the SL01s activities included prostitution. *Perfect*.

As soon as Sean left the building he called Elsa back to tell her he changed his mind… he wanted to take a girl from Slovanic not Flint.

"That'll be easier. The girls hate him. He's viscous," Elsa answered as she watched Jazzi and Alexia climbing the slope to the garden. "Our girls said they'd share a room. They're pretty excited about helping you."

"Awesome… that's great." Sean grinned. "The net is closing."

"Sean, you know this isn't going to stop them. They will just get more girls to replace these ones."

"Did you ever hear the story about the little boy walking down the beach? He kept stopping to pick up starfish and throw them back in the ocean. After awhile an older man asked the boy what he was doing. The little boy said he was saving the starfish. The old man laughed and said, 'There's thousands and thousands of starfish on this beach! How is what you're doing going to make a difference?' The little guy picked up another starfish and flung it into the ocean and said, 'It made a difference to that one!'"

Elsa chuckled and said, "I get it. I'll come up with a name by tonight."

He thanked her and hung up. On impulse he passed his SUV and walked the two blocks that put him in Slovanic's territory. He circled several blocks casually looking for a good meet-up place for a prostitute.

He drove back to the travel agency in deep thought. He would be exceeding his little mountain home's capacity very soon. He'd need a bigger place or a second place... maybe a phase two situation. Pulling into the space in front of the agency, he sat thinking. Catching movement in the rearview mirror, Sean saw Megan waiting at Brindles.

He hopped out and waved to her. She waved back and pointed to herself and the bar. Sean gave her a thumbs-up and went into the agency to check for messages from Carolyn. After glancing at the notes he locked the door and headed over to see Megan.

She was sitting at the bar with a wadded-up scarf holding his seat for him. Sean picked it up and swept it around his neck. Fluttering his eyes, he asked, "You're too kind... purple is perfect for my eyes."

Megan laughed at him and took her scarf back. "Goofball!"

Sean ordered his beer and turned to face her, his legs straddling her.

She sat up straighter at his attention and fluffed her hair. A slight blush crept up her neck.

Sean wisely didn't comment. He had sisters. He knew it wasn't considered amusing to a woman to be teased for blushing. "How was your day?"

"It was long," Megan said, thankful for the change in subject. "We've got a little glitch in one of the programs. My boss has been in a really, really bad mood lately."

Sean suppressed a smile of pleasure.

"I'm thinking about quitting, honestly. The tension is starting to get to me. I'm thinking about applying at the Intel in Folsom."

"It can get old working somewhere stressful, day in, day out," Sean said. "Especially if you don't like your boss."

"It's fun working with a small team on program development, and I like it when I learn from my boss. But things have changed. The comradery is gone." Megan let her knee rest against Sean's thigh. Time flew as they talked. Finally Sean asked if she was hungry. She was, so he suggested another restaurant nearby. Agreeing, she paid her bill and wrapped her scarf around her neck with feminine skill.

"Are you cold?" Sean asked as he held the door for her.

"Just slightly. The evenings are starting to get a little nippy," she answered. "Where do you want to go?"

Sean pointed across the parking lot, "The Firebrand, or do you want to go somewhere away from here?"

She hesitated.

Sean grinned. "Let's go somewhere else. I'll drive. I know a great little restaurant you'll love." Sean led her to the 4-Runner and again held the door for her. Walking around to the driver's side he questioned what his motives were. *Keep it casual, dude.*

***

They were sharing a dessert when Sean's phone gave a prolonged vibration in his pocket. Pulling it out, he checked the caller ID. "I have to take this call. Don't hog the rest of the dessert… I'll be right back."

Megan teasingly pulled the plate to her side of the table. Sean gave her the snake-eye and hurried away as he answered Elsa's call. "Hey?"

"Hi, I talked to the girls and we narrowed it down to one girl. She's very ill, and they think she has some sort of disease."

"Can you handle that, Elsa? Seriously… that's a huge responsibility."

"I know, but I want to do it. It breaks my heart to think of a young girl dying alone in that world. Plus I think it would be good for Jazzi and Alexia to take care of her," Elsa explained.

"We're going to need a bigger place at this rate, huh?"

"That's your job. Just keep bringing me girls. Have you looked into getting Alexia home? She claims she was taken from a fairly respectable home and her parents would want to have her back."

"Oh that's excellent news, Elsa! Get the details from her and I'll get started on it."

When Sean returned to the table, he was still smiling.

"I take it that was a happy call… good news, I hope," Megan asked as she forked a corner of the huge chocolate cake between them.

"It was just an old friend of mine. She has a friend with an illness and they think they may have found a solution—a place for the friend to live while she heals."

"That is good news."

"You've been eating the best part!" Sean waved his fork threateningly at her.

"Don't leave me alone with chocolate," Megan responded primly. "I can't be trusted."

"Duly noted." Sean took a huge chunk and popped it in his mouth.

Megan giggled and pointed to the blob of icing on his cheek.

"When are you going to apply at Intel?" Sean asked as he wiped his mouth.

She shrugged.

"Well, I hope you do."

"Why?" Megan asked as she concentrated on the cake.

"I don't know, I guess I'd like to see you happy with your work." It was Sean's turn to shrug.

***

A week later Sean invited Red into a coffee shop for a hundred dollars. Red followed him into the café and took a seat. "Do you want some tea?" Sean asked the skinny redhead.

She nodded.

When the tea arrived she cradled it gratefully. The weariness and sadness permeated every aspect of this emaciated girl. Sean wondered if she would survive the extraction. Not knowing where to start, Sean asked her if she was well.

Looking nervously at the door, she answered, "Yes, of course… I'm fine."

Sean detected another Slavic accent.

"How long have you been in the United States?" he asked.

"A long time," she answered laconically.

This wasn't going to be easy, he decided. Sipping his coffee, he noted her dirty hair of an un-likely shade of red. The roots showed brown hair peeking out. Thick make-up poorly concealed the deep circles under her eyes. Pale skin, dilated pupils, dry lips, rotting teeth. This little girl had been through the wringer. He gave her six months max.

When they were done with their coffee and tea, Sean suggested they go to a nearby hotel. She nodded as she stood and put a sexy smile on her face… only it wasn't sexy. When he led her into the motel room and locked the door behind him, she just stood in the center of the room.

Red had much worse Johns lately, since she'd been sick. Maybe they scented weakness. She was too tired to care. *Hopefully death will come to get me soon,* she thought as she watched this big man. She wasn't surprised when Sean took a firm grip on her arm and led her to the next room, and locked the door behind him.

He handed her a big hooded sweatshirt and baggy sweatpants. "Put these on," he ordered.

Red sighed and pulled on the clothing and stood waiting for the next bizarre command. Her brows drew together when Sean pulled out a flannel shirt, a wig, and a baseball cap for himself.

"If you say one word, you will regret it for the rest of your life," Sean threatened. At her nod, he guided her from the room and they exited out the back door into an alley. He led her to his rental and pushed her in.

She stared dejectedly out the passenger's window of his SUV as he pulled onto the north-bound freeway twenty minutes later. Nothing mattered anymore, not even this strange man. The pain in her stomach contorted her features.

"Are you hungry?" Sean asked, noting her hand on her concave stomach.

"No," she whispered.

"Not even a cup of soup?" Noting her quick glance his direction he pulled off at the next exit and pulled into a fast food restaurant he knew had soup.

An hour later he glanced over at her flaccid features in the flickering lights of the oncoming traffic. Sean gently placed a hand on her wrist to feel for a pulse. Detecting a faint rhythm, he sighed in relief. She was just asleep.

When he arrived at the mountain cabin, he held a finger to his lips as he rounded the hood of the SUV. Elsa came forward in concern as he gently lifted the limp body in his arms. Rushing back up the steps past the girls she held the door for him. "First door on the right," she whispered and followed him down the short hall. Sean carefully laid the young woman on the bed and backed out of the room as Elsa took over. Jazzi and Alexia crowded past him to help.

Sean was standing in the kitchen, leaning against the counter, when Elsa and Jazzi came out. Seeing his worried face, Elsa rushed forward and took his hand. "She'll be okay... for now. Alexia is going to stay with her tonight and then we'll see what happens tomorrow." One arm slipped around Jazzi's waist. "We're so thankful for what you are doing, aren't we Jazzi?"

Tears sprang to the teens eyes. "Fur sure. I hope she'll be okay."

"Probably not Jazz, but at least she'll be amongst kindness," Sean replied sadly.

The next day, Sean came back by to see how Red fared through the night. Elsa handed him a cup of coffee and bustled around the kitchen quietly.

Nodding to the rooms, Sean whispered, "How's she doing?"

SAVE THE GIRLS

"She's still asleep. Jazzi is with her now, and Alexia is sleeping. It was a rough night. The poor thing is in a lot of pain, on top of coming down off a high."

"She kept clutching her stomach last night on the way here." Sean watched Elsa scramble a pan of eggs. "Should I get a doctor to come see her?"

Elsa looked surprised. "You can do that? I mean a doctor would come here? A female doctor?"

"I don't know about a female doctor, but I'll try."

After eating a plate full of eggs and toast, Sean left for Weaverville. He loved the drive through the forest. Slowing for a deer, he let the tension of his daily life sift away. In the old mining town he stopped at the little hospital and asked for a list of doctors and Googled where their private practices were. Next he went to the first female doctor on the list. She was out of town. He went to the next one and was greeted by a tall heavy-set woman seated at a desk. Sean stated his request for an in-house appointment. She lumbered to her feet and went through a door without a word. A little nonplussed, Sean entertained himself by inspecting a tiny fish tank while he waited. Five minutes later a short muscular woman dressed in khakis and a tee-shirt came out with her hand extended.

"Hi, I'm Dr. Dressel. Margaret says you're needing a home assessment."

Sean nodded.

"Well, that's a little unusual for me to see someone at home... especially when they're not one of my patients. Maybe this person should go to the hospital if they are that ill."

"I understand, but this is a special situation. She is traumatized and I don't think she'd handle going public

183

just yet. But, you see, I'm concerned about her. So could you come over to Lewiston to assess her?" Sean asked.

Intelligent eyes peered up at him from the petite doctor. Giving a nod, she said she would. "I'll follow you over. Can you come back in an hour?"

"Perfect, I'll grab some groceries and be back."

When Sean returned an hour later, Dr. Dressel waved from a Jeep in the small parking lot. He whipped a u-turn and she pulled in behind him. They pulled into the cabin driveway twenty-five minutes later.

Elsa came out onto the porch with a worried look on her face. Sean couldn't tell if she was worried about meeting a doctor or about Red. Probably both he decided.

"Dr. Dressel," Sean started as he accompanied the doctor up the steps. "This is Elsa. Elsa is the house-mom of this home for... for young women in need of protection and recovery."

Dr. Dressel extended a hand to Elsa. "Pleased to meet you, Elsa."

Elsa took a deep breath and shook the doctor's hand. "Thank you for coming out. I'm really worried about our recent girl."

"Can you tell me anything before I see her?"

This was met with confused silence. Sean and Elsa looked at each other. "It's your choice, Elsa," Sean finally said.

Elsa, seeming to come to a decision, said, "We're all rescued from prostitution. This girl, called Red, arrived last night. She's very sick and hasn't spoken since she got here. I don't know much about health stuff. Maybe you could tell me what I can do for her."

"Okay, so she is probably withdrawing from drugs too. I imagine she's been abused." The doctor looked from Sean to Elsa. "Do we know how old she is?"

"I would guess mid-twenties, but it's hard to say," Sean offered.

"Well, let's see her," Dr. Dressel smiled encouragingly to Elsa. "Show me the way."

Elsa led her into the house. The doctor inspected the home as she went to the girl's room. Everything was immaculate and tidy.

Sean followed them in and took a seat in the kitchen.

Jazzi and Alexia were sitting in bean-bags chairs next to the bed. They both scrambled to their feet at the entrance of the doctor and Elsa. Before they could escape, Dr. Dressel held out her hand and asked for an introduction. Jazzi gave a limp inexperienced handshake, whereas Alexia gripped her hand and made eye-contact.

Turning her attention to the wisp-of-a-human barely showing under the fluffy comforter, Dr. Dressel sighed. Indeed, Red did not look well. Her skin had a parchment quality, and her cheeks were bright-blotchy pink. She laid a hand on the girl's forehead. She pulled a thermometer out of her pocket and placed it in Red's mouth. Pulling the comforter back, she placed a stethoscope on her boney ribs to listen to her breathing. The doctor nodded to herself while Elsa watched anxiously. She lifted the girl's eyelid and held a small penlight to the blank eye. Rubbing her knuckles expertly over the girl's sternum, she watched for the reaction, which was a restless movement and fluttering of eyelids.

"What do you think," Elsa ventured to ask.

"Well, without an x-ray or blood tests, I'd say she has pneumonia." The doctor continued to inspect the girl's body... rolling her back and forth to see her back. A large greenish bruise covered her upper back. "Probably pneumonia. This is quite a bruise. She may have a broken rib, making her breath more shallowly. That might have contributed to her not fighting the pneumonia a little better, but who knows." Turning to Elsa, she said, "I think an antibiotic should do the trick. We'll start there."

She slid a needle into Red's arm, amongst the scars, and drew a blood sample.

Dr. Dressel covered the girl up and tucked the comforter around Red's skinny shoulders. With a wave, she indicated she wanted Elsa to follow her. In the hallway, out of earshot of the teens, she confided, "It kinda concerns me that she isn't coughing. The way her lungs sound, I'd expect her to be coughing a bit."

"Sean said she was coughing on the drive here. Last night she had a few coughing fits, but she seemed too weak to really do it proper-like."

"Did she cough up anything?"

"Yeah, yucky greenish stuff." Elsa answered.

"Okay. There is of course, the possibility of something more serious underneath it all... you know, maybe AIDS, or another immunity disease."

Elsa's sensitive eyes welled with tears.

"Don't worry about that right now. Let's focus on getting her started on antibiotics. Have you ever taken antibiotics?"

"Oh yes," Elsa nodded. "In our profession, being sick is common. But we couldn't take time off to be sick, so we were always on antibiotics."

"Oh dear, that's not good," Dr. Dressel shook her head. "I'll have to make it a strong antibiotic. You must make sure she takes the entire prescription, exactly as prescribed… all the way to the end, no matter how good she feels. Do you understand me?"

"Yes, ma'am. I will, I promise."

"Good," she said as she turned down the hall. Speaking a little louder to include Sean, she said, "She's very dehydrated and needs lots of water. I'll write a prescription for antibiotics for her. I'm guessing it's pneumonia. There's no pharmacy over here, so you'll have to go back to Weaverville to fill it. Do you have any aspirin, acetaminophen or ibuprofen for her fever? She's at one-o-three now."

Elsa looked blank.

"No problem, I'll go get the prescription now, before I head back to… home." Sean grabbed an apple from a grocery bag and followed the doctor and Elsa back out onto the porch. "I'll pick it up in half an hour. And I'll get something for her fever. Is that enough time for it to be filled?"

"An hour's more like it. You've got to give me time to get back to the office and submit the order. By-the-way, pick up a box of masks for everyone who goes in her room. We don't want to be inhaling her bugs."

"I'll swing by your office afterwards and get the bill for this visit." Sean said around a mouthful of apple.

She agreed and was down the driveway leaving Sean and Elsa standing on the porch. Jazzi and Alexia came out and stood waiting to see what the news was.

"Well, it's good news," Sean said with a grin. "She's just sick and the antibiotics should help. I'll be back in an hour or so. I'll get a few supplies for her. Could you make me a sandwich for my drive home? I'll have to leave right away."

CHAPTER THIRTEEN

Sean's cell chirped, drawing his attention from the computer screen. Looking at the screen he tapped it to read the text from Dr. Dressel.

"When will you be back?"

"I don't have a plan for returning right away. Why? Is our pt not getting better?"

Sean watched his cell until she answered, "She's getting better. I have a business proposition for you."

This got his interest. *A business proposition? What could that mean?* He texted back, "How urgent is it that I come up now? I'm backed up with work."

"Not urgent… when convenient," she wrote back.

"How 'bout Saturday?" he dreaded making the three and half hour drive so soon.

"That's actually a perfect time. I'll meet you In Redding."

Sean scratched his head and stared at his smart phone. "Okay, I'll text you when I leave Saturday morning."

The week dragged by slowly. Saturday morning, Sean texted the doctor and headed north yet again… this time without a girl.

In two-and-half hours he pulled into the restaurant parking lot in Redding. Dr. Dressel was standing out front waiting. They went in, sat down and ordered coffee before talking.

"What's up," Sean asked with a smile.

"It's a long story," she started.

"Okay, I've got plenty of time," he said, leaning forward with elbows on the table.

"Once upon a time…" she laughed. "No seriously, I was raised on a ranch over by Lassen. My brother and his wife have an even bigger ranch than my folks. Thirteen hundred acres of cattle land."

Sean schooled his features to not show his wonder at where this conversation could be going.

"My parents are quite old now, and I've been considering moving back to the ranch to take care of them. The two ranches are adjoining." She paused.

Not knowing what to say he prompted, "You're thinking about retiring?"

She laughed, and said, "Well, taking care of my aging and stubborn parents and running an eight-hundred acre ranch isn't exactly retired."

They ordered food and she continued, "So, you're probably wondering what this has to do with you?"

"The thought did cross my mind."

Taking a nervous breath, she said, "I'd like to help you with the girls."

"Really?"

"Yes. I've been talking to Elsa, and we both think you should be moving the girls from the house to make room for more. My brother and his wife are empty-nesting and they want to offer their property for a recovery program for these girls after they spend time with Elsa." She rushed on to explain before Sean could respond, "I know we'd need training, but it's a super healthy environment for them. They could stay as long as they need to, and they'd be given chores like helping take care of the animals."

"Wow… I wasn't expecting this." Sean leaned back and stared at her in awe. Leaning forward again, he said, "I could really use the help, but there's no way I could afford that kind of operation, no way. I'm stretched thin as it is trying to take care of four people and a second house."

"You won't have to pay for our end of things. And your place could go back to two girls plus Elsa."

"Dr. Dressel--"

"Lisa," she interrupted.

"Lisa, I don't know if you understand the danger. This is a very serious and dangerous game we're playing!" Sean raked his fingers through his short hair impatiently. "For these girls it's a life-or-death risk. I mean, I don't know if you realize… they don't have some pimp from a Hollywood movie. These are dangerous mafia-type gangs spanning several countries."

"Then why are you doing it?"

"Revenge," he answered simply. He didn't want to romanticize his motives.

"Revenge?" she asked with one brow raised. "I don't believe you. Maybe that's part of your motive, but it's not all. You could've just stolen the girls and dropped them off in a different city to fend for themselves, or just killed them."

They sat looking at each other.

"Look, I'm a little more savvy than you give me credit for. My late husband was a cop. Narcotics division in South Central LA. He was brutally tortured and murdered five years ago... by a gang."

Sean sighed. "Okay, so let me think about it."

Lisa waved a hand in the air for their bill. Pulling out her wallet, she said, "My treat. You'll have plenty of time to think about it and to ask questions on the drive."

"What drive?"

"The drive out to the ranch," she said as she stood. "Come on. We haven't got all day."

A couple of hours later and a lot of conversation, Lisa pulled off the small rural road onto a gravel road. A massive gate loomed before them. She rolled down her window and punched the code into a computer panel. The gate slowly slid open. The first mile was narrowly fenced with vast rolling hills on each side. Cattle grazing peacefully looked up at the passing truck. They came to another fence with another computer panel. She punched in the code and they continued another mile or so. The fence still hemmed in the road, but a huge white dog trotted alongside the truck on one side, while a trio of border collies barked and raced in circles on the other side.

"What kind of dog is that?" Sean asked pointing to the ferociously barking white dog.

"That's an Akbash. They've been sheep dogs since at least five-hundred years before Christ."

"It certainly looks mean," he commented.

"They are... to anything and everyone besides their precious sheep."

Lisa turned a smug smile on Sean.

"All right, you win. This is a great place, but that doesn't mean you won't have trouble," Sean warned.

They came over a small hill and a medium sized ranch spread out before them. Lisa pulled around the circular driveway and stopped at the porch where a wiry short man with a gun on his hip and a woman with carrot-orange hair stood waiting. A golden retriever stood at her side.

Lisa embraced them both and introduced Sean.

"This is my brother Todd and his wife Agatha, and their dog Riley."

Todd reached out for Sean's hand and pumped it manfully. Agatha gave him a firm handshake and smiled with giant dimples. The freckles across her nose crinkled with her grin as she greeted him. "So you're the hero Lisa has been telling us about?"

Lisa and Todd both laughed at Sean's embarrassed blush.

"Come on in," Todd waved Sean into the spacious entry hall. "We've got some fresh brewed coffee, or some iced tea?"

Sean followed Todd into the kitchen. "Coffee sounds great."

Agatha bustled over to the pot and filled a mug. "Do you want milk? It's fresh."

"That sounds heavenly. I haven't had fresh milk in ages." Sean's mouth watered as Agatha poured the milk from a chilled ceramic pitcher.

"Come out back, Sean. It's a beautiful day." Todd indicated the giant deck extending away from the home.

Sean stood silently admiring the majestic Mount Lassen looming over them. Turning he looked at the east side of Mount Shasta. "I have never seen Shasta from this angle. This is beautiful."

Todd pointed to the south. "That's where Ma and Pa live on their ranch. Lisa's going to move in with them next month. That'll help us a lot. We've been running ragged trying to manage both ranches."

"I can imagine," Sean replied and took a long sip of the delicious brew. "Are you off the grid here?"

"No, not truly. We don't have cell service, but we have WiFi. We have a land line. No television at all, but we have radio. Food-wise we are mostly independent—buy our flour and such from town. We're not hiding from the world, we're just ranchers... we're busy," Todd explained in his crisp rapid fire way.

Sean nodded. "Todd, I don't know if Lisa has told you why I'm here--"

"She has."

"Okay, well I don't really want to involve other people. What I'm doing is dangerous to say the least."

"We can handle it," Todd answered abruptly. Pointing to his right, he said, "That's where we're going to build the girl's home. Agatha wants to call it *Daybreak*."

"Daybreak?"

"Yeah, nice huh? She's a good woman. We can't run no halfway house for young women, 'cause we don't know how, but we know how to love. You provide the rules and a manager and we'll do everything else." Todd sipped his coffee as he gazed with squinted eyes across the horizon.

Sean didn't say anything. He was still feeling overwhelmed. He wasn't sure if he was being cautious or if he wanted to keep the glory to himself... he could hear his mother asking him what he was afraid of?

"Right then, it's settled," Todd stepped off the porch and waved Sean to follow. "Let me walk you around the proposed site."

Sean followed Todd and Riley silently. Lisa stood next to Agatha on the porch.

"I hope we're making the right choice," Lisa said quietly.

"Of course we are, honey. It's always the right choice to do the right thing." She smiled her big smile and added, "Besides, I don't have any children to worry over with the kids married off and moved on."

Lisa watched Todd and Sean walking the flat area proposed for the structure. She felt sure she was doing the right thing. Working with Elsa and the girls had grabbed her heart like nothing ever had. She'd never been able to have children of her own and she was okay with that... but this felt like her purpose... what God had planned for her. She linked her arm to her sister-in-law's arm and blinked back tears.

**

Sean scrolled through his emails a week later and clicked on the one from Todd. It had an attachment of the architectural plans for the Daybreak Home. Sean looked them over wonderingly. It looked like a small hotel to him. Lots of big bedrooms. Every two rooms sharing a large bathroom. It had a large kitchen and two separate gathering rooms.

Sean responded to the email and shut the computer down. He locked his office and took a seat at the travel agency desk to follow up on some reservations. His cell beeped. It was Sam wanting to go for a run. Sean put his forehead in his palm and groaned. He hadn't worked out in two weeks. He texted back, "Sure, where?"

Two hours later he was jogging alongside Sam. "How're the wedding plans going?"

"Good, I guess," Sam huffed as he scrambled up a trail. When they came alongside each other again he continued, "I think Mary's finding out what it's like to marry into a Filipino family. My mom wants her to invite everyone, including relatives I've never even met. We're gonna have people flying in for the wedding from the islands."

"Is it stressing Mary out too much?"

"Too much? I don't know… I think she thrives on this stuff." Sam grunted. "Not me. I can't wait until it's over."

Sean laughed at his morose friend.

As they stood panting and walking circles in the parking lot, Sam asked, "Hey, do you know anything about this recent inter-gang rivalry? It's getting crazy. Petrov's gang has been targeted by two other gangs, now he's retaliating."

"Really? How's he retaliating?" Sean asked innocently.

"He stole one of their girls and he threw an M-80 into one of his cousin-gang's warehouses. No one was hurt, but they sure had a mess to clean up… and a posse of police inspecting the place," Sam added with a grin.

"Well, I hope they destroy each other." Sean hid his intense satisfaction at this news. *The M-80 had been effective then.*

When he left Sam, he went home, showered, changed, and went out to the CIA office downtown. It was late, but he wanted to get in and catch Heckle and

Castle before they left. He lucked out and they were still working.

After an hour of talking about the gang situation, Heckle asked Sean if he'd considered switching from Pantell to their team. "We could use some help with the prostitution angle of this and you seem to be kinda passionate about it."

Sean sat back and looked at them in surprise. He'd never thought of that. His eyes swiveled from face to face to see if they were serious. They were.

"Think about it," Castle said.

"Yeah, talk it over with Pantell," Heckle said as he closed his laptop. "Let's call it a day. I've got a date tonight."

"A date?" Sean asked.

"With his niece," Castle teased.

"She happens to be the most wonderful girl on earth." Heckle held the door for them and flipped off the lights. "See you guys tomorrow."

Castle and Sean walked the opposite direction and stopped on the sidewalk. It was six o'clock and the Delta breeze was stirring the hot air, bringing the promise of a thirty degree drop in temperature.

"It was a hot one today," Sean commented, "I think it hit one o-five."

"I wouldn't know. I've been in the cave since this morning."

"The days are getting shorter." Sean watched one of Boris' guys drive by.

"You know who that is?" Castle asked.

Sean shook his head. "I know he belongs to SL02, but I don't know his name."

"He's next in line for Petrov's job. Name's Maksim Bykov."

"That's very interesting," Sean said thoughtfully. "Very interesting."

"You're not a lone ranger type are you? We don't want that on our team. I've had a hard enough time reigning Heckle in."

"I've been called that before. Why don't we both think about this," Sean said as he patted Castle's broad back and turned away. He needed to think about Bykov and the implications. Could this be used in his plan to destroy Boris? His cell buzzed. It was a text from Megan. He texted her back and walked slowly back to his SUV—through Slovanic's neighborhood. He needed to figure out how to set Petrov against Sokolov. Then he could achieve his goal without getting his hands dirty. He would take another of Sokolov's girls as soon as he had room for one. Red was healing and starting to come out of her shell. Alexia wanted to go home, but she was still feeling too dirty to face her family. Sean was sure Jazzi was ready to reach out to her mother. It would be months before the Daybreak could be operational.

It was a serious Sean who walked into Brindle's half an hour later. Megan was out in the courtyard sipping her martini. She waved. Sean skirted the plant barricade and placed a friendly kiss on her cheek. Catching the bartender's eye, he raised a finger and sat down across from her. "So, how's the job hunting?"

"I have an interview next week, Tuesday." Megan uncrossed her legs and re-crossed them in a smooth motion and re-arranged her skirt. A flick of her head sent her silky dark brown hair shimmering down her back.

It occurred to Sean that she looked prettier than usual.

"What?" she asked as she watched his expressive face.

"I was just thinking how pretty you look," he grinned to take the flirting down a notch. "You always look pretty, but today it seems more so. Do you think it's because you may be working somewhere different?"

"It's probably because I just came from the hair salon," she laughed. "You know... clean hair and all. It's the new sexy."

Sean barked out a laugh. "I'll have to give it a try."

They smiled contentedly at each other. Sean added, "Our friendship's a good one."

"Yeah, it is," Megan agreed as the bartender set Sean's frosty mug down.

"Should we start dating?" Sean asked lightly.

"No, I don't think so. Honestly, at this point, I don't think I could bear losing your friendship." She held her martini up in a toast.

"To good buddies," Sean said and clicked her glass with his mug. "Let me know when you change your mind... I'd like to kiss that mouth some day."

She laughed and shook her head. "Don't tempt me."

They lapsed into conversation as the sun set and the temperature dropped.

***

Elsa sat next to Jazmine on the bench facing the little garden they'd grown together. She sensed the girl wanted to talk and she guessed it was probably about her mother.

Jazzi glanced sideways at Elsa and back to the garden. She fiddled with her baggy tee-shirt. One of Sean's rules was loose clothing. He felt they should have time away from their looks for awhile. At first she'd hated the clothes, but now she felt her physical beauty losing its hold on her. Slowly her self-confidence was growing. Maybe she wasn't stupid after all?... maybe.

"Elsa?"

"Yes," Elsa turned to her little charge. She marveled at Jazzi's beautiful skin and fine bone structure.

"Do you think I should find my momma?"

"Honey, your momma has already been found. It's you who needs to be found. She's been looking for you for a long-long time. The question is; is she a good mother? Will you be in good hands?" Elsa felt her throat tighten at this huge responsibility she'd been given. Jazzi was her first girl. She couldn't imagine life without her.

"Oh, Elsa, she's the best mom. She took real good care of us, but she had to do it alone. My dad left right after I were born. I have an older sister. She must be twenty now." The floodgates were open. Jazzi turned and straddled the bench as she continued, "My daddy was in the military. I think the Air Force, but I'm not sure. My momma is a secretary for a big company in Las Vegas. I don't remember where. I didn't care at that age. I was kinda rebellious. I used to like to go down to the strip and hang out with my friends. We'd pretend we were famous dancers from one of the casinos. I didn't understand what it must've looked like to the men." She looked down at her bare feet. "Now I know."

Elsa wrapped her in a motherly hug. "Oh sweetie, I'm so sorry."

Jazzi's shoulders trembled and then heaved as she sobbed against her mentor's soft shoulder. After a good cry, she pulled away and scrubbed her face dry with her palms. "I guess I should let Sean call her."

Elsa didn't trust herself to speak, so she nodded.

The girls weren't allowed to use the WiFi unchaparoned. Elsa made a point of signing off after each use since the last time she'd caught Jazzi's text. Elsa went to the tool shed and texted Sean to let him know Jazzi was ready to be in contact with her mother.

"Excellent," was the brief reply. Elsa leaned against the rough wood door and let the tears slide down her cheeks. Looking up, she wondered if there really was a God. She laughed at herself, *Why're ya looking up? If there is a God, he's not in the rafters.*

***

That Saturday morning Sean was at the airport waiting to board a flight to Las Vegas. He'd decided to speak to Donna in person. He couldn't imagine telling her this over the phone. Besides, he wanted to see this mom for himself. He didn't want her to go into a toxic situation. He also needed to tell her she would probably need to move away. He'd called and told her he needed to talk to her about a job opportunity... not a complete lie. She was very professional, yet skeptical.

Once he arrived in Las Vegas, he went straight to their meeting place. A café far from the casino strip. He recognized her from the photos. She was a large woman. Tall and heavy-set. Her hair was slicked back into a professional bun. Sean stood and waved a hand to her. She walked straight to him with a confident stride, and held out her hand for an introduction.

"Hello, my name is Donna Taylor," she said as she set her giant purse in the chair.

This was not what he'd expected. Somehow he'd pictured a poorly dressed, unhealthy teen mom. Instead he was faced with a business woman. "I'm Sean."

"Sean?" Donna asked with an admonishing tone. "No last name?"

"Just Sean," he answered with a grin. She reminded him of his oldest sister.

They sat facing each other, while Sean tried to figure out how to drop this bombshell.

"So, what can I do for you?" she encouraged with a grin. "This is about a job?"

"Sort of. The job of motherhood."

"You want me to have your child?" she asked sarcastically as she began to lose patience with this stranger.

Sean laughed. "No, but I have located your daughter, Jazmine."

She gasped so loud, several customers looked their way curiously. She didn't notice as she stared at Sean like he'd grown another head. "What?"

"Jazmine would like to be reunited with you, if you're interested," Sean decided he was going to like this part of his job.

She sat there in stunned silence for a full minute. "I can't believe it. It's—it's so crazy... do you know how long I've looked for her? How many tears I've shed for my baby?"

Sean slid a recent photo of Jazzi across the table to her.

Donna made a sound somewhere between a hiccup and a gasp. Slowly, she slid the photo closer. "She's beautiful. Where did she go? Is she okay?" Donna looked up at Sean with large tears streaming down her cheeks.

He handed her a napkin and gave her a moment to dab at her face.

"She's not good," Sean started. "I mean she doing pretty good now, but... well, it's been pretty bad. You see, she was kidnapped and sold into prostitution."

Donna's eyes grew dark with motherly rage at this news.

"It's going to be a long journey for her. She's been abused and it will take time for her to heal."

"Abused?" Donna whispered through clenched teeth. "What do you mean?"

"Physically and psychologically. She was drugged on a regular basis and has had to battle the withdrawals. She is recovered from that now, but she'll need counseling for a long time. But she's decided she wants you, if you'll have her."

Donna silently mopped her tears and nodded.

"Here's the problem; I kidnapped her from her... boss. That, obviously didn't go over very well. They want her back, and it won't be good for her if they do get a hold of her."

"What are you saying?" she asked, staring at him wide-eyed.

"If I bring her back to you, you should move. Far away. Don't tell anyone why you're going. *Then* I'll deliver her to you." Sean tapped the tabletop emphatically with his forefinger.

"Leave," she repeated. "I'll need time. I have to see if I can get a transfer to another site. Or maybe another job. Where should I go?"

"That's up to you."

The first hint of a smile appeared as she fingered the photo. "My baby is alive."

"Yes, and I want to keep her that way," Sean added wryly. He handed his card to her. "Contact me when you're ready."

"Can I speak to her?"

"I can arrange that when I get back," Sean answered with a smile.

***

As Pantell and Sean were walking down the hallway, Detective Allen leaned out his door and flagged them down.

"Hey Sean," Allen started as he hurried back to his table of computers. "The last twenty-four hours have seen a lot of action on the site you had me monitoring." He waved them closer. "See here..." he pointed to a bunch of symbols, letters, and numbers. "This is big. It means they've had a change in leadership."

Sean and Pantell looked at each other blankly.

Seeing their expressions, Allen explained the way he could tell it was a new person running the show. His technological talk was not enlightening them, so he finally just said, "Trust me." Pointing to another screen, he added, "I've been able to locate their shop based on the information you gave me regarding Megan. I narrowed the circle down to an area within ten minutes of your travel agency." He tapped the screen on a glowing rectangle. "This trailer is off the charts with electricity usage."

Sean snapped a photo of the screen and thanked Allen. "Come on Pantell, we have work to do." As they retraced their steps to the parking garage, Sean explained his theory that they had to strike right then... In the moment, before they could close shop. "You drive," he said as he skirted to the passenger's side. As he buckled up he was already zooming in on the location, using the photo as a reference. He called back to the office for back-up as they bounced out of the lot.

"Get on H Street and head towards the river," he told Pantell.

Sean used the time to zoom in to a ground level view of the spot the trailer was now located on. "It's on private property!"

"Crap... we'll need a warrant to even walk around it."

"Turn right on fifty-seventh and it's on the left. It's a warehouse parking lot, so we can go in."

"You just said it's private property... make up your mind!"

"Sorry, it's privately owned. I was hoping it was on the street. We can at least scope out the area. Should I call off our back-up?" Sean asked.

"No, we may still see some action, especially if they bug out," Pantell advised as he turned onto fifty-seventh.

"Okay, turn left into the parking lot," Sean pointed. Pantell slowed as he approached the lot. As they circled the large warehouse complex the trailer came into view. Several cars were parked next to it. One was Megan's.

Pantell passed it and pulled into a spot in front of an antique showroom. They both adjusted their mirrors to watch.

A non-descript sedan pulled into the parking lot and parked near their vehicle. Sean pointed to the trailer. The agent in the other car nodded and slouched down to where he was barely visible. Half an hour later a semi-cab pulled into the driveway and went around the building to the trailer. As it backed up to the hitch three men and a woman came from the back of the trailer.

"Megan," Sean commented, watching the little cluster.

They stood for a few minutes talking and watching the hitching process, then they turned towards their respective cars.

A police cruiser drove past them on fifty-seventh and turned into the lot. As it circled back towards the CIA group Sean groaned.

"You've got to be kidding me!" Pantell rolled down his window as the unit pulled in next to him.

Sean leaned forward and laughed as he saw the officer was Sam. "Sam! I thought you would be taking time off preparing for the wedding?"

Sam's face lit up when he realized it was Sean. Putting the cruiser in park he answered, "Women take time off... not the guys, dummy. All we have to do is show up." Sam looked around the lot and back to Sean and Pantell. "Whatcha doing here? We got a call saying there were some creepy guys sitting in a sedan in the lot. Are you the creepy guys?"

"Yup," Sean laughed. "That's us. We're getting ready to go into the antique shop and buy some stuff."

Sam just stared at him, deadpan. "Right."

The semi truck and trailer was on the move.

Pantell fired up the engine.

On an impulse Sean leaned over again and asked Sam, "Does everything about that semi look legal to you?"

Sam turned his attention to the truck lumbering past them. He looked back to Sean and replied, "There's always something illegal with every vehicle, you know that."

"Could you pull it over and question them?"

Sam made eye-contact with Sean for a moment and answered, "Sure, if you think I need to."

"I do, but don't involve us and be extremely careful. The driver is probably armed."

As Sam pulled away he flipped on his lights. Pantell turned to Sean. "Are you sure that was a good idea?"

"No, but it may be the break we've been waiting for."

They watched as Sam approached the driver's door. Sean kept his attention on Megan's group, who all stood watching. The older male in the group spoke to them, and the two younger males and Megan dispersed to their respective cars. Looking back at Sam, he saw him reach for the driver's license. Sam waved the driver to get out. As the man opened the door, the older male approached from the shadows.

"Not good," Sean pointed to the approaching man. "Can we get involved?" he asked Pantell.

Pantell nodded as he pulled out his service weapon and opened the door. Sean got out and stepped up to the other agent's car. "This is about to go south on us. That's Boris Petrov's brother, Derik. That trailer is valuable evidence. Circle around the front."

The agent nodded and backed out of the space and disappeared around the building. Sean and Pantell stood casually waiting for them to reappear in front of the stopped semi. Simultaneously the truck driver had stepped down to Sam and was answering Sam's questions. The man shook his head no. Sam glanced towards Sean. Big mistake... the man followed Sam's eyes. Within seconds the driver was back in the semi cab. Derik was running towards Sam. Sean and Pantell approached from the back. The other agents came around the front.

The first bark of gunshot was wild, the second connected with Sam. Sean saw red as a haze of anger flooded his vision. Pulling the trigger as he ran, Sean dropped the driver. Then he felt the bite in his thigh. It suddenly sounded like a war zone. Sam was firing from the ground, the driver lay motionless. Derik was firing wildly. The two CIA agents found cover behind their car and fired with precision at Derik, who took several shots before he finally went down.

Sean was at Sam's side in seconds. He grabbed Sam's radio and called for an ambulance. A police unit skidded into the parking lot followed by three more. Sean put his hands up in the air from his kneeling position at Sam's side. "Officer down!" he shouted.

The other three agents laid their guns down and held their hands up. Pantell yelled out, "CIA."

Police officers rapidly approached and grabbed the pistols. "Identification?"

They all slowly reached into their pockets for their badges. One recognized Sean. "McGee?"

"Micky! Hey give me a hand here. I already called it in." Sean turned his attention back to Sam. "You okay buddy?"

"Yeah, I think so." Sam reached up to touch his chest. "The vest stopped the bullet. What in the hell just happened?"

"You just got a couple of days off before your wedding," Sean teased.

"Boris doesn't stand a chance now," Pantell commented as he nudged Derik's dead body.

***

"Hey boss," Sean sat next to him in the computer lab. "I have a question."

"Shoot," Pantell responded as he pivoted toward Sean.

"Can I temporarily assist Heckle and Castle? I mean, can I do that? Or do I have to officially transfer to their team and transfer back to you?"

"You don't need to officially transfer. I can handle everything we've got going right now. If I run into problems, I'll ask for your help," Pantell suggested.

Sean looked relieved. "Good, because I don't want to give up my partnership with you."

"Not yet, but you will," he answered with a slight smile.

"Maybe, but not yet." Sean laughed. "Catch ya later." *This will give me more freedom*, he thought as he walked to the gang-office. *This will make it less obvious when I disappear.*

CHAPTER FOURTEEN

Sean stood solemnly at the front of the church next to Sam's brother. Out of the corner of his eyes he could see Sam's knees quivering against his rented tux. He could understand why as Mary was slowly swept up the aisle by her father. Her narrow train slid with a whisper behind her. Behind the sheer veil he could see her elegant smile. She was perfect for Sam... petite, classy, smart. Sean wondered what his perfect type was as Mary's father placed his only daughter's hand in Sam's hand.

He envisioned Megan, but then his mind wandered to Tasha with her battered face and bullet hole in her forehead. Kim's face drifted past the ceremony next, equally dead. Then came Evangeline's beautiful face with her mutilated body. Elsa, Jazzi, Alexia, and Red...

Pressure built behind his eyes as tears threatened. This healthy, lovely wedding was torture. Sean forced himself to focus on the couple kneeling next to him, the sonorous tones of the Irish priest.

At the reception he inspected the crowd. Someday he'd find a woman tough enough to handle him. Someone like his sisters. Right now he just needed to stay awake. Exhaustion was dragging him under. He noted the coffee urn and headed that way... coffee would be good.

***

The following Monday Sharice sat cross-legged on the floor of Sean's Travel agency. She'd picked a spot near the plate-glass windows to sort the cruise pamphlets. Her short-shaggy blonde hair curled around her face as she stuck the tip of her tongue out in concentration. Sean smiled at the sight.

She glanced up at him. "So how's Elsa doing?"

"She's doing great. I think the responsibility has actually been good for her." Sean swiveled his chair towards her. "Thanks for helping her get adjusted."

"Thanks for letting me. I really enjoyed it. I'd like to do more, if you'd let me."

"Nope," Sean answered. "Way too dangerous. I can't lose you. You're already in danger."

Sharice sighed, and turned her attention back to the brochures. "Does she have any girls there yet?"

"Three."

"Three? Wow, that's awesome," she remarked.

Sean desperately wanted to tell her about the ranch, but he didn't. He hadn't told a soul. Once the Daybreak was officially ready, he'd tell Elsa. At least he could talk to Lisa.

"It *is* awesome. I wish I could tell you all about it. It's hard to keep it all in."

She looked at her brother with adoration. "I love you so much Sean. I'm proud you're my brother."

The doorbell chimed as the door opened. They both glanced at the door. Megan stood just inside the door and looked at Sharice uncertainly.

"Megan," Sean stood and went to her. He gave her a hug and turning to his sister, said, "This is Sandy, my part-time helper. Today's her first day."

Sharice hid her look of surprise at being introduced as Sandy. By the time she'd gotten to her knees, Megan had approached with her hand out.

"Nice to meet you, Sandy," Megan said dutifully. "You didn't answer my text, so I thought I'd pop in and make sure you're okay."

Sean pulled out his phone. "Oh bummer, it was on silent-mode."

"Well, I'm heading over to Brindle's if you want to come over and have a drink together."

"Are you okay?" he asked, though he knew exactly what was wrong.

Megan looked pointedly at Sharice. "Maybe we can wait until we meet up over there." She tipped her head across the parking lot.

"Sounds good. Give me ten minutes to wrap it up here."

Megan said good bye and left. Sharice let out a low whistle. "Wow, she's super pretty. Is she your girl-friend?"

"Nooo…." Sean ruffled her hair and went back to his desk.

"Why'd ya introduce me as Sandy?"

"None of your business," he retorted as he went into his office. Coming out, he shut and locked the door. "Come on, time to close."

"I can stay and close up the shop," she said from the floor.

"I can't do that, sis. I can't explain, but it's dangerous right now."

"Dangerous?" she asked. "How so?"

"Move it little girl! I'm not going to explain it to you," he said as he stood waiting for her to gather her stuff.

"Meany," she said.

"I thought you loved me and were proud of me?"

"Not right now. That was like five minutes ago." She walked past him with her nose in the air.

Sean laughed at her as he locked the door. "I'm not giving you a hug, but you know I love you."

"Yep, I know," Sharice grinned as she unlocked her car door and slid in.

As Sean watched her pull out, he realized he had to keep her away from the agency for the time being.

Brindle's was crowded and noisy. Megan waved him to go outside. He found a seat and she joined him with her martini. A waiter approached and took Sean's order.

"You look stressed out," Sean commented as he gazed at the circles under her eyes. "How's the job hunting going? Did you hear back from Intel?"

"I've had a horrible couple of days. My boss was murdered." She watched his face.

"Murdered?" Sean looked shocked. "What happened? Home invasion or something?"

"He was shot by a cop."

"Why in the world would a cop shoot him?"

"I don't really understand everything, but it had to do with our work. We were moving the mobile site to a new location. Derik was always moving the trailer I worked in to save money on renting an office." She sipped her drink. "Day before yesterday we had finished our day and the trailer was going to be moved to its new location when the police stopped the truck. I'd already taken off, so I wasn't there when it happened."

"I heard about it on the news. Something about the driver shooting the cop, right?" he asked innocently.

"Yeah and I guess they opened fire on him and Derik somehow got caught in the crossfire." Sighing, she added, "It's a good thing you'd talked me into changing jobs because they confiscated the trailer with all the equipment in it."

"No wonder you look stressed out," Sean said gently.

She smiled weakly at him. "I don't like change. I would rather boil like the frog than jump out when it gets hot."

"Lots of people are like that. When do you start your new job?"

"In a week."

"You should get away for awhile. Maybe go see your dad," he suggested.

Her expression changed as she thought about it. "That's not a bad idea. I think I'll do that. He's been after me to come for a visit." She pulled out her cell and texted her father.

They visited long into the evening after her father had responded. "Well, I'd better get home and pack, if I'm gonna leave in the morning."

"Where does your father live?" he asked, relieved she was leaving.

"Napa."

"Tough place to go visit, huh?" he teased.

"I guess I'll have to drink wine."

"Poor thing!"

She laughed, "Well, I was raised there. I've had enough wine to last me a lifetime."

***

A couple of nights later, when Sean was heading to his SUV, he walked through Slovanic's territory again. He passed a black Mercedes similar to the one he'd blown to smithereens. He memorized the plates and noted a bodyguard in the shadows. Glancing back, he could see a man sitting in the back seat. Instinct screamed it was Boris' cousin, Slovanic. He glanced back again like he was checking traffic and then crossed the street.

It had been over a week since he'd met with Jazzi's mother, Donna. Just as he was wondering about her progress with moving away from Vegas, she texted him. "Call me when you get a chance."

He drove straight to his secure office at his agency. Once in his office, he called her.

She answered on the first ring. "Hello Sean. I've got good news. I've been transferred to Atlanta. When can I have my daughter?"

"When you move there, I'll bring her to you."

"Okay, two weeks from tomorrow I'll be there. I'll call you when I have an address."

"I'm looking forward to it." He answered, though he wished it was sooner, so he could grab another girl. He realized now, more than ever, how much he needed the home on the Dressel Ranch. Things were moving too slow.

He checked the plates on the Mercedes. It was registered to an unknown man in Rio Linda. Probably the same system as the grandfather in Rancho Cordova. He sat in his office chair, feet on desk, and chewed his thumbnail. *Should his next abduction be one of Boris' girls or his cousin's?* He decided to hit Boris again.

"Give me a call when you get this text," Sean typed to Elsa. He paused for a moment, then tapped send.

Elsa replied right as Sean was pulling into his driveway. "Give me about ten minutes."

He went straight to the fridge and pulled out two beers. He put one in the freezer and popped the other one. The pool looked low, so he went out back and turned the water on to fill the pool. Stopping, he looked inquisitively at a footprint in the soil near the spigot. The neighbor's dog barked at him through the fence. Sean looked from the footprint to the dog barking through the slits of fencing.

"It's okay Bouncer, it's me," Sean explained to the dog. Bouncer sniffed the fence to make sure he wasn't being tricked. Satisfied, he trotted away to investigate another possible menace.

Sean's phone chimed. He went back inside and hung up the call from Elsa. He texted back, "Not secure. Will call you in twenty."

"Okay."

Sean sighed as he pulled the beer out of the freezer and put it back in the fridge. Driving back to the travel agency, he decided he'd get a dog. He was fairly certain someone had been lurking around his property and could easily have placed bugs at his home.

"Hey Elsa, I'm in a safer place now," Sean said when she answered the phone.

"Okay, what's up?" Elsa asked.

"I'm looking to take another girl in about two weeks... which is about how long it will take Jazzi's mother to relocate," Sean commented as he gazed at his foil lined walls. "Can you handle that?"

"I don't know, Sean. Red isn't as close to Alexia as Jazzi is. I'm not sure if Alexia will take another girl into her room. I'll ask her, but give me a couple of days to see how things progress with Red. She's slowly coming out of her shell. The girls are being real patient with her." Elsa fiddled with a string hanging from a nail in the shed as she talked. "Have you heard anything more from Jazzi's mom then?"

"Yeah, she's relocating so she can get her daughter back, but it's a bit of a process to change jobs and move."

"I can imagine. I'm having a harder time with this than I expected. I didn't realize how attached I would get," Elsa said quietly.

"That's a good thing... it means you care."

"I do," Elsa answered.

"Start thinking of a girl from Boris' gang."

Sean hung up a few minutes later and called Dr. Dressel. "Hi there."

"Well, hello there Sean. What's up?" she asked as she watched her ninety-year-old father struggle to get out of his favorite recliner.

"Now that I'm committed to this home you're building, I'm anxious to get it done. How's it coming along?" he asked.

"Good. They laid the foundation a couple of days ago. We decided to buy a few prefab homes and attach them. Todd is pretty handy with stuff like that, so it'll be good."

"Oh, so it'll be much faster then, huh?"

"It should go pretty fast. We've already ordered the homes... three of them. That'll give us nine bedrooms and three kitchens, which we won't need, but we can use the space for gathering and for a classroom," she said.

"Classroom?"

"Yeah, It's Agatha's idea. She actually has her bachelor's in education. She's excited, to say the least."

"That's great. Let me know as soon as I can move someone in," Sean said.

She promised and they hung up. Sean went back home to his empty house and pulled his open beer out and took a gulp. The second beer went back into the freezer. He grabbed a can of chili out of the cabinet and started a package of hot dogs to boil. This was his comfort food. For some reason, he felt melancholy. He flipped all the lights on and turned the TV on for company. The pool was a little too cool for comfort with the cooler nights, so he flopped on the couch. Five minutes later he jumped up and turned off the burners and went out and swam laps for thirty minutes. Feeling much calmer, he restarted his dinner and relaxed at the table.

He picked up his phone and called one of his sisters. "Hey Beth," he started.

"Hi Sean. How's the house?" she asked in her rapid way of talking.

"It's great, but it's kinda lonely. I was wondering if you know of anyone giving away a dog?" he asked his rescue-dog crazy sister.

"There's always dogs to be rescued! What kind of dog do you want? How old?" she asked.

"A medium-sized dog, not a puppy. I don't have time to train it. It'll be outdoors during the day and inside whenever I'm home. I like dogs that have soft fur."

"Soft fur sheds," she commented.

"I can deal with hair. I'm not a clean freak," he added.

"Okay, I'll ask around," she assured him. They chatted until his food was ready.

The next morning she sent him a photo of an ugly brown dog with half its ear missing. "Wow, that's one pathetic looking mutt," Sean texted back.

"He's a sweetheart and loves to be a running buddy. He was brought to the pound by his owner's parents… apparently the boy went away to college and the folks didn't want it."

"Jeez, that's mean!" Sean shook his head in disgust. "Is he at the pound out on Bradshaw?"

"Yep. I asked them to hold him for you to come by and see him."

"Thanks sis, I'll go by this afternoon. Will you be willing to dog-sit when I'm out of town… which is often?"

"Sure, I can always squeeze one more into my house."

That afternoon, Sean pulled into the pound. An employee showed him to the dog's cage.

"His name's Jet," the girl said as she unlocked the dog's cage door.

Jet stood leisurely and ambled over to take a sniff of Sean's hand. He gave it a lick, then sat down to study his new owner. Sean squatted down to study his new dog. "Jet seems an ambitious name for such a calm dog."

"Yeah, not sure how he got that name."

Jet's mouth curved up at the corners and he bared his teeth into a ridiculous smile. Sean started laughing and ruffled Jet's hair. "What mix is he, do you know?"

"No, I don't know, but I'd put money in it that he's part Border Collie. Maybe a bit of Irish Setter or something long haired and slim. Look at that tail." She pointed to the six inch long hair coming off his tail like a fan.

"Is that ear a fresh injury?" Sean asked.

"Yep, he got in a fight with a dog right after he arrived. He's been here a week. We had him slated for destruction tomorrow.

That decided it. Sean caressed the silky hair and Jet fixed his chocolate-brown eyes on Sean. "I'll take him."

"Okay, that's great," she smiled. "But first you should take him out into the yard and see if you get along. I'll set you up. Give me a couple of minutes."

She left Sean with his new dog. Jet panted in anticipation of he knew not what. He gave a little inquisitive whine.

"Let's go show this lady that we'll be a good pair, okay?"

***

The next two weeks flew by for Sean as he settled Jet into his new home, worked at the travel agency and the CIA office. He'd been loaned to the drug and gang team. He and Heckle hit it off well and exchanged ideas for how to slow down the sex-slave trade. Sean never even hinted at his rescued girls up north.

Lisa called and told him the homes had arrived and the process to get them attached to each other had begun. The plumbing would be in by the end of the week and the electrician was scheduled for the next week to make sure everything was attached properly. "What exterior color do you want it to be?"

Sean was surprised at the question. "Color? I don't care. Make sure it looks good with their house. Let Agatha choose."

"Okay, I'll tell her," Lisa said and added, "Todd thinks it'll be ready for one or two girls by the end of next week."

"Oh that's great. I'll send Alexia to you, but I'm not sure if Red will be ready."

"I hope Red can make it. It would be so much easier for me to have her here, where I can keep an eye on her. I'm afraid she's going to relapse. I don't think she'll survive for long. She's really damaged."

Sean sighed and pinched the bridge of his nose. "That's too bad," he murmured.

"We're not looking at quantity of life, Sean. We want to give them quality," she reminded him.

"Yeah, I know. You're doing a great job, doc," Sean said.

"What about Jazzi?" Lisa asked.

"She's returning to her family."

"Really? That's awesome!"

The following day Sean got a text from Elsa. Alexia and Red would share a room to make a way for a new girl. A lump lodged in Sean's throat at their generosity and kindness. What started out as revenge had turned into a passion.

He called Elsa to get a name, Katie.

Two nights later he was driving north with a stunned teen prostitute in his SUV. She talked non-stop until he fed her then she suddenly fell asleep. Her head angled toward Sean, showing heavy make-up over delicate features. She looked to be from Eastern Europe.

Earlier, when Sean asked her where she was from, she'd grown quiet and said she didn't remember. "I think I lost my memory. I don't remember anything from before, but I speak Russian, so I guess that's where I came from," she had answered simply.

Now that she was asleep, he could think. Elsa had told him the girl was considered mentally slow. She never complained and never questioned anything done to her. "She's a little slow, you know, kinda simple-minded," Elsa had told him.

PTSD shows itself in many different ways. The shock could have altered her mentation, he thought. He was intensely curious to see how she would be in six months or a year. He hoped she would remember where she came from, otherwise she'd be difficult to place. Jet placed his muzzle on Sean's left shoulder and looked out the front window.

The dog had been so silent, Katie hadn't even noticed the dog until they went through the fast food drive-through window. Jet gave a short bark when he smelled the burgers wafting through the air. Katie squealed in surprise, but immediately showered the dog with attention. Sean decided she must've had dogs around when she was younger.

When they pulled into the driveway of the mountain home, Elsa stepped out onto the porch to greet them.

Katie jumped out of the vehicle before Sean even had it in park.

"Mom," she yelled as she raced up the steps and threw her arms around Elsa. "I've missed you so much."

Elsa patted the girl's back as she clung to her. Sean grinned at Elsa's look. "Mom?"

"Lots of girls called me mom," Elsa said as she stood rocking the girl back and forth.

Jazzi opened the front door and peered out, Red looked over her shoulder. Sean greeted them, causing Katie to break away and look with shock at the two girls in the doorway. "Oh my god! Candy and Red!" she shouted as she dove into Jazzi's arms, making everyone laugh.

Alexia stood back a little, as she didn't know Katie. They faced each other after the introductions were made. Making a guess, Alexia spoke to Katie in Russian, to which Katie responded. They switched back to English after a couple of awkward minutes. "She doesn't know where she's from," Alexia said sadly.

"Yeah, I know," Sean said. "But Katie's safe now."

"I know where I just came from and I don't wanna ever go back." She looked in alarm at the group.

"Shh-shh, don't you worry about that... we're not sending you back. Like Sean said, you're safe now." She patted the frantic girl's back soothingly. "Let's get inside. It's starting to sprinkle."

They all followed her in and Red sat at the kitchen table, obviously still weak. She looked lovely though, with her cheeks filling out a little.

"Are any of you afraid of dogs?" Sean asked the group. They all shook their heads no, and looked at Sean curiously as he went back out to the SUV and let Jet out. He trotted up the steps next to Sean with tongue lolling out to one side. The girls squealed in delight at the mangy dog. "This is Jet," Sean introduced the dog to them as they showered it with attention.

Elsa led Katie back to her room. Alexia had decided to sleep on the couch that night and they'd moved Red in Jazzi's room since Alexia would be leaving with Sean the next day for the ranch.

"So Red," Sean asked the delicate girl as he sat. "What's your name?"

"Lynette, but I've gone by Red so long, it sounds strange," she answered. "After talking to Elsa, I understand why it's important that I use Lynnette, or Lynn. It will help me break from this recent past, if that makes sense.

"Makes sense to me. It's one of the reasons I made the rule of baggy clothes only and no guys here—except me. I want you to have a complete change until you heal."

"*If* we heal," Alexia commented.

"Oh you will heal. But you'll never be the same… you'll be different than you'd have been if this hadn't happened to you. It'll take time." Sean stood and stretched. "Tell Elsa I'll be back in the morning with groceries."

Sean called Jet to his side and asked Alexia if he could speak to her privately for a moment. She looked nervous as she agreed.

"So," Sean began as they stood under the eave out of the rain. "Did Elsa talk to you about moving to the ranch?"

She nodded silently.

"Are you okay with that?"

"No, but if it means more girls can be rescued, then I will do it," Alexia answered.

"I admire your strength Alexia. One of the reasons I chose you first is because I want you to help us make the ranch a good place. Your maturity will help so much."

"Thank you for compliment, but I don't feel strong," she answered quietly. Jet nuzzled her hand.

"We leave in the morning, okay?" Sean asked.

Her eyes showed her fear, but her chin went up a notch. "Yes. Why can't Jazzi come too?"

"I'll explain it tomorrow," Sean said. "But Alexia, you must say goodbye to her. I can't guarantee you will ever see each other again."

Alexia couldn't respond, so Sean respectfully left her with her thoughts.

The next day he arrived in the afternoon to give them all time to say goodbye to Alexia. She had circles under her eyes, but she looked resolved to this next step.

Katie stood on the porch with tears streaming down her face. "Why does she have to go?" Elsa gave her a chiding look. "Where are you going?" she asked next.

"That I can't tell you," Sean said cheerfully. With a playful wink, he said, "It's a secret hide-away!"

Jazzi and Alexia hugged long and hard. "I hope you'll be happy with your mom," Alexia whispered.

"Me too. I'll miss you and think about you all the time." Jazzi gulped back tears as she made room for Lynn, then Elsa. Turning lastly to Katie, she spoke to her in Russian. The girl nodded and hugged her hard.

"Come on you cry-babies," Sean teased, "We've got a long drive ahead of us." He opened the door for Jet and went around to the passenger's door and held it open for Alexia. She got in solemnly. Jazzi trotted down the driveway to open the gate for them. She stood waving with a smile on her face and tears on her cheeks.

Two hours later they pulled into the large circular driveway of the Dressel Ranch. Todd, Agatha, Lisa, and two elderly people stood on the porch waiting. Riley sat with tongue lolling to one side, but he snapped to attention when he spotted Jet.

"Jet, you get to stay in the car, okay buddy," Sean told the excited dog.

As they got out Lisa came forward with both hands outstretched. "Welcome Alexia."

"Dr. Dressel!" Alexia's surprise made her usual reserve drop a little.

"Lisa, to you." She kissed her cheek and stepped to the side to make introductions.

Agatha was beaming with joy at the sight of her first rescued girl. She impulsively wrapped Alexia in a bear hug. Alexia melted into the soft woman's arms. "I hope you help us make this a great place for young ladies. I'm so excited you're here!" Ignoring everyone else, Agatha led Alexia into the ranch house.

At the same time the men encouraged Sean to introduce Jet and Riley. When the two dogs got done sniffing each other, they raced around in circles barking and tackling each other.

The women went straight to the kitchen and Agatha poured Alexia a glass of iced tea. Then she led her out to the back deck. Pointing, Agatha said, "That's your new home." Arm-in-arm, she grinned at the girl. "You can help me decorate it."

Alexia looked in wonder at the rambling structure. It looked enormous to her. "Me? I don't know how to decorate."

"Sure you do, honey. Everybody knows how to decorate. You just say 'I like this color and I think that carpet looks pretty,' and there you go!" Agatha pulled the stunned teen along as she walked across the freshly mown grass. "I got you a bed and some bath stuff."

Sean looked at Lisa and laughed. "Well, she seems made for this job."

Lisa shook her head in wonder. "Apparently."

***

"I know this is McGee!" Boris barked at Alec.

Alec shrugged. "Maybe... maybe it's your cousin getting even with you for taking one of his girls."

"I didn't take one of his girls!"

"I know, but he feels differently."

"I don't care what he thinks," Boris retorted.

"Maybe it was Maksim," Alec commented, referring to the man who would take Boris' place when Boris was gone... Maksim Bykov was a patient man, but it was well known he was ready to take over SL02.

"Maksim? Is he trying to get rid of me? Is that what you're saying?" Boris demanded with a flicker of concern.

"I haven't heard anything, but you know how it is." Alec answered.

After a moment, Boris shook his head. "No, it's Sean McGee... I know it is."

"Do you want me to get rid of him?"

"Not yet, I want to know where he took my girls."

"I could make him talk," Alec assured his boss.

"He has sisters, right?"

Alec smiled. "Yes, boss, he does."

***

As Sean came through his front door, his cell phone beeped. It was Sharice wanting to know if he needed help the next day at the agency. "No Sis, I don't think it's safe for you to come to my work for awhile."

"Fine! □"

Sean smiled at her petulant emoji. He knew this latest rescue was going to really piss off Boris. "Don't be mad. Maybe we can have lunch this week."

She texted back a thumbs up emoji.

Chuckling, Sean let Jet out the back door. The dogs hackles rose and it dashed out into the night. Sean pulled his gun out of his holster and followed the dog. "What's up Jet?" Sean surveyed the dark yard and then flipped on the flood lights. Jet was at the side gate barking ferociously. Sean slid around the corner with the gun ready for business, but there was no one there. Sean searched the perimeter and called the anxious dog into the house. Jet searched the house and finally came into the kitchen to beg.

Sean ruffled his fur and congratulated him on being such a good boy. They curled up on the couch together and watched TV until Sean fell asleep. He woke up with a start. Turning the TV off, he and Jet went to bed.

The next day, Sean was back sitting next to Pantell at the CIA office. They worked in silent comradery at neighboring computers.

"It looks like someone is working on Petrov. Heckle and Castle have it from the streets that he's had several of his girls kidnapped," Pantell commented glancing at Sean.

Sean kept his eyes glued to his own screen. "Good, I hope he's miserable."

"Yeah, first a girl gone, then his car blown up, now two more girls have been taken. They even took one of

Slovanic's girls." Pantell continued to stare at Sean's profile.

Sean glanced over at him and asked, "Why'ya staring at me?"

"Are you involved in this?"

"What kind of question is that?"

"It's the kind of question I want answered," Pantell persisted.

Sean saved his work and stood. "I'm gonna go see what Heckle and Castle are up to."

Pantell watched him walk away. Shaking his head, he went back to his work.

Heckle waved him in. "We've got a lot of action right now." He showed Sean several familiar spots on the map. "Here's the spots Boris' girls were nabbed. Here's where one of Sokolov's girls was taken."

Sean attentively inspected the map. "What does that indicate? Obviously they were in this area. That's where they worked."

"True," Castle said. "Word is that Boris Petrov knows who is after him."

"Really, who?" Sean asked with interest.

"A cop, or an ex-cop," Heckle answered, looking at Sean curiously.

"That makes sense," Sean agreed. "But I'm surprised he isn't more concerned about it being an inside job. Let me know if you find anything. I'm going to be out of town for a couple of days," Sean added.

"Another vacation?" Heckle asked.

"Sort of, family time."

"Must be nice to have so much vacation pay," Castle commented sarcastically.

"I usually just do three day weekends." Sean answered and decided it was time to talk to Becker about his plans. He headed down the hall and tapped on Becker's window and waited for him to get off the phone. When Becker hung up, he waved Sean in and indicated the office chair.

"McGee, how are you? We haven't talked for awhile." Becker closed his laptop and leaned back comfortably to chat.

"It's been awhile for sure," Sean sat opposite his boss. "Do you have time to talk? Privately?"

"Sure." Becker glanced at the door pointedly.

Sean closed it and sat back down. "So here's the deal… remember when we first met? It was over the Boris Petrov case."

Lieutenant Becker nodded.

"Well, as you know it's progressed a lot. We found his internet source—his brother. He was killed in the process, but we managed to get the semi trailer that the entire computer system was in. We are this close to closing the noose around this scumbag's throat." Sean held his fingers a centimeter apart.

"Yes, I've read the reports," Becker held a palm up. "Is there something new?"

"This is complicated. You see, I connected with one of his old-time prostitutes. She helped me, so I removed her."

"Removed her?" Becker interrupted in his raspy voice.

"Yes. I took her someplace safe where he couldn't find her."

"You didn't run that by me," Becker's placid face was darkening. A storm was brewing.

"True, that's because I did it for personal reasons, not related to the case," Sean added.

"What? Are you in love with her or something?"

"Something like that," Sean answered. "Anyway, it gets worse, or better, depending on how you look at it. I have since rescued four more girls. This is on my personal time."

"All Petrov's girls?" Becker's brows were practically connected as he tried to follow where Sean was going with this story.

"One is Slovanic's, four are Petrov's." Sean paused.

"So, you've had a very busy private life," Becker said.

"Uhm, yeah," he answered sheepishly. "The problem is, I think he's figured it out... that it's me doing it."

"Wow, really?" Becker's voice dripped with sarcasm. "And now he's targeting you and threatening to blow your cover as a CIA Agent? Brilliant! Does Pantell know about this?"

"No, sir," Sean answered in frustration. This was not going as well as he'd hoped. "Look, if helping these women be free from a life of terror and abuse is going to cost me my career with the CIA, then so be it. I can't just stand by and do nothing. Everything I did was on my own time and using non company resources. I'll continue to help these girls one way or the other!"

"What do you want from me then?" Becker asked in a calmer tone.

"I mainly wanted you to know," Sean answered. "At some point they can be used as witnesses. Not all of them, but the stronger ones."

"Please tell me you didn't blow up Petrov's car?"

Sean squirmed uncomfortably.

"Are you friggen kidding me?" Becker's voice rose. "You're suspended until further investigation of your actions."

Sean walked out and headed to the garage. Twenty minutes later he was at the travel agency. He called Randy from his foil-lined office.

"Hey, do you have a minute?" Sean asked.

"Not right now. I'll call you in about an hour," Randy said and hung up.

Sean sighed heavily. *Suspended.* That had never happened to him before. A part of him acknowledged it was justified, but he knew he'd done the right thing. Well, maybe not the car bombing... or the warehouse bombing.

CHAPTER FIFTEEN

"Randy," Sean greeted. "You gotta minute?"

"Yep, what's up?" Randy's deep voice boomed across the phone.

"I need help."

"Okay… what do you need?"

"I need to have a girl secretly escorted to Atlanta."

"Plane or car?"

"Plane."

"Is she under-age?"

"Nope. Her mother will be waiting at the other end. Problem is I need you here in Sac. How soon can you get here?" Sean pulled up the flight information on his laptop. "There's a flight that leaves at eight o'clock in the morning."

"Lucky for you, I'm in Houston. I'll get there tonight. That way I'll be in time to get her on the plane," Randy answered.

"Thank you, buddy. I owe you," Sean's faced relaxed slightly.

"Yeparoo, that's why I'm doing it," Randy laughed. "Send me her flight details, and her name."

"I'll send you the flight numbers, not the name, but make sure no one sees it but you," Sean ordered. "Hey, do you want to do it tomorrow morning or the day after tomorrow?"

"Day after tomorrow… that way we can catch up. I can stay with you right?"

"Absolutely, do you need me to pick you up from the airport?"

"Nope, I'll rent a car," Randy answered. "See ya tonight."

Next he called Dr. Dressel. He couldn't think of anyone else who could deliver Jazzi to Sacramento Airport. She agreed and promised she wouldn't come into the city with the girl.

"As a matter-of-fact, we won't stop anywhere on the way, except maybe a rest stop," Lisa assured him.

"If you see anything suspicious at the rest stop, keep moving."

"I promise," she assured him.

"Okay, thanks doc. I'm pretty excited for Jazzi and can't imagine having to put this off until I'm free."

***

That night Randy arrived in the midst of a torrential down-pour. Jet barked boisterously at the newcomer, his tail wagged wildly. "Well hello," Randy said with surprise. "What's your name?"

"Jet," Sean answered as he pushed the eager dog back enough to get Randy through the door. He took his dripping coat to the garage. "Your room's first door on the left," he said over his shoulder.

Randy threw his duffle on the bed, and went straight to the refrigerator. "Please tell me you have some decent beer?" he asked as he bent over to rummage through the shelves.

Jet sat with tongue out, dripping saliva in his excitement.

Sean laughed at his friend. "I stopped and picked up a couple of your favorites. There's one in the freezer."

Randy pulled out the slushy beer and smiled. "You are officially my best friend!"

"I know," Sean tapped beer cans with him and grinned. "Did you eat?"

"No, do you have any grub, or should we go out?"

"I've got a pot of spaghetti and garlic bread," Sean answered with a nod to the stove.

"Oh man, really? Is it your famous spag with the spicy meatballs?" Randy lifted the lid and sniffed appreciatively.

Sean leaned around him to turn on the broiler. "Yep, my mom's recipe." He threw a couple of placemats on the kitchen bar counter. "Get outta the kitchen you mangy mutt." Sean pointed. Jet reluctantly obeyed. "Good boy."

Randy circled around and sat down. "When did you get him?"

"It's been a couple of weeks. I've had a couple of times when I suspected someone was lurking around my property. He's been a good watchdog."

"So, ya gonna tell me what's going on?" Randy asked as he sipped his beer.

"It's a long story," Sean said as he opened the oven to check on the garlic bread.

"I've got time."

"It all starts with a scumbag named Boris Petrov." Sean pulled on oven mittens and began a story that went long into the night. Randy had intelligent questions and teasing insults.

The next morning, Randy sat on the couch with Jet's head on his lap and a cup of coffee. "The more I think about this project of yours the more excited I get. One of my friends was just telling me about this mission group in Cambodia. They have been rescuing little girls from the sex slave trade. Since they've involved the police, asking them to bring them the girls they arrest, they've had a population explosion in their dorms... they'd taken over an old apartment complex. Now they're having to build a new complex to make room for all these girls... thousands and thousands of them, Sean. My buddy was saying they have a ninety-nine percent success rate with keeping the girls from prostitution."

"How?" Sean asked eagerly as he envisioned his girls being free.

"I think it's because they have, like, three phases. They get them healthy and then something else and finally a skill so they can move out and earn money."

"That's so cool. I think that's what Todd and Agatha want to do," Sean said.

"Well, apparently the Cambodian government has a recovery plan of their own for these girls, but it's less than forty percent successful." Randy pondered the depths of his cup for a moment. "I think it's because the government doesn't have the reintegration phase, where they train them," he said, looking up at Sean.

Sean nodded. "I think that's a biggie. You know, I never thought about involving the PD."

"Well, if you do, you'd better be prepared," Randy warned.

"Yeah," Sean agreed.

"You know, I think the coolest part is when the little Cambodian girls arrive, they throw a princess party for them... tiara and everything." They sat silent for several minutes as they visualized the girls being rescued from countless rapes and unimaginable abuse.

"Hey," Sean leaned forward. "You wanna see the homes where I take them? We could go get Jazzi ourselves."

"Sure, I'd love to see it."

Sean pulled out his cell and texted Lisa to tell her. Then he texted Elsa. "Let's go." Sean stood. "It's a long trip. We'll have to stay the night up there." Sean called the little hotel and made reservations for them.

"We're staying the night?" Randy asked as he followed Sean down the hall.

"Yeah, I can't risk bringing Jazzi into Sac. I'll follow you out to the airport, so you can drop off your rental."

"What about him?" Randy looked down at the ever-present dog.

"Oh, I'll have Sharice come by and feed him," Sean answered. "I'm going to take a shower. Come on Jet."

Randy smiled at the pair as they disappeared into the master room.

***

That afternoon Sean turned into the first part of the Dressel Ranch. The giant shaggy dog barked them through the first phase. The border collies herded them through the second part and Riley stood watching them intelligently as they rounded the driveway. He let out a couple of barks as a greeting.

Agatha stood on the porch with Alexia at her side. A cloud of dust in the distance heralded the arrival of Todd on horseback.

"Alexia!" Sean shouted in his usual exuberant way. "Look at you... wow. You've changed in just a week. You look like a cowgirl," Sean teased.

"Agatha is turning me into one," she grinned. Her hair was pulled back into a ponytail, accentuating her sharp cheekbones. She wore a pair of dusty blue jeans with a tee-shirt and a pair of mucking boots.

"I called her in from tending the horse's stalls," Agatha said proudly.

"That's why you smell so awful?" Sean asked. Alexia stuck her tongue out at him. "This is my friend Randy. He'll be helping me out from time to time. He's going to escort Jazzi to be with her mom tomorrow."

Alexia impulsively clapped her hands and turned to Agatha for a quick hug.

"Honey, will you show them the house for us while I put on some lunch?" Agatha asked. "Ya'll're hungry, right?"

"I'm always hungry." Sean laughed. He and Randy followed Alexia around the corner of the ranch house. The girl's house loomed before them. "Man! Look at that... this looks great. I love the color."

"I picked it out," Alexia said shyly. "We're going to paint the name right there." She paused to point to the wall where the word *Daybreak* was sketched out in a marker pen. "We just have to get the paint."

Todd trotted up on his horse. Hopping down he shook hands with Randy and Sean. "I'll see you up at the house."

"This is the front door here," Alexia explained as she continued her tour. She led them into the giant family room. "This is our community room. We're going to have games and a TV for watching movies in here. We got these couches from a thrift store in town." She led them into the kitchen. "We'll be doing our own cooking in here. Agatha is teaching me how to cook."

They followed her down the hall to a series of bedrooms. "These are our rooms. They're all double or triple, depending on what the girls want. We don't like to be alone at night," she said and turned away to hide a blush. They came to another large room.

"I like the way Todd attached these houses." Sean inspected the juncture where Todd had removed part of the outer wall to blend it with the adjoining house.

Alexia nodded and continued her description. "This is our classroom. We will eventually have desks in here to study. Most of us didn't graduate from high school. Agatha is going to help us get our GEDs... our diploma, I think it's called. She said that's real important here in the United States. That way we can get jobs when we move out. But, I don't want to move out," Alexia added seriously. "I want to stay here and help all my sisters as they come through."

"You don't want to go back home?" Sean asked gently.

"No, I don't think so. If I go, I won't be able to come back." She lifted her delicate shoulders and added, "This is my home now. Maybe my parents will come visit someday, maybe. My family is a very important family. This would bring shame on them... we'll see."

She bravely showed them the rest of the place as they followed in respectful silence.

Back at the ranch house, Alexia bustled around, taking orders from Agatha like a mother and daughter. Too much food was served for lunch and a pot of coffee was emptied. Standing and stretching his bloated stomach, Sean told them they had to go. It was time to get over to Lewiston before it got dark.

They drove in silence for half an hour before Sean said, "It's a lot to take in huh?"

"I'm trying to come to grips with how little I knew about something so terrible. I mean, I knew, but it seems so much more real now that I've met Alexia."

"Wait until you see Elsa, Jazzi, Red and Katie," Sean warned teasingly.

Randy just rested his head against the headrest and gazed out the window at the passing scenery.

***

When Sean pulled up the driveway he waved to Jazzi as she opened the gate for them. He pulled around to the front and told Randy, "This is Elsa," he indicated the lady standing on the porch. "That was Jazzi, the one you're taking to Atlanta tomorrow." He pointed back to Jazzi, who was walking up the driveway.

Sean made introductions to Elsa and Jazzi and asked where the girls were. As he asked they both came out the front door. Lynn looked much stronger and Katie calmer. Sean thought of the tiaras and could see them shining on their pretty heads.

"Hello ladies," Sean greeted them with a grin. "This is my friend Randy."

All four women looked suspiciously at this male. The only time they'd been around a male was when the landlord had come over to fix the toilet and an elderly neighbor who'd come over to bring them cookies from his wife.

Randy wisely began chatting about the dormant garden he'd seen coming around the driveway. He admired the front yard which still had snow in the shady areas. Elsa invited him into the home. Sean had warned him to not talk about Daybreak and the ranch. Elsa knew about it, but they chose to not tell the others unless it was time for them to go there.

"Can I get you some coffee or tea?" Elsa asked like a regular little hostess. Jazzi sat at the table with the men. Lynn sat on her lap and Katie sat on the arm of their chair. They looked like frightened kittens.

"Sure, some coffee sounds good," Sean nodded to the already brewed pot. Katie jumped up and fetched two mugs for them and held them for Elsa to pour. She cautiously carried the cups to the guys and sat back down.

"So what's happened to my Chatty-Cathy dolls?" he teased.

They shyly looked at Randy.

"He doesn't bite... so how's it going? Did you like the snow?"

"Yes," Jazzi bravely answered. "I never seen no snow before."

"It was like living in a fairytale world yesterday," Lynn quietly added.

"I had my first memory, kind of... I remembered seeing snow, but I don't remember where." Katie shook her head. "I can't believe I don't know anything about myself."

"You know all about yourself," Elsa chided in her motherly way. "You're Katie who loves to work in the yard and is learning to cook, who loves to watch old-fashioned movies and cries at all the sad scenes."

"The one who always braids my hair without having to ask," added Lynn.

"And gives me the best part of her waffles with all the syrup." Jazzi hugged the girl's waist.

Katie grinned at them. "And the one who talks all the time."

"All the time!" Lynn laughed.

"Even during movies." Elsa took the third seat with steaming mug in hand.

They all fell silent for a moment, then Jazzi spoke, "So, I'm leaving today? Is that why you're here?"

"Tomorrow morning," Sean corrected her. "Tomorrow night, you'll be with your mother." At Jazzi's forlorn expression, he asked, "Aren't you excited?"

She was quiet for a moment. "I'm just nervous is all. It was my fault this happened--"

"No it wasn't," Sean interrupted firmly. "A girl should be able to be silly with her friends and not be attacked. You didn't deserve this."

"Well, I know that now." She nodded her head towards Elsa. "But my momma may not feel that way. What if she regrets getting me back?"

"Then call me and I'll come fetch you and bring you back," Sean answered sincerely. "I'll give you Randy's number. He'll contact me."

Jazzi looked relieved and Katie leaned into her. Lynn got up and transferred herself to Elsa's lap to make room for Katie.

They stayed visiting for an hour and then Sean told them he'd be back in the morning at four o'clock.

As they got in the SUV, Elsa said quietly to Sean, "Thanks a lot, Sean. They'll not sleep a wink tonight and keep me awake with their chattering."

"You love it," he answered, to which she rolled her eyes.

Sean and Randy checked into the tiny hotel, where Sean was becoming well known. He brought in a fishing pole and a tackle box.

"We going fishing?" Randy asked.

"Nope, it's just a cover. You gotta have a reason for being up here. People notice."

"What? You don't think they notice you coming and going from that house?"

"Maybe, but to the casual observer, I'm a tourist," Sean said.

"You're delusional, that's what you are," Randy grunted as he threw his meager belongings on one of the stiff beds.

"Whatever. You hungry?" he asked.

"Not much, but we ought to eat. Is there anyplace to eat in this little town?" Randy wondered.

"Oh yeah, they have a great restaurant over at the old hotel."

***

Randy shook Sean's hand in front of the airport.

Jazzi impulsively hugged Sean and started crying. He patted her back as he gently held her. "Don't worry Jazz. Your mother is so excited to see you, she even moved to a new city and changed jobs and everything."

Jazzi leaned back in wonder. "Really?"

"Really, you're not going to Las Vegas," Sean said and tweaked her wet nose. "Now get going, little one. I'm proud of you for being so brave," he added as he turned her over to Randy. "You can trust Randy, he won't hurt you. He'll protect you, so don't stray far from him," he warned.

"I won't, I promise," she said and sniffed back another torrent of tears.

"Come on, we've got a plane to catch!" Randy interrupted cheerfully. "Grab your bag and let's get a move on."

"Take care of her, or I'll wring your neck myself," Sean said semi-jokingly.

"Jeez… where's the trust?" Randy asked Jazzi as he guided her into the airport. Sean stood trying to swallow past a knot in his throat as they disappeared. He felt his phone vibrate. Looking at the screen he smiled a little at Elsa's text. She had another girl for him to rescue.

"Okay, I'll call you when I get to a secure area to get the details," he texted back.

***

Sean tapped on Captain Grant's office door. Grant looked up in surprise. "Come in McGee, how the hell are you?"

Sean wondered at the sense of belonging he always felt when he came to the Sac PD. It felt like home. "Hey boss, how are you?"

They sat facing each other across the serviceable desk. "So, seriously, how are you doing? Shut that door for me," he added with a wave of his hand. "Now that you're all top-secret and stuff we need to be careful."

"Thanks," Sean closed the door. "As a matter-of-fact, I do need some help."

"What can I do for you?"

"It's a long story. Let me start by telling you about a missionary group in Cambodia…."

Grant grinned. "Cambodia? I'm dying to see where this goes."

Sean explained the sex-trafficking rescue efforts and focused on the help the police gave to the missionaries. "So, here's the thing. I'm kinda doing that on a very small scale. The problem is I've been taking these girls from under their pimp's noses. Then it's hard to get them away without the pimps finding them. I was wondering if you could help me by offering the girls you bust an option." Sean sped up as he saw the furrowed brow of his old boss. "All I want you to do is offer the girls an option, and if they accept it, call me and I'll come get them… then they're my problem."

Grant was silent as he thought. As this was his normal style, Sean didn't interrupt. Grant never made rash decisions. "Who knows you're doing this, and how many times have you done it? Tell me more about your end of it."

Sean explained that Randy knew, and so did his boss. He didn't mention he'd been suspended. As far as Sean was concerned it wasn't related to the girls. Then he told Grant about the girls and how unique each was. How they'd grown and begun to recover. How the Dressel's had decided to build a recovery home for the girls.

Grant watched the passion flash across Sean's face, and knew Sean would stop at nothing to accomplish his goal. When Sean finally wound down, Grant steepled his fingers. "You know, I think we can do this. But first I want to make sure it's a good solution, that you're doing the right thing for them."

"Okay, I have photos here of the two properties. And if you'd like, I can call Dr. Dressel for you to talk to."

Grant leaned forward and typed into his computer. "How do you spell Dressel?"

Sean told him and watched.

Grant asked Sean for her address. Sean gave it, but explained that she'd retired.

"She's still listed at that address." He typed some more. "She's a legit doctor, family practitioner… Give me her number and I'll call her myself."

Sean told him and waited on the edge of his seat.

"Hello, may I speak to Dr. Dressel?" Grant leaned back and observed Sean as he spoke.

"This is she," Lisa answered.

"Excellent, this is Captain Grant with the Sacramento Police Department. I'm sitting here with a recent acquaintance of yours."

"Sean McGee?" Lisa wondered out loud.

"Yes ma'am, how do you know him?"

"She's not going to answer that question, boss," Sean grinned.

"Why do you want to know?" Lisa asked with an edge to her voice. "We met in northern California."

"Okay, I've raised your hackles. How about you say a quick hello to Sean and then we can talk some more?" He handed the phone to Sean.

"Hey Lisa, this is Sean," he said. "I'm working on Captain Grant to see if he'll help me with rescuing our girls. I've heard it works to have the PD offer the girls an escape. He's just doing a little background checking to make sure I'm not lying through my teeth."

"Oh, okay," Lisa answered, though she still sounded a little ruffled. "Put him back on."

Grant took the phone back and gently interrogated her for twenty minutes. After he hung up he looked at Sean thoughtfully. "I'll tell you what, I'll give this a shot. But I'm only going to have Sam work with you at first. We'll see how that goes."

"Sounds good."

"Do you want me to brief him or do you want to do it?" Grant asked.

"I think it'd be better coming from you." Sean stood and shook his hand.

"I have one request," Grant asked. "Can I go up and see this place someday?"

"Absolutely, but not the first stage house. I don't want too many people knowing where that is, since the girls go directly there from the streets," Sean answered. "So when can we start?"

Grant laughed. "I'll talk to Sam next time he's here… maybe today."

"Thanks boss." Sean stopped at the door and turned to Grant. "I can't tell you how much I appreciate this."

"Well don't make me regret it," Grant said with a serious look.

"I won't."

***

Donna stood at the luggage pick-up waiting for her first glimpse of her beloved daughter. A man came out and looking around walked over to the wall and stood watching her covertly. After ten minutes, he approached her. "Donna?"

She looked in surprise at him, and then asked, "Are you Randy?"

"Yes ma'am," he answered, shaking her hand politely. He continued to survey the surroundings.

"Are you waiting for someone?" she asked as she glanced around. "Where's my daughter."

"Let's get the luggage first, not that we have bags, but I want to go over there," Randy said as he turned towards the spinning luggage claim. She followed. Standing side-by-side, she controlled her anxiety as well as she could. Her eyes kept sweeping back to the terminal exit. The crowd of travelers gathered their bags and wandered off leaving just the two of them. "Okay, let's give this a go," Randy said cryptically as they headed back to the area he'd come from. Pulling out his phone he sent out a text and when the next group of travelers came out, Jazmine was amongst them.

As soon as their eyes connected, they both broke into a run. They hugged in the middle of the flow of people, causing the crowd to part like water around a boulder. Randy guided them away, which wasn't easy considering they were still attached to each other.

CHAPTER SIXTEEN

Sean approached the woman standing in the doorway. She smiled encouragingly. Sean slowed as he came near.

"Well, hello handsome," she said pleasantly.

"Hi," Sean said as he stopped in front of her. She was different than the others. Much older and much more hardened. Her jet black hair was swept back in a bun. Fake eyelashes blinked back at him, as she seemed to sense this wasn't your normal john.

"You a cop?" she asked with a sexy smile.

"Not any more… how 'bout you? You a cop?"

She laughed, showing clean teeth. "Yeah, do you wanna go *undercover* with me?"

It was Sean's turn to laugh, then he told her, "Your name is Tetyana, but you go by Yani. You're Boris Petrov's top earner after he tired of you. You had a child from him, but Boris killed the infant. Your best friend, Elsa, disappeared."

Her face had turned pale at this. "Anything else?"

"Yeah, you hate Boris and would love to get even with him. Elsa is alive and wants me to rescue you," Sean added gently.

Yani looked up and then down the street as though looking for the trap she was sure this was. "Elsa's been gone a long time."

Sean nodded. They stared at each other for several minutes before she pushed away from the wall. Putting an arm through his and leaning into him she said, "Let's go *talk.*"

"Okay, where?"

"Your choice, honey... coffee shop or motel?" she asked as she strutted next to him in her stiletto heels.

"Let's start with coffee until you give me an answer," Sean said as he let her lead him to a little café. Half an hour later, he escorted her to the motel of his choice. Once in the room, she stepped away from him.

"Now what?" she asked looking about the dumpy little room with an adjoining room.

Sean tossed her a small bag from the bed. "Go change."

She went into the bathroom and opened the bag curiously. A change of clothes and a wig. She was ready in five minutes. When she came out she was unrecognizable. She'd removed her long fake lashes and her make-up. A fluffy blonde wig swept towards her face, making her look ten years younger. For the streets, she was old at twenty-eight. Her standard issue baggy sweatshirt and loose jeans completed the transformation.

Sean had also changed, making her laugh. "You look completely different!"

He grinned back at her from under a mop of black and purple hair. His black hoodie with a dread-locked Bob Marley plastered on the front completed the disguise.

"You even walk different," she commented.

"You're shorter than I realized," Sean looked at her shoes with the heels broken off. "That was a good idea."

"I've thought through this many times. I'm so ready."

"Let's do this." They went through the connecting door and out into the hallway with a giggle. Someone turned to look at these silly kids trying to sneak out of a motel without getting caught. Sean slung the back pack over his shoulder.

Once in the rented SUV, and clear of Sacramento, she sighed in relief. She surprised him by not talking until they'd reached Williams.

"You hungry?" he asked.

"Yes, I haven't eaten since a roll this morning." She turned to look at his profile in the dark. "I plan to get fat," she informed him with a laugh.

"Well, you've got a long way to go, so let's get started." Sean pulled into a truck stop with multiple food choices.

She carried two bags full of junk food out to the rental. They got in and Yani tore into her hamburger like a ravenous wolf. Before Sean had finished his burger, she'd eaten all her fries and was working on a burrito.

He pulled back onto the highway and turned up the radio. In half an hour she was sound asleep, wig askew. He sipped his coffee and thought about this girl... his final take. He was surprised at how sentimental he felt. He admitted he liked being part of the initial transformation. Part of their first shock. He decided he'd talk to Sam, and see if he could be the one to tell the girls.

Elsa had many reasons for choosing Yani. She considered Yani to be very smart and compassionate. Plus, Yani spoke Russian and Polish. She was a natural leader. If everything went as planned, Elsa hoped to have Yani at the second stage to manage the girls.

When Sean arrived at the cabin, Elsa was at the gate to open and close it. A puppy frisked about her feet as she followed the SUV up the driveway. Sean nudged Yani awake. "We're here," he said with a smile. Opening the door, he asked, "Who's this?" he bent and tried to pet the head of the yapping fluff ball. "*What* is it?"

He was ignored as the two women stood rocking back and forth quietly at the bottom of the steps. Sean went around them with the bouncing dog.

"Hi Sean," Katie said from the porch. "That's Annabelle, she's a mix of Pomeranian and terrier. She's only six months old. Mr. Parker, the old guy down the street, gave her to us. He said she was too much for him." Katie had picked up the little dog as she talked. She nuzzled its neck and accepted grateful kisses from Annabelle.

Sean followed her through the front door as Lynn came down the hall. "Wow! Who is this young lady?" Sean asked teasingly.

"Hello, my name's Lynnette, but I go by Lynn." Lynn smiled calmly up at him as she held out a hand in introduction.

"Look at you! You've got some color now and your cheeks aren't sunken. You look so healthy."

"Thanks to you," she smiled prettily. "I'm not well yet, and may never be, but I'm much better. I can eat now without throwing up… so that's a start."

"Are you all packed up for tomorrow?" he asked with concern.

"Yep, I'm ready," she reached for Katie's hand, who looked downcast. "Don't worry little one. We'll be reunited soon. Just work on getting better and remembering."

"I will, I promise."

"Who's the lady outside with Elsa? Is she a new girl for us?" Lynn asked.

"Yeparoo," Sean responded looking out the screendoor. "Her name is Yani."

"Here, Annabelle wants you to hold her." Katie held the squirming dog out to him.

"She doesn't look like she wants me to hold her... she looks like she wants to bite me." Sean backed away cautiously, but Katie followed with the pup held out. He gave in and took the dog under its armpits. Holding it at arm's length they surveyed each other.

"Cuddle her, she likes to be cuddled," Katie insisted, much to Lynn's amusement. She pushed the dog closer.

When Elsa and Yani came in they stopped in surprise. Sean looked like he had the little puppy in a neck-lock with its back legs hanging down... wiggling. She was letting out a series of growls and snarls. After the second high-pitched yap, Sean handed her back to Katie with a shudder.

Annabelle growled from her perch.

"Apparently Mr. Parker was right. She doesn't like guys," Elsa said with a laugh.

"Apparently," Sean responded sarcastically. "I'll see you in the morning. I've gotta check in."

When he came back the next morning, he smelled the air appreciatively. "Is that maple syrup I smell?"

"Have a seat," Elsa ushered him out of the kitchen, "Shoo."

Annabelle hopped into Lynn's lap to better growl at Sean. Katie came yawning down the hall in her fluffy house slippers. Stopping in the kitchen, she poured herself a cup of coffee.

"Offer some to our guest, honey," Elsa ordered as she flipped pancakes.

"Want some?" Katie asked.

"Yeah, sure." He smiled at this domestic little scene.

Yani came next, wearing her outfit from yesterday... looking like a tomboy with her hair pulled back in a ponytail. She asked If Elsa needed help. Elsa told her to get the plates down and put out silverware, to which Yani looked bewildered. "Lynn, will you please show Yani where everything is?"

Lynn came to Yani's rescue and showed her the cupboards and drawers. Then she pulled out the placemats that had mysteriously appeared from Amazon last week. "Do you want coffee Yani?" Lynn asked. At her nod, she pointed to the cupboard with the cups. "Creamer's in the fridge. Sugar's right there."

Sean felt a burning sensation behind his eyes at this touching scene. He leaned back when Elsa placed a plate of three pancakes in front of him. She put butter and syrup next to his plate and bustled back to the stove.

Sean smothered the pancakes with syrup and waited.

The girls noticed. Glancing at each other, Elsa asked him if he needed something else. He told her no, that he was just waiting for everyone to have their food before he started.

"Why?" Katie asked.

"Because it's not polite to start eating until everyone is ready to eat...." Seeing their confusion, he added, "Unless you tell me to get started before my food gets cold."

"Oh," Elsa said. She glanced at the others and turning back to Sean she said, "Go ahead and eat. I don't want your food to get cold."

"Thanks," Sean said as he shoveled a forkful of pancake into his mouth.

Yani shrugged at this bewildering lesson in manners.

After he and Yani had eaten as much as they could, Sean rose to his feet, causing Annabelle to go crazy again. She snapped and growled until Katie finally put the dog in her room. They all hugged and cried, including Yani, though she didn't know exactly why. Finally the tiny girl went bravely down the steps to the waiting SUV.

When she got in, Sean asked her, "Ready?"

"Yep." She put her seatbelt on and waved to her friends. "Let's go before I change my mind."

As they pulled away, Yani turned to Elsa and asked, "So where're they going?"

"I actually don't know," Elsa answered with a laugh. "Sean's extremely protective and secretive about this place and where you go from here." She watched Sean disappear down the gravel road. "I will stay here, but you will go if you recover."

"Recover?" Yani asked as they turned back to the cabin.

"Yes, recover to become who you are... who you are now."

"Not who I was?" Yani asked intelligently.

"No, Yani," Elsa stopped in front of the door. "That little girl is gone. Now you need to decide if you're going to say goodbye to the woman you were forced to be?"

"I'll happily say goodbye to most of her, but I've learned some things also. I don't want to lose the strength I've gained," Yani spoke tentatively. She found it difficult to explain her feelings so soon.

"You'll figure it out." Elsa put her arm across Yani's shoulder and gave her a reassuring hug. "You've got plenty of time. Right now, you just need to focus on healing."

***

Lynn sat awestruck in Sean's passenger seat as they entered the Dressel compound.

"Look at that beautiful dog!" she said as they passed the serious Akbash who was seated on a knoll watching his goats.

"That's a guard dog," Sean told her. "Next come all the border collies." As they passed the second gate the band of collies raced back and forth barking as usual. "Here's the main house. Yours is around back." Sean pulled up to the welcoming committee.

Lynn leaped into Alexia's arms. Agatha and Todd watched with happy smiles. Lisa came out on the porch. A horse tied to a post neighed at her.

"Hello Lynn, welcome," Lisa opened her arms to receive a hug. "This is my brother Todd and my sister-in-law, Agatha. And this handsome boy is Riley." She indicated the gentle dog who stood waving his tail hopefully.

Lynn squatted down and held out a hand to him. Riley took the invitation and walked right into her embrace, knocking her over. Lynn laughed as she fended off the slobbery tongue.

Agatha gave her a hand up. "It's so nice to meet you, Red," she began.

"My name is Lynn," she corrected as she shook Agatha's hand. "Red was my old nickname."

Agatha fought the urge to comment on her delicate beauty. She had been warned by both Sean and Lisa to not focus on their looks. Their beauty is what endangered their lives.

Todd politely shook her hand, "Pleased to meet you Lynn."

Agatha ushered them into her home and served them her usual glass of tea. Alexia struggled to remain patient as long as she could before she burst out, "Come on... I want to show you our new home."

They all followed the two girls to the Daybreak home. Todd and Sean stayed outside talking. "We decided to follow your idea to keep men out of the house, unless it's for repairs, and never without me present," Todd explained.

"I'm glad to hear it. I think they will have the best recovery if they can just be girls for awhile. As far from sexuality as possible."

"I get ya." Todd nodded as he squinted over the plains. "We do have a problem I need your advice on. I have a couple of ranch hands who help out with the cattle and the goats." He pointed to the horizon where a herd of cows could be seen grazing. "Lisa and I were discussing it and we decided to explain the situation to them, but say they are runaways and they come from another state. What do you think?"

Sean was silent. It seemed somehow wrong to place any wrong-doing label on the girls. "I agree and disagree. They are not runaway girls who are defying their parents. I don't really want them labeled as prostitutes to perfect strangers… how about we say they were rescued from abusive situations."

"You're right, that's a great solution and it's not a lie. It also explains our desire to be secretive."

"I may be getting girls more often now. The police department has sorta partnered with me to get them out," Sean told him.

Todd turned his eyes to Sean. "Lisa told me, Agatha will be thrilled when I tell her."

When the women came back out, Sean said goodbye and hopped back into the SUV.

"Did you get a new ride?" Lisa asked.

"Nah, it's a rental. I thought my SUV was getting a little too familiar to Boris." Sean put it into gear and added, "Take care of our girls."

She smiled and promised to do her best. Lynn and Alexia waved goodbye as he pulled away.

***

Sean meekly entered Becker's office a week later. He silently sat down in front of his boss's desk and waited to hear the verdict. Becker let him suffer for a full minute. "So, what do you think, McGee? You going to blow up any more cars?"

"No, sir," Sean answered solemnly. "I shouldn't have blown up that one."

"I've come to a decision. I'm placing you on a different job. You'll have a new partner."

Sean flinched at this separation from Pantell. "Yes, sir… what job am I going to?"

"I've been wanting to come up with a team to deal with this explosion of sex trafficking into Sacramento.

I'm putting you with Heckle. Castle will work with you when there's crossover to gang activity." Becker leaned back and pointed one long slim finger at Sean. "No more rogue crap. I will fire you the next time you go off on your own."

"Speaking of that, the rogue crap, I wanted to tell you that on my own time I'm still working to get girls off the streets," Sean began. "Only this time the Sac PD is partnering with me."

Becker pinched the bridge of his nose and squeezed his eyes shut as though he had a sudden headache. "Do they know you're CIA?"

"Only Grant, sir."

"Make sure you keep it separate from the Agency."

"Yes, sir." Sean stood. "And thank you for giving me this project… I can't wait to get started."

"Good. Go get Heckle and get started!"

Sean went straight to Heckle's office. Rapping on the doorframe as he entered, he said, "Hey *partner.*"

Heckle looked up with a laugh. "Man, you lead an enchanted life, dude. You get suspended, then you get to head up your own project!"

"I know, right?" Sean knuckle bumped him and shook Castle's hand. "So, do we get to work in here together," he asked Castle.

"Yep, if you don't mind," Castle's pride was ruffled.

"No, working with you would make it perfect. We'll need your advice."

Castle relaxed a little at this. "Okay, but keep it down. You two get too noisy at times."

"Okay, dad," Heckle teased. "So McGee, while you've been loafing around, I've been busy."

"You have no idea," Sean started.

Castle looked up from his work. "Oh, you mean the girls you've been kidnapping from Boris Petrov and taking to a cabin in Lewiston? Or do you mean the ranch in Lassen County?"

Sean looked shocked for a moment, and then burst into laughter. "You got me."

"So, let's start with Boris Petrov. Head of SL02," Heckle began. "How many girls have you taken from him and where are they from?"

"I've taken five from Petrov and one from his cousin, Slovanic," Sean said.

"Why did you take one from Slovanic?" Heckle asked as he wrote on a white board. He placed Petrov at one side and next to him he wrote Slovanic.

"Well, originally I thought I'd try to make it look like the girls were being taken as retaliation for Petrov taking one of his girls. That's also what motivated me to blow up Petrov's car."

"Yeah. Heard about that."

"As much as I enjoyed that, it was a mistake," Sean admitted. "Since I started this recovery process, I've had a family partner with me. They built a giant recovery house for these women on their ranch in Lassen," Sean said with a nod to Castle. "The Sac PD is going to help me get the girls out legit. So now I can focus on stopping this before it happens. We've gotta figure out how they get them here."

"What do the girls say?" Heckle asked.

"The girls from Eastern Europe were offered modeling jobs in California. Once here, they're drugged, raped, and emotionally destroyed by shame."

"Hmm... any chance they're from the same region? Could we trace a pattern?"

"Good question, I don't know where each one is from. The Americans are basically kidnapped and transported here... mostly African American girls."

"How're they getting the European girls here?" Heckle asked.

"I don't know. If they come one by one on a plane, how are they slipping through the cracks and staying here past their visitor's visa?"Sean felt the rush of the chase course through his veins. "Are they coming by ship in groups?"

"Stashed away in cargo like slaves?" Heckle asked.

"Maybe. We need to figure out exactly where Petrov is from. Criminals have a habit of staying close to home."

"They're from Biclovichy, a po-dunk little town east of Berlin." Castle answered. "Slovanic and Petrov are cousins, remember?"

"Yeah, I remember," Sean wrote the town on the side of the white board. They worked for several more hours on research and the correlating evidence.

***

Alec watched the pretty blonde drop her children off at school. In two weeks he'd figured out her routine. She was up at six o'clock, on her power-walk by six-thirty, back by seven. She left at seven forty-five on the dot to take the kids to school and then she usually ran errands and met friends for coffee or lunch.

He pulled in behind her. If she went to the coffee shop with the parking lot in the back, he'd grab her. That one had the best cover.

He grinned when she went to that one… his patience was finally going to pay off. As she pulled in and got out of the car, he pulled into the lot and parked.

An hour later Sharice came out. She'd had a lovely visit with her sister, Barb. Barb's husband had picked her up out front, so Sharice was alone as usual. She glanced up at the approaching man. He was opening the passenger's door of his car, so she waited at her trunk for him to get whatever it was he wanted from the passenger's side.

With a swift glance around the lot, Alec stepped to her and grabbed her wrist. She was so shocked she didn't get a chance to scream before he clamped a damp cloth over her mouth. Sharice sank into oblivion as he thrust her into the back seat of the sedan.

***

Sean was sitting at his computer working on a reservation for a cruise when his cell phone rang. He glanced at the screen and rolled his eyes. Judy, the pushy sister, was calling. *Now what?* "Hey Sis, what's up?"

"Sean, we can't find Sharice! Her car's at the coffee shop she and Barb were at, but she's nowhere," Judy's voice sounded frantic as she speed-talked.

"Whoa, whoa, slow down," Sean demanded as he stood abruptly. "What do mean, she missing?"

"She never showed up to pick up the boys, so the school called Barb and Barb went back to the coffee shop they'd been at, and there was her car."

"I'm on my way," he answered after he got the address of the café.

He was in his SUV and on the freeway in a couple of minutes. Putting the phone on speaker mode he called Becker's office. He rapidly told him he suspected Sharice had been kidnapped in retaliation. Becker sighed and said he'd put Pantell on it. Sean told him he'd get a hold of Pantell himself.

He felt relief wash over him at the sound of his mentor's voice. He quickly explained what he thought had happened as he wove through traffic. Pantell agreed to meet him there. By the time Sean arrived, the police where in the lot, inspecting Sharice's car and the ground for clues.

His entire family was present. When he got out of his vehicle he was met with an onslaught of emotions. Sean went straight to his father. "What's up Dad? Have they found anything yet?"

"No, nothing," Mr. McGee's voice shook as he tried to maintain his composure. "These guys are good though. They've talked to each one of us and scoured the area for clues."

A city police officer approached Sean with her hand extended. "Your father tells me you are ex-Sac PD?"

"Yeah," Sean answered. "What've you found so far?" They walked away from the grieving group of women leaning into his father.

"It's strange, there doesn't seem to be any sign of struggle. Could she have gone willingly?" the officer asked.

Sean knew this question was coming, so he was prepared. "She may have not struggled if she thought someone else would be hurt. Or if she knew the person, I suppose. But she definitely wouldn't have left her kids at school and not answered calls from her family. We're pretty tight."

"So you think she's being held against her will?"

"My gut says yes, but I suppose she could be ill or unconscious or something," Sean answered calmly.

"Does she have any medical diagnosis, like seizures or something that would render her unconscious?"

"Not that any of us are aware of." Sean looked around the lot at the surrounding buildings. "Do any of these places have security cameras?"

The officer pointed to a nearby building and said, "That looks like a camera. I sent my partner to check it out. As soon as we're done, I'll check each building and ask."

"Go ahead, I want to look around... if you don't mind?" Sean asked politely.

"No, go ahead," she answered, turning away.

Sean held a palm up to his family to silence them. It worked. They watched him from their cluster. Ignoring them Sean stood perfectly still and stared at Sharice's car. This was a method that used to drive his fellow officers with the Sac PD nuts. He slowly scanned the scene. His eyes rested for a long time on the space next to her car. Her car was locked and the keys were nowhere to be found.

Thoughtfully he envisioned how the assailant would have approached her without alarm being given. Sharice was a cautious woman. The kidnapper must've had a valid reason to be that close to her. He must've been parked next to her. Squatting down he stared at the space next to hers. A slight square of tread pattern was left from liquid of some sort. Without destroying it, Sean touched the grease and sniffed his finger. Rancid cooking oil.

Looking across the rectangle back lot, he spied the garbage dumpster.

Standing he followed the trajectory to the dumpster with his eyes. He could envision a vehicle parked there, waiting. Another tread mark, slightly bigger showed the direction the car had come. Knowing it could be from any car, he still followed the path. It led to the littered space next to the dumpster. A stream of oil had meandered from the dumpster to the space. Sean squatted down again and stared at the mess. Pulling his phone out he snapped pictures of the tire treads of the car that had also been parked next to his sister's car. He also took multiple pics of the area.

A bright white object caught his eye. A cigarette butt, lay next to the driver's side. Sean circled around to look at it. He snapped a photo of it as an officer approached.

"McGee?" he asked as he stretched out a hand.

Sean nodded as he shook it.

"My partner told me you were back here. Did you find anything?" he asked looking at the ground.

"This cigarette looks fresh and these tire-marks lead to the space next to her car." Sean pointed to the faint trail.

"Good eye," he remarked as he pulled on a pair of gloves to gather the evidence.

"Did the camera show anything?" Sean asked.

"No, see the lens is broken." The officer pointed up to the camera. "They said it had been damaged last week."

"Can I see the footage from last week, before it was broken?"

"I'm sure they'd be okay with that. I'll go with you," he said and led Sean around the building. The camera belonged to a Chinese restaurant. They followed the manager through the dingy back room to his office. Sitting down, he pulled up the footage last taken. A gloved hand reached around from the side and tapped the lens with a sharp object. The screen went black.

"Back it up... stop! Can you see that? Is that a rock, or what?" Sean asked.

"Looks like a rock to me," the manager said staring at the image. "It's uneven looking."

"Yeah, I think you're right," Sean agreed in disappointment. "If this was a pre-meditated kidnapping then we should be able to spot a repetitive car in the lot."

"Let me burn you a thumb drive, so you can look at it on your own," the manager suggested.

"Okay, that'll help," Sean agreed as he watched the guy download the surveillance footage.

Back in the lot, they found Pantell waiting by his car.

Sean went straight to him. "Thanks man, how do I handle this without giving away who I work for?"

"We used to work together at Sac PD. We've stayed in touch. You called me," Pantell said this last part as he turned to the approaching female officer.

"Hi," she looked questioningly between Pantell and Sean.

"This is one of my friends from my police days, Dale," Sean introduced him using his first name.

"Nice to meet you. I checked each business and we lucked out. That one," she turned and pointed to a small house, "has a camera. It's behind some leaves, but we may still be able to get something from it. We have to wait until the owner comes in because the employee doesn't have the key to her office."

"Excellent, is she coming in?"

"Yes, I spoke to her. She lives half an hour away."

"So, McGee, what've you come up with so far?" Pantell asked.

Sean went through the scenario as he imagined it and showed him the tracks. "Looks like a car."

Pantell stood silently staring at the oily mess by the dumpster. "Needs an alignment. Tread is worn on the inside. This was made today."

"How do you know that?" the officer asked in surprise.

Pantell pointed to piece of a receipt partly under the pool of oil. "That's dated today. The oil is on top of it, so the oil came second, there's a series of paw prints from raccoons around the garbage." Pantell pointed to the paw prints on each side of the oil. "The trail is covered by the oil, so the raccoons were here before today, probably last night." He looked around the area. "It was a stakeout. There's no recent disturbance on the ground around the doors, so he didn't get out of the car. Why didn't he get out? No one got in and no one got out. That means this was premeditated."

The other officer had arrived in time to hear Pantell's theory. They glanced at each other in awe. "Wow, that was good," the female commented.

Pantell shrugged. "Worked crime scenes for a long time. You pick up stuff."

They left the officers to their write up and measurements. Sean introduced Pantell to his family and they stood talking to Sean while Pantell silently observed them. He turned his attention to the buildings and finally the car. A car squealed into the lot and Sharice's husband leaped out. He went straight at Sean.

"What happened? Where is she?" John demanded in his aggressive New Yorker way. His eyes betrayed his emotional state.

Sean knew these two adored each other, even if John was a little rough around the edges. "We don't know what happened or where she is, John. That's what we're working on."

Pantell scrutinized the husband. In his experience most cases of missing people had something to do with family. But he respected Sean's judgment, and he didn't look suspicious of the husband.

"Does this have anything to do with you, Sean?" John asked abruptly.

That got everyone's attention, especially Pantell's. All heads swiveled to Sean, who looked uncomfortable.

"What makes you say that?" Sean asked.

"Because she's been mysterious about you lately. She went on that trip with you and wouldn't tell me about it. Then you told her you didn't need her at the travel agency any more, even though you know she loves it there." John paused for a breath. "Dude, I know you. You wouldn't have hurt her feelings unless you had a good reason."

"I don't know why she made our little road trip a mystery." Sean raised his hands, palms up. "But as far as the agency goes, I've had some threats lately from a case I worked on when I was with the police. I didn't want her to get hurt, so I told her to not come into the office until it blew over."

"Well, she did get hurt. She's gone!" John shouted.

Sean couldn't blame John for how he felt, it was how he felt about himself. "I know, John, and it's my fault," he answered quietly.

This seemed to take the wind out of John. His shoulders drooped. "Do you have any idea where she might be?"

Pantell spoke for the first time, "Yeah, we have a pretty good idea who's responsible and we know where to start looking."

John turned to look at this stalwart older man, and decided he'd said enough. "What can I do?"

"Take care of the boys. We'll get her back, trust me," Sean said with the first indication of the rage he was feeling.

A grandmotherly woman came around the corner and went directly to the police officers. She apologized for taking so long and led them into her book store. The four of them crowded around her computer screen as she booted it up. She nervously searched the screen crowded with icons. Finally, with a shaking hand she clicked on it. It took every ounce of restraint on Sean's part to not snatch the mouse out of her hand. She slowly navigated through the program, with a finger on the notes she'd written to herself on a piece of paper. "I can never remember how to do this, so I wrote notes to myself."

"Smart," the female officer complimented.

The elderly lady looked up gratefully.

Sean sensed a distraction and jumped in, "Is that the right button?" he asked touching the screen.

"No, it's this one." She clicked on it and the camera footage came up. "This is right now. This one is rewind." She clicked on it, and they held their breath waiting for it to get to the right spot.

"There!" Pantell ordered. "Now pause it."

She complied and they all leaned closer to get a better look.

"Right there." Sean tapped the screen. "Can I have the mouse ma'am?"

She nodded and let go of it. Sean expertly zoomed the image. Pulling out his cell phone he snapped a shot of the screen. The angle didn't allow for an image of the license plate. But they could easily see it was a recent model silver Mercedes. They silently inspected the half of his face visible.

"Thank you, ma'am. This was extremely helpful. You may have helped us solve a crime." Sean stood and indicated to Pantell he wanted to leave. "Here's my contact info if you need me for anything. I've got to get back to my family."

They went back to the lot and Pantell nodded his head to the cars and said, "We've got work to do."

Sean hugged his family and went to his car where Pantell was standing, waiting.

"I'm gonna kill that bastard!" Sean growled fiercely to Pantell.

"Yeah, probably," he answered calmly. "First we have to find your sister. What's her name?"

"Sharice."

"Okay, we'll find Sharice, but right now you're going to tell me what's really going on." Pantell opened his car door and told Sean to meet him at a nearby park.

They found a bench in the middle of the park and sat facing each other.

"You know everything except that I stole six prostitutes and created a rescue-house for them in Nor-Cal. Five of 'em are Boris', one is his cousin's. I originally did it to torment Boris, but now my heart is in it. These girls are amazing, and they're getting a chance to get free of this slavery. I've had a doctor and her family design and build a large home on their ranch up north. They're all in. They are planning to take up to ten girls at a time. I delivered the first girl to them last week."

Pantell said nothing as his eyebrows slowly rose during this recital. "What does this have to do with Sharice?"

"Sharice helped me get the first girl settled in the house. She stayed with her for the first week to explain household stuff and be there at night. I stayed at a local hotel. So, anyway, I felt Boris had figured out it was me, so I told Sharice to stay away from the travel agency. She knew why, sort-of."

"Is this why Becker suspended you?"

"Uh, no… I blew up Boris' car." Sean looked abashed.

"Yeah, I figured that was you. Why didn't you tell me any of this before now?" Pantell asked.

"Why do you think?" Sean laughed harshly. "If you knew about it, you would have been implicated and suspended too!"

"So what's your plan? What do you hope to achieve?"

"You know there's several ways to destroy a person."

"The wallet, the mind, and the body," Pantell nodded. He and Sean had had this discussion before. "So by taking his girls, you are going for the wallet. Blowing up his Mercedes and taking Slovanic's girls is messing with his mind."

"Exactly, but I didn't realize how much it would mean to me to help the girls. I feel like it's my mission… I'm obsessed." Sean knuckle-rubbed his eyes.

"Okay, enough chit-chat. Where do you think Boris took Sharice?"

"Don't know. The guy caught on camera didn't look like Boris, but I think I've seen him before. Maybe one of Boris' men." Sean began.

"Okay, okay... I'm going back to the agency to talk to Becker. I'd like to get some more agents on this case. It's something we've been working on for a long time and this may be our break." Pantell stood. "I'll let you know." Pantell paused with his hand on the car door. "We'll get her back."

"When?"

"Today, tomorrow at the latest."

***

Sharice lay shivering on the narrow bed in the dark room. She acknowledged she wasn't cold, so it must be shock. *Is shock the best choice right now?* She rolled onto her back and stared hard at the ceiling. At first her mind was a blank, but she kept a determined eye on the dark ceiling. It crept into her awareness that there must be a light source, or she wouldn't be able to see anything. Her small chin set with resolve, she sat up and inspected her prison... *temporary prison.*

Light streamed in weakly under the door. The room was bare except the bed, more a cot really, and a chair. An open door across from her was probably the bathroom. She jumped up and started toward the door, but a wave of dizziness washed over her making her stumble. She bent over and waited until her blood flow was stable and continued to the door. It was a bathroom with a tiny shower. *Is this a cheap hotel?* She looked around wonderingly, and then a thought crossed her mind... *Is this where they bring the girls after they are kidnapped?*

Sharice stared bleakly at her reflection in the cheap mirror.

***

"I've got an idea," Sean barked into the phone.

Pantell held the phone away from his ear. "Okay."

"I'm going to head north and talk to the girls and see if any can shed light on where Boris takes the girls to hide them and prep them." Sean started his engine as he spoke. Jet scrambled to the front seat to sit looking out the front window. He'd have to swing by Beth's place to drop off the dog.

"Sounds good. I'll pick Heckle and Castle's brains for leads," Pantell said as he stood and exited his computer.

"Thanks man, I'll keep you posted." Sean hung up and put it in drive. Three-and-a-half hours later he pulled past the gate at the Lewiston property.

Elsa closed it behind him and followed the SUV up the driveway. She couldn't help but wonder at the seriousness of Sean's call earlier and his set jaw now. He was out and walking her way before she made it to the house. "Hey Elsa, can we talk up at the garden?"

She nodded, but as she was turning she noticed the girls watching them in nervous concern. "Let me tell the girls not to worry... right? They don't have anything to worry about?"

"No they don't have to worry," Sean answered.

Little Annabelle was barking her high pitched yap that made the hair stand up on the back of Sean's neck. Elsa noticed and turned away to the girls. "We'll be back in a minute. Can you calm her down, Katie?"

Katie grinned and gently placed her fingers over the dogs muzzle. It instantly stopped barking and flopped out its tongue to pant.

"Wow, that was impressive," Sean remarked.

"She has a way with dogs, for sure." Elsa led the way past a giant tank to the trail. "By-the-way, before I forget to ask. What's this tank for?"

"Oil for the heater."

"Oh, how do I tell if it's full or not?"

"Probably has a dip stick." Sean backtracked and showed her the long metal rod hanging next to the tank. "I'll check it before I leave."

They sat on the bench and Sean cleared his throat.

"Sounds pretty serious Sean. You're making me nervous."

"Well, honestly, it's so important I'm afraid you won't take it seriously… I really need your help… and the girls." Sean looked up into the canopy of pine trees.

"Sean, I promise I will take it very seriously." Elsa put a hand lightly on his broad shoulder. "What's happened, you can tell me."

"Boris kidnapped my sister, Sharice," Sean answered simply.

"Oh no! No," Elsa gasped.

"I don't have proof, but I'm positive he's responsible." Sean knuckled his eyes fiercely as he fought exhaustion. "Putting myself in his shoes, I think he would get revenge with me by forcing her into prostitution… or at list the preliminary steps."

"I see. You took us, so he takes her," Elsa said.

"Yes, but I don't know where he'd take her. I need your help," Sean asked, allowing his desperation to show.

"Do you know where Boris takes the girls when he first gets them?"

"He changes the location occasionally to keep a step ahead of the cops. I know my location is long gone." Elsa stood. "Let's ask the girls. We've got no time to lose… he'll destroy her."

Sean followed her to the house. Katie and Yani sat at a picnic table on the porch waiting. The dog had been put in Katie's room. They both looked concerned when they saw the haggard face of their friend who was usually smiling. Sean and Elsa sat quietly.

"You're not going to get rid of us are you?" Katie blurted out with tears welling in her expressive eyes.

"No, no, I'm sorry to scare you. Nothing's happening to you or this house," Sean reassured the frightened teen.

She took a deep shaky breath. Yani silently took her under her wing for a cuddle.

"Sean's sister has been kidnapped by Boris. Sharice is one of the sweetest, purest souls there ever was. She helped me when I came here… taught me to cook, clean, and care for a home. Sean thinks we can help him find her," Elsa ended and turned to Sean.

"Do either of you know where Boris brings his girls when he first gets them?"

Yani and Katie looked at each other.

"I know of a few places he's used, but I don't know if he still does. It's been a long-long time since I was taken," Yani answered.

Katie started crying. "I don't remember," she sobbed.

Sean tried to hide his disappointment. "It's okay Katie. I forgot you'd lost your memory."

Elsa tapped the wooden table top with her knuckles. "Stop crying. We're here to help Sean, not make him feel sorry for us. We're tough women! Just calm down and think," Elsa commanded.

Katie sat up straighter and bit her trembling lip. They all sat silently as she tried to calm herself and think. "It was dark… a small room."

Sean nodded encouragement to her.

"Uhm, it had a bathroom."

"Could you hear anything from outside the room? Or smell anything?" Elsa asked.

***

Pantell stood next to Heckle and surveyed the map.

"These areas are outside of the gang territory, but they've been spotted coming and going from these buildings." Heckle pointed to five different areas.

"Okay, I'll start here," Pantell tapped West Sacramento.

"I'll cruise around South Sac over by Florin."

***

Sharice stopped munching on the stale cheese puffs and listened intently as footsteps echoing on a wooden floor approached. Holding her breath, she waited to see what would happen next.

A key slid into the door lock and the old round handle rotated abruptly. The silhouette of a tall man entered. She knew it was her kidnapper. He was followed by another man, a little shorter. The deference he was shown made her think he must be the boss.

"Sharice?" The boss asked in a cultured voice. Slight Russian accent.

She'd already had a long debate with herself about her response. Should she remain silent, speak reservedly, or drive them crazy with chatter. Since she didn't know anything, silence seemed a waste of time. Speaking rapid fire babble seemed exhausting somehow. She went with curt. "Good lord... you have to ask? So you could have abducted the wrong woman?"

Boris paused and threw her an annoyed glance. "Sean McGee's sister."

She folded her arms across her bruised ribs and glared at him. "Did my brother hurt your feelings? Is that why you kidnapped his sister?"

Boris didn't answer as he approached.

"So, I take it you're afraid of him," she sneered.

He back handed her across the face, sending her backwards onto the bed. She scrambled up and darted across the room.

"No, but you're afraid of me... or you will be," Boris answered with a sinister smile.

"Well of course I'm afraid of you, you idiot! You're a *man* with a protective bodyguard and I'm a helpless half-starved female. That's why you chose me... you're afraid of my brother." Sharice circled backwards as Boris moved closer. "A real man would've gone directly after his enemy, but you... you are a coward!"

Boris' only reaction was the flaring of his nostrils. Without another word he crossed to the door. As he opened it he turned back slightly and said, "I have time... as you said you're only *half* starved."

After the door slammed a scent of used frying oil wafted in the room. It reminded Sharice of her teens when she worked at a greasy-spoon restaurant. Going to the door, she pressed her ear to the door... just footsteps.

Going to the other side of the room, she pressed her ear to the thin wall. Faint clattering and conversation could be heard in the distance. Maybe a restaurant was nearby.

***

Elsa stood up after several minutes of Katie's attempts at remembering. "I'll put a pot of coffee on. You staying the night?"

Sean shook his head. "I have to find my sister."

"Look, it's getting pretty late. You're not going to be much help to your sister if your body is spread out all over the highway because you fell asleep." Elsa paused at the door. "Come in here and lay down on the couch for thirty minutes while we talk to Katie... that way she won't feel rushed, okay" she waved him to follow her.

Sean stood and stretched. "Okay, thirty minutes."

He went straight to the couch and lay down.

"I'll have a pot of coffee for you when you wake up." Elsa set up the coffee and quietly went back to the front porch. Sitting down at the table, she asked, "Anything?"

"I remember smelling food. I was so hungry."

Elsa smiled encouragingly. "Did it smell delicious?"

"No, it smelled rancid and gross, but I was so hungry I thought I'd eat it... whatever it was.

"Was it like rotten fruit or meat?" Yani asked the girl.

Katie sat silently for a minute. Her eyes drifted shut as she tried with all her might to remember. "It didn't smell rotten. I think I've smelled it before, back home I think."

Yani and Elsa exchanged a surprised look. "Like a kitchen, maybe a restaurant?"

Katie's eyes flickered under her eyelids as she tried to break through to her past. "Mmm... I don't know... maybe a restaurant. I feel like my mother's kitchen would have smelled good." She breathed in through her nose as though she were sniffing. "Bread."

"Bread?"

"My mother made fresh bread I think."

"What about the rancid smell?" Yani asked gently, not wanting to break the almost trance-like state Katie was in.

"I don't feel anything bad about the smell... like a bad memory. Maybe it was just a restaurant." She popped her eyes open. "You know, like the food bank sometimes smells like old oil when we get our meals?"

"That's good," Elsa said. "What about noises? Was it noisy?"

"No, it was very quiet... almost silent." Her face blanched at a memory. "I remember the sound of steps in the hallway. It had an echo, like wood or something."

Katie's breathing was becoming more rapid and her heartbeat could be seen in her delicate throat. "Okay, Katie. That was a lot."

"It was super helpful!" Yani patted her hand.

"Do you think you maybe lived in the country or the city when you were a kid?" Elsa asked.

"Maybe the country. Up here, when I hear a dog bark or a horse make its sound, it's familiar. And this house and you guys remind me of something." She shrugged. "Sometimes I feel I could chop firewood... weird huh?"

"Not weird at all honey. You must've lived in the country. Since you speak Russian, we know you probably lived there, though other countries speak it." Yani added.

"I'm almost sure I'm from Russia. It just sounds right."

Elsa stood and said, "Let's get Sean moving. He's probably going to want to visit Alexia and Lynn too." They followed her into the house causing Sean to jolt awake. They gathered around and told him what Katie remembered while he gulped down a cup of strong coffee.

As soon as he had cell service, he called the Dressel's ranch to let them know he was coming and would need to sleep there. Then he called Pantell, just to be told that they'd uncovered nothing so far. "Well, it may be near a cheap smelly restaurant in a quiet part of town."

"Okay, I'll head over to Del Paso Heights and check that out."

By the time Sean arrived at the ranch it was well past midnight. Todd was waiting on the porch for him. He silently ushered Sean in and led him down the hall to a guestroom. Sean heard the door shut quietly as he crawled on top of the bed, fully clothed. He was asleep in moments.

***

Sharice strained her ears to her the faint sound of people talking. Someone laughed. The smells of cooking food... onions? She sniffed the air like a hound dog. It was very late at night, maybe even morning, but this restaurant was open for business. She drifted back to sleep.

***

The next morning Sean made his way down the narrow hallway to the bathroom. He could hear the girl's voices in the kitchen. A fresh towel was set on the counter and the shower looked too inviting to pass up. Hurriedly, he jumped in the shower for a quick rinse and re-dressed. In ten minutes he stepped into the kitchen. They stopped chattering and turned their attention to him.

Agatha jumped into the silence. "Come on! Pour yourself a cup of Joe." She held out a giant mug with a horse on the side of it.

Sean poured it and sat down.

Before he could speak, Agatha set a plate of waffles in front of him and Alexia handed a plate to Todd. Lynn set a pitcher of syrup and a dish of fresh butter in front of them.

"Talk while you eat," Agatha commanded. "You're of no use hungry."

Sean chuckled slightly and took a bite. They all sat down at the giant ranch table and waited while sipping scalding hot coffee strong enough to tar pavement with. Sean munched thoughtfully. "Is Lisa coming?"

"Should be here any minute," Todd answered.

Sean nodded and took another bite.

"You're not here to take us away are you?" Lynn asked quietly.

"No, I'm not," Sean looked her straight in the eyes. "I need your help, and when Dr. Dressel gets here I'll tell you all about it. I don't want to repeat myself again."

"Did you go to Elsa's first?" Alexia wanted to know.

"I did, and they helped me some. Believe it or not, it was Katie who remembered some things for me."

"Katie?" Lynn asked. "Wow, that's amazing. Maybe her memory will come back some day."

The sound of tires crunching on gravel announced the arrival of Lisa. She entered and went straight for the coffee pot. "Oh thank goodness you have coffee!" she said to the room in general.

"I made an extra pot." Agatha beamed with joy at her crowded kitchen.

"Okay, spit it out!" Lisa demanded as she flopped into the chair.

"Boris kidnapped my little sister."

This announcement was met with profound silence.

"Yesterday around noon." Sean lay his fork down. "Boris did this because I took his girls from him."

"That sick bast--" Alexia started.

"Now, now, let's not get side tracked with emotions," Lisa cut in. "What can we do, Sean?"

"I know this may be very hard for you two, but do you have any idea where he may have taken her? Do you remember where you went when you first were abducted… kidnapped?" Sean tried to control his emotions, but it showed in his eyes. "I think he may be planning to put her on the streets, or at least making her go through the process of being beaten into submission."

"He won't beat her unless she refuses to cooperate," Lynn said quietly.

"She won't cooperate. I know Sharice."

"Does she have children, because he'll use whatever he has to break her," Alexia warned.

Sean groaned.

"This isn't helping," Agatha said. "He needs to know where to look for her."

"I don't know where I was when I was first brought here," Lynn said.

"Me neither," Alexia added.

"Okay… think back. Do you remember any lights, smells, sounds, anything?" Sean pleaded.

The two girls sat silently thinking. The clock ticked loudly. A chicken crowed.

"The place I was in was very quiet I think. It was super dark, but a light came under the door constantly." Alexia pressed her fingertips to her forehead in concentration.

"It had a bed and a bathroom," Lynn said.

"Yeah, the light came under the door to the hall," Alexia continued.

"The hall?" Sean asked. "Was it in a house or maybe a motel?"

"It was a hall with wood floors, because I can remember them walking and it made noise."

"So, it had to be a house or a hotel," Lisa commented.

"That's what I said." Sean looked exacerbated.

"No, you said motel. Motels have exterior doors, hotels have interior hallways," Lisa answered calmly.

"It could've been a wood exterior walkway… it creaked," Lynn added.

"Interesting, Katie recalled the sound of the wood as well…" Sean leaned back in his chair.

"It was the scariest thing to hear them coming," Alexia whispered.

"Yeah, really scary," Lynn's lips trembled.

Everyone was silent for a moment. "Okay how about other sounds or smells?" Sean asked.

"I think there was a restaurant nearby."

"I could smell the food sometimes."

"I think it was a diner, like a twenty-four-hour place."

"If I behaved good, they brought me a plate of food… like the way food is served at a café."

"Did the plates have anything special about them?" Sean asked.

They both shook their heads looking at each other. "They were white. Sometimes chipped."

***

Sharice glared up at her assailant as the drug was injected into her vein. "Coward," she hissed between gritted teeth.

***

Sean dialed Pantell and put the phone on speaker mode as he waited for the electric gate to open. Seeing movement in his periphery he glanced towards the house to see the whole group waving goodbye to him. Sean surprised himself by grinning and waving… he didn't know he had a smile left in him.

Pantell picked up on the second ring. "McGee."

"Boss," Sean greeted. "Have you looked in the Del Paso or Rio Linda areas?"

"No, but it's on the list. His guys have been seen coming and going from a couple of different places. I'll head over now."

"Let me know where you are in three hours. The girls remember footsteps on a wooden surface leading to their room. They all recall the smell of rancid cooking oil, restaurant noise at all hours." Sean impatiently waited for the second gate to let him through. "So we're looking for a wood structure, probably an interior room because there was minimal light coming in under the door. It will be next to a twenty-four hour restaurant—most likely behind it because they said the smells were gross. Oh, and they occasionally heard chickens."

"Gotcha, I'm on it," Pantell answered.

Sean turned the radio to a hard rock station and cranked it up. After about thirty minutes his testosterone and heart rate were at an all time high. "Idiot!" Sean said out loud as he changed the station to K-love. The music soothed his soul and calmed him. Driving down I-5 at ten miles over the limit, he reviewed all he knew. He tried to consider what his next move would be if he were the team leader in Recon. The problem was he depended on his team. They knew each other and could be relied upon to follow orders explicitly. Pantell didn't operate like his team, and Sean didn't want to go solo.

***

The room swirled slowly, lazily around the bed. She didn't feel afraid, but she held onto the bare mattress just the same. A ghost moved slowly about the dark room… but there was more light than usual. Lolling her head to the side, Sharice tried to identify the source of light, while wondering why it was interesting. A rectangle in the wall was the source… *Heaven?* She giggled at this random thought. That couldn't be Heaven, but maybe it would lead her there.

The ghost approached and pushed her back onto the bed as she struggled to rise.

"Heaven," she croaked and weakly held a hand towards the exit.

"Heaven?" a voice asked.

Sharice thought maybe it was the ghost who spoke. Peering up at her jailer, she wondered who this could be. "You're a girl."

"Yes," it answered gently. "Don't fight it... relax."

"No," Sharice said simply. "I will fight it until I get to Heaven."

"They'll kill you," the girl whispered fiercely.

"They can't kill me...I'm, I'm invincible." Sharice's voice trailed off as she lost consciousness.

***

"Boss," Sean said as he answered his phone.

"McGee, I'm staking out the place. Halfway down Cycad Street, between Bliss and Flanders. You take the ally. Come around the back of Elvira's Diner and it's the third dump on the left. You'll see the back fence broken down. I've got a guy in a utilities van working on the electricity pole on the corner of the lot. A woman wearing a pink t-shirt will be walking her dog. There're two of our guys at the diner. We were just getting ready to move in. How far away are you."

"Ten minutes, if I don't get lost."

"Okay, we'll wait. I'll text you the exact address so you can paste it to your GPS."

Sean's phone chirped a text message. He copied and pasted the address and mounted his phone. In less than a minute he was exiting the freeway.

About a block from target, Sean pulled off the road and took deep focusing breathes. He pulled the Sig P220 out of the leather pouch and slid it into his holster. He pocketed several magazines and pulled back on the road.

"Boss, I'm turning onto Cycad. I see the utilities truck. I'll pass by and walk back."

"Gotcha," Pantell responded just above a whisper.

Sean parked and headed back down the litter-strewn one lane road. A woman came from the opposite direction with a pink top and a medium sized dog. She had a radio blaring in one hand and was bobbing her head to the music. The electrician closed the giant metal box he'd been working on and stepped toward his van.

At that moment a dark blue Mercedes turned down the street.

The electrician pulled out a walkie-talkie and spoke as he appeared to be looking for something in his van. The girl nodded to Sean and kept walking. Sean's text vibrated. Sean dropped to his knee to tie his shoe. He was thankful he'd thought to wear the silly visor he'd gotten at the State Fair last year. It had a tuft of grey hair standing straight up on top like an unruly flat-top. He heard the car stop and two car-doors open and close. Standing, Sean pulled his phone out and looked at it as he kept the two newcomers in his periphery. He read Pantell's group text, "Hold until we identify new threat."

Sean rotated like he was trying to shade the screen to read it, and took a selfie. Zooming he could see the face of both men behind him. Sean strolled away as he texted, "Boris and his goon, Alec."

"Let them lead us to the exact room and then we take him."

Five thumbs-up emojis appeared in rapid sequence.

Two men rounded the corner from the diner. The woman circled back, the electrician grabbed a clipboard and started toward the house.

"We're in the house. Entry hall," from Pantell.

"West side," came another.

"Back approach," came from Sean and the two others.

The woman's dog was obviously trained. She took it off its leash and it dropped its head and sniffed the air expertly. Making eye-contact, they took Sean's lead as he pulled out the Sig and tipped his head to the old wooden back porch. He sprinted across the lawn and squatted in the hydrangea bush next to the house. Pulling out his cell he typed, "Wood floors creak loudly."

Glancing at their devices, the other two nodded. Five thumbs-up bounced onto the screen.

It looked like it was a mansion at some point in the distant past. A couple of windows were widely spaced along the eastern wall. They must've divided the rooms so some had windows and some didn't. Sean noted an additional door on the far end. He headed towards it. This could be a possible escape route.

As he squatted amongst the overgrown bushes and weeds, he listened to the sound of creaking wood and low masculine talk. A female voice responded occasionally, but it wasn't Sharice. Belatedly, Sean realized Pantell didn't know what Sharice looked like. He quickly downloaded a recent photo of her to the group text. A moment later five thumbs ups appeared.

Pantell texted, "Ready, we silently enter on 3. ...1."

Sean rose to his feet with eyes almost shut, giving him time to adjust to probable darkness.

"2"

Sean put his hand on the knob and slowly turned it.

"3"

It was locked. He slid a lock-pick file into it and released it. He entered the dark room silently. He slowly panned the room over the sights of the Sig. A sliver of light showed the location of a door. A bed in the corner appeared to be empty. A toilet flushed and a silhouette appeared. The small figure was walking back to the bed when Sean slid his hand over her mouth. He knew instantly that it wasn't his sister. Now he had a dilemma. If he let go of her she could scream and jeopardize the entire operation.

He turned her around so her back was to him and pressing her head back onto his chest, he maintained the vice grip over her mouth. The girl was so weak she just submitted to his dominion. He pulled out his cell phone and rapidly typed with his free hand, "I'm in first room to Pantell's right. Wrong girl. Can't release her."

Pantell shot him an okay emoji. "I'll take first left."

"First right south end," an agent typed.

"First left south end," came another text.

"Male voices in third room on left to north entrance, need back-up."

Five responses bounced across the screen. Sean groaned in frustration. He grabbed a threadbare bath towel from the bathroom and gagged his girl. She collapsed. Sean carried her to the bed and double-checked to make sure he hadn't cut off her air supply, then he opened the door to the hallway quietly. Remembering, he texted a thumbs up to keep from getting shot. Pantell crept past him. Sean fell in behind him. Several shadowy figures materialized along the hallway. A cupboard door slammed in the kitchen area, followed by a man appearing at the end of the hall silhouetted by the dim light flowing in the dirty front windows.

He walked right past the first agent who'd flattened herself against the wall.

She peeled away from the wall and placed a hand over his mouth from behind. The big man instantly collapsed, making Sean wonder what she had in her hand. Stepping over the inert body, she continued toward him. The dog materialized in front of her. It silently stood at the door in question and stared at the door, hackles raised.

Pantell took point and stepped in front of the door. With a glance at his team, he whispered, "Shoot high, Sharice will be low," and he kicked the door. It didn't give. Sean was ready. He threw every ounce of his angry, infuriated self against the door. It splintered the frame and crashed open along with the blasting of gunfire from inside.

Sean spun from the impact of the first bullet, but kept his feet and entered the fray. Explosions coming from so many firearms, it was hard to keep track. In a pause from the shooting, Pantell whispered, "Check."

Two agents responded. Sean whispered, "Check, hit."

"Hit," echoed a familiar voice—Heckle.

Suddenly the room was flooded with a faint light. Alec lay in a pool of blood. Boris was on the bed with an arm wrapped around Sharice's throat. He'd been hit in the thigh. His steely eyes fixed on Sean and the gun barrel held against Sharice's temple didn't waver.

An agent groaned from the hallway.

Sharice kept her eyes on Sean.

"Drop it," demanded Boris.

Pantell slowly lowered his gun to the floor. The solo explosion from Sean's Sig startled everyone. Boris' eyes registered shock as he stared at Sean in death. Slowly his lifeblood drained out the back of his head and his body went limp.

Sharice scrambled away in hysterical terror. She fell off the end of the bed and crawled to Sean. Sweeping her up in his arms, he carried her from the room. In the shabby front room he sat down with her in his arms and rocked her slowly while making hushing sounds.

Three wide-eyed girls were escorted down the hall to the front room.

Pantell called for a paramedic as he held a towel to the gushing wound of an agent in the hall. Another agent approached Sean to press a towel against the hole in his arm.

Police sirens competed with ambulances and fire-trucks. The police won. They leaped out of the vehicles with guns drawn, shouting orders to come out with hands up. An agent stepped out with his hands up. "CIA!" he called. "Permission to show my ID, sir?"

"Slowly," ordered the nearest deputy as he approached with his gun leveled at the CIA agent's chest.

"Are my babies okay?" Sharice asked in a whisper.

"Yes," Sean answered as he rested his chin on her head. "Are you okay?" He leaned back to look down at her. "Did they... ?" he trailed off.

She shook her head slightly, "I don't think so, but I was pretty high at times."

Sean silently pulled her torn purple flowered shirt up over her bruised shoulder.

"How long has it been?" she asked with her head burrowed into his chest.

"One day... the longest day of my life."

CHAPTER SEVENTEEN

It was a full vehicle on this trip. Sharice sat in front next to Sean, and three teenage girls sat in back. They talked non-stop. It was an expensive order when they stopped at the fast food drive-through, but the expense was welcome.

The older teen on the driver's side was quieter than the others. It had been a year since she'd been kidnapped from Vegas. Her battered face proved she'd not been an easy sex slave. She was Chloe.

The other two were barely fourteen and slipped into speaking Russian frequently. Both had been abducted from the same region, but had never met before. They munched their hamburgers and fries with the enthusiasm of youth. They'd both been raped repeatedly, but having each other seemed to give them courage. They were Mila and Nadia.

When they arrived at the Lewiston house, Elsa was at the gate. Sharice jumped out and embraced her. With their arms around each other's waists, they followed the SUV up the winding driveway. Yani and Katie were on the porch.

The three girls timidly got out to meet their temporary family. Katie, looking mature, greeted the two younger ones in Russian. They glanced at each other in surprise and grinned at Katie. All three began a rapid fire dialogue while Yani took Chloe under her wing. Sharice and Elsa arrived on the porch as introductions were made.

Katie took Chloe's hand and said, "We're going to share a room. Come on." She dragged Chloe into the house. Elsa smiled tenderly at the younger teens. "Let me show you the room you guys will share."

"What about Yani?" Sean asked.

"You two can talk about that," Elsa said with a nod at Yani.

They leaned hips against the kitchen counters as they talked. Sharice followed Elsa to the girl's room.

"If you think I'm ready, I'd like to go to the next house," Yani said nervously.

"I think you're ready, if you do." Sean reached for the coffee pot and offered her some. She shook her head no. As he poured himself a cup, she reached into the fridge and got the milk for him.

"I love it here, but you need the room for the girls. I'm ready… I think. Lynn is there right?"

"Yes, and Alexia." Sean sipped his coffee. "I think you will love it and will be a great asset to the household. I'm glad you're going."

She let out a shaky sigh of relief. "Okay, I'll go pack."

When Sharice came out he asked her if she minded a detour to the ranch. Sharice clapped her hands together in excitement. Pulling out her cell phone she grimaced and held her phone out. "No signal!"

He laughed and handed his to her. "Mine's on the WiFi." He held a finger to his lips and pointed to the back of the house.

She went up on her toes and kissed his cheek before rushing out the front door to call her husband.

Sean stood by himself in a sunbeam slanting through the kitchen. His eyes wandered to the décor of a feminine hand. A houseplant in the window frame with a metal ladybug in it. A flowered table cloth. A delicious odor emanating from a crock-pot on the counter. It was a home now.

Yani returned with Elsa and the four girls. Katie held Yani's free hand and fought back tears. "Don't worry Katie-girl, you'll be next," Yani was saying. "We'll be together soon."

"Promise?"

"Promise." She kissed the tip of the girl's nose.

Yani and Elsa hugged tightly, murmuring encouragement quietly.

"Let me throw some sandwiches together for you guys," Elsa said as Sharice came back in. The kitchen was a bustle of activity as Elsa and Katie expertly worked together.

Tears slid down Sharice's cheeks as she accepted the bundle.

"What's wrong?" Elsa asked with concern.

"Nothing's wrong… I'm just so incredibly proud of you Elsa," Sharice said as she wrapped her arms around her friend and rocked back and forth.

"Good grief! Do you women ever stop crying?" Sean teased as he walked out the front door.

On the front porch, Sharice took Katie's hand. "Katie, I can't thank you enough for helping to rescue me. It was horrible for me, but I kept thinking how terrible it must've been for you guys." Sharice held a hand towards the three newcomers. They instinctively nestled close to this mother. Katie translated for the two younger ones and they nodded. "You're all so brave," Sharice whispered as she gently kissed each forehead in turn. "Now it's time to heal and move forward," she told Chloe. "Thank you for taking care of me... I know it was you who fed me and looked after me."

A couple of hours later Yani watched the process of the gates and dogs in wonderment. "Wow, I ain't never seen nothing like this before."

Sean smiled.

Sharice rolled down her window and breathed in the farmland air. "Reminds me of when we were kids," she commented.

The family was on the porch as usual, with Riley panting between Agatha and Todd. They greeted Sharice warmly, but their attention was for Yani. To the Dressel's, the new girls would always be the focus of their love and attention. Tough as Yani was, she melted in the circle of love. Sharice and Sean followed quietly behind, taking back stage. Agatha invited Sharice to come in the girl's home for a tour, leaving Sean with Todd.

Todd walked around the home showing Sean his plans for a private back deck with a view of the mountains. A garden would be placed next to the porch with steps leading to it. Agatha thought there should be a little area for reading amongst a flower garden. They walked up to the big house and sat in the shade on the giant porch. Todd pulled out a cigar and Sean declined the offer for one, but settled into the first relaxing moment in a long time.

Sean squirmed and took his gun out of his hip holster and set it next to Todd's.

"So, things're gonna change a bit huh?" Todd asked squinting across the valley.

"Not from your perspective." Sean stretched his legs out in front of him. "It may get even busier for you, but now I won't have to steal the girls and sneak them off in the middle of the night. That was exhausting, exciting, but exhausting. Now that the police are working with me, I can bring them to Elsa's in broad daylight.

The women spilling out of the Daybreak drew their attention. The two men silently watched the women they were committed to protect. Yani was wearing a little crown of flowers they'd made for her. Lisa strolled along with Lynn, her favorite.

"Beautiful sight," Todd said as he puffed his cigar.

"Yup," Sean responded laconically.

***

Standing at his kitchen sink, Sean gazed out onto his own little bit of paradise. Jet nuzzled his leg. Sean ruffled his head and said, "You're a good boy, Jet."

His cell rang from the granite countertop. Sean looked at the lit up screen... Megan. Much had happened since he'd last seen her. A smile lifted his cheeks as he picked up the phone and popped a beer. "Megan?" he asked.

"Hi Sean," her soft voice floated across the waves to him. "I went by the travel agency, but you weren't there, so I decided to call. How are you?"

He slid the glass door open with his toes. "I'm good. It's been a busy couple of weeks." Sean smiled at the understatement as he settled into a lounge chair by the pool. "How's your dad? Did you have a good visit?"

"I did. He was so happy to have me there. I didn't realize how long it'd been since I'd been down to Napa." She laughed lightly. "We even went wine tasting."

"You make that sound unusual?" Sean watched Jet sneak up on a squirrel. "Doesn't everybody in Napa go wine tasting?"

"Not when you own one of the oldest and largest wineries in the valley," Megan answered with a laugh.

"I didn't know that about you," Sean took a gulp of his beer.

"Yeah, well, it never came up."

"Whatcha doing tonight? Want to come over for a barbeque?"

"Sure, but as a friend right?" she asked.

"Friends, but bring your swimsuit," he ordered. "Five o'clock?"

"Okay, I didn't know you had a pool," she said.

"See… we're learning all kinds of things about each other." He gave her his address and went in the garage to rummage through his freezer for meat. He pulled out a couple of steaks and found some potatoes in the fridge. On a hunch he decided to make twice-baked potatoes. When she arrived a couple of hours later he had everything ready.

She stood at his counter and watched him follow directions for making an apple martini.

Later that night, when she finally left he felt like a wet noodle. He flopped onto a floatie in the pool and gazed up at the stars.

Sean jolted awake at two in the morning. As he slid his leg over the edge of the bed he encountered water. A flash of images blurred past his mind as he saw the stars above, the trees, a roofline and then the floatie flipped over and dunked him. Sean came up sputtering. The water rippled around him like gentle laughter. Seeing the humor, Sean chuckled as his feet found the cement bottom of his pool. He got out, dried himself off and went to bed.

The next morning he woke up thinking about church. Glancing at the clock he decided he could make it to mass if he hurried.

As he came in the side entrance, he scanned the pews his folks always sat in. He slid onto the bench next to his mother. She turned to smile politely at him and realizing it was Sean, let out a little squeal of delight. His father shushed her as he reached across to shake Sean's free hand while his wife hugged their son. A few parishioners shot glances their direction. The father of one of Sean's high school friends nodded a greeting. Though Sean couldn't understand half what the ancient priest was mumbling, he felt enveloped by the comfortable old church routine.

THE END

ABOUT THE AUTHOR

H. Schussman currently lives in Northern California with her husband of thirty years and their cats Loca. She travels six weeks a year throughout Italy, Mexico, Central America, and the Caribbean. Heidi is a retired Physical Therapist, having specialized in psychiatric disorders, dementias, and geriatrics.

H. Schussman's first three conspiracy novels, Counterpart, El Tiburón, and In the Crossfire of Revenge, (published by Smashwords & Vinspire Publishing) can be found everywhere online. H. Schussman is currently writing screenplays for the full feature adventure/detective genre and an epic Christmas film.

Discover other titles by H. Schussman at Smashwords.com
Counterpart
El Tiburon
In the Crossfire of Revenge

Connect with her online on one her three blogs:
Author H. Schussman
A Dashing Bold Adventure:
The Wine Tribe

Or
Parler: @HSchussman
Instagram: h.schussman

Or email her at H.Schussman@yahoo.com

www.ingramcontent.com/pod-product-compliance
Lightning Source LLC
Chambersburg PA
CBHW030649260626
47157CB00007B/2563